Murder on the Rebound

An Amicus Curiae Mystery

Published by ECW PRESS
2120 Queen Street East, Suite 200, Toronto, Ontario, Canada M4E 1E2

LIBRARY AND ARCHIVES CANADA CATALOGUING IN PUBLICATION

Miller, Jeffrey, 1950–
Murder on the rebound / Jeffrey Miller.

(An Amicus Curiae mystery)
ISBN-13: 978-1-55022-793-2
ISBN-10: 1-55022-793-9

1. Title. II. Series: Miller, Jeffrey, 1950– . Amicus Curiae mystery.

PS8626.145M875 2007   C813'.6   C2007-903492-6

Cover and Text Design: Tania Craan
Cover illustration: Gordon Sauve
Production and Typesetting: Mary Bowness
Printing: Webcom

This book is set in Solstice and Garamond.

With the publication of *Murder on the Rebound* ECW Press acknowledges the generous financial support of the Government of Canada through the Book Publishing Industry Development Program (BPIDP), the Canada Council for the Arts, and the Ontario Arts Council, for our publishing activites.

DISTRIBUTION
CANADA: Jaguar Book Group, 100 Armstrong Avenue, Georgetown, ON, L7G 5S4

UNITED STATES: Independent Publishers Group, 814 North Franklin Street, Chicago, Illinois 60610

PRINTED AND BOUND IN CANADA

ECW PRESS
ecwpress.com

Murder on the Rebound

An Amicus Curiae Mystery

JEFFREY MILLER

ECW PRESS

Also by Jeffrey Miller

Murder's Out of Tune, 2005

Murder at Osgoode Hall, 2004

*Where There's Life, There's Lawsuits: Not Altogether
    Serious Ruminations on Law and Life,* 2003

Ardor in the Court: Sex and the Law, 2002

The Law of Contempt in Canada, 1997

*Naked Promises: A Chronicle of Everyday Wheeling
    and Dealing,* 1989

For details see www.jeffreymiller.ca

For Phyllis,
and she knows why.

The crime of spreading false news dates back to 1275, in the *Statute of Westminster*. It survived in Canadian law until 1992, when the Supreme Court heard the Holocaust revisionism case discussed briefly in this novel. By a margin of four judges to three, the court struck the offence out of the *Criminal Code* as an unreasonable limit on free expression. See [1992] 2 *Supreme Court Reports*, page 731. Via appeal by poetic license, I have reinstated the offence for the purposes of this book. (For more discussion of the crime's recent history, see the afterword.)

Details concerning the life of Sir Francis Bacon are taken from the standard works (especially Catherine Drinker Bowen's highly readable *Francis Bacon: The Temper of a Man*), and at least one idiosyncratic volume of historical revisionism. Amicus's quotation from Sir William Blackstone in Part IV, Chapter Two may be found in the *Commentaries on the Laws of England*, IV, 314–15; his other information regarding outlaws comes from Pollock and Maitland, *History of English Law*. Amicus's summaries of the "Blackie the Talking Cat Case" are drawn, as he says, from genuine American case reports, which can be found via the citations he provides (and, perhaps more accessibly, on the Internet). The cases cited as epigraphs to Parts I and V (that is, the cases concerning the Socratic method and judicial notice) are also genuine cases, reported in the volumes cited.

This book was originally called *Dead Cat Bounce*, but by the time it began to see the light of day there were several books styled the same, at least two of them novels. Gabriella Papic, readers of my column in *The Lawyers Weekly*, and my long-time (and ever-thoughtful) editor, Edna Barker, provided useful suggestions as we searched for a new title.

"What is truth? said jesting Pilate; and would not stay for an answer."

— Francis Bacon, Essays, *"Of Truth"*

CONTENTS

PART I

The Socratic Method

Socratic method: Teaching law by cross-examining
students on the cases and principles, as opposed
to lecturing, conducting discussions, or
answering student questions.

"Only a person trained in an American law school
under the Socratic method could postulate . . .
that a firearm transported in a drug trafficker's
car on the way to a sale is not 'carried' by him."
— Judge Stephen Trott, dissenting,
in *U.S. v. Foster*, 133 Federal Reporter, 3rd, 704 (9th
Circuit U.S. Court of Appeals).

"A popular judge is a deformed thing, and plaudits are fitter for players than magistrates."
— Francis Bacon, *Essays*

ONTARIO COURT OF APPEAL

BROSSARD, MARINER, and FIERSTEIN, Justices of Appeal

B E T W E E N:

HER MAJESTY THE QUEEN

Appellant

- and -

IAN LUTHER PASTIES

Respondent

The judgment of the court was delivered by:
MARINER, Justice of Appeal

What is interesting about this case is that it takes nothing — literally nothing — for granted. It strikes at the

*very bedrock of our legal system, challenging a basic pre-
sumption, the presumption that a trial in our law courts is
the search for truth.*

In undertaking this search

*A quest for the truth. That is how our law defines a trial
in court. But this appeal raises something even more funda-
mental, insofar as that is philosophically possible. This
appeal challenges*

We accept that a trial is a quest for the truth.

*We accept that a trial in our law courts embodies a quest
for the truth. And this appeal digs deep And this appeal
dredges And xxxx*

*Like the knights of King Arthur's Round Table, the par-
ties in a law trial undertake a quest, a quest for the parties
in a legal proceeding attempt*

Like the search for the Grail Like

Fortunately or not, someone is ringing at the front door of 1415
Elysian Fields North, interrupting His Lordship's vexed reasons
for judgment in *R. v. Pasties*, a nasty little matter of what our
Criminal Code calls "spreading false news." The accused Mr.
Pasties has published pamphlets, web logs, and whatnot stating
that North Americans of French heritage — the French-speakers

of Quebec, the Acadians of the Canadian maritime provinces, the Cajuns of Louisiana — are engaged in a terrorist conspiracy to extort money and other advantage from the Canadian and American governments, and possibly from Britain. But the more immediate problem for Justice Theodore Elisha Mariner is this messenger at the door of his house in Forest Hill Village, a messenger bearing altogether true and literally weighty tidings of your nomadic narrator.

If, as in Justice Mariner's library, your shelves groan under much-thumbed volumes of *The Norton Anthology of English Literature*, you will recall that in 1797 the poet Samuel Coleridge was interrupted by someone knocking at the door, "a person on business from Porlock," frustrating Coleridge in his composition of the poem *Kubla Khan*. Mind you, the testy old bard was off to a more propitious start than my own ancient Mariner, writing *chez lui* on this particular day, circa autumn, 2005. "For he on honeydew that fed," says *Kubla Khan*, of the poet who has found his voice, "And drunk the milk of Paradise."

Full of hope and glory in Justice Mariner's foyer, and accompanied there by Animal Control Officer Wayne S. of the Toronto Humane Society, I have similar expectations of milk and honey. But as another judge once said — Sir Francis Bacon, it was, the English lawyer and essayist who will poke his nose often into the tale that follows — "Though hope makes a good breakfast, it is a bad supper."

"Mr. Marinara?" The Porlockian Wayne is an overweight, greasy-haired underachiever of about thirty-two years, and he is pungent with human perspiration. Justice Mariner nods grimly, and the redolent animal control officer sets the carrier holding

Your Correspondent on the lip of a great clay pot that houses a laurel tree just inside the Mariners' door, which door is elegantly framed by lintels of undulating leaded glass. "We found your cat."

"My cat?" His Lordship asks, peering in at me and scowling like we'd never made one another's acquaintance, never mind our peripatetic association, professional as well as intimate, of several years' standing.

"Lucky you put that transmitting device collar on'm. GPS is it?"

"Not exactly, no," the judge replies, still eyeing the carrier. "More like DNPS."

"Never heard o' that one."

"Never heard of Damned Nuisance Positioning System, have you, . . ." His Lordship squints at Wayne's name tag, "Wayne S.?"

Hi, Dad, I'm home!

"Well, anyways, caught'm tryin'a hightail it off a bus at the Kennedy subway station. Otherwise, he'd'a been roadkill for sure." Wayne sweats with determination.

His Lordship sighs, shaking his head. "Ah, yes, the prodigal returns. Amicus Overly Curious." He furrows the judicial brow at Yours Nomadically, and then, unfurling himself to his full six-foot-two at Wayne of the Humane, says, "He probably would have been better off as roadkill, all things considered."

"You don't mean that, chief," Wayne chides, and I begin to warm to him in a more personal way than one generally feels is appropriate respecting the hired help, such as chauffeurs, animal control officers, and sundry delivery persons.

"You haven't met the top judicial officer at 1415 Elysian Fields North," the judge replies. "Chief." The officer in question would be Justice Mariner's wife, Penny.

Shaking his head, Wayne is unsympathetic. "And you shouldn't let the little guy roam at large." *Roam at large.* Professional jargon, no doubt, the official language of Her Majesty's Doghouse a.k.a. the Humane Society shelter. "Not in a city this size, anyways. It's pretty dangerous, for all kindsa reasons. As a general rule, we recommend you keep your domestic animals inside, felines included, or on a lead in the yard. Ya know, like off your clothesline or whatever."

"My clothesline," the judge repeats.

"I know people don't much like to hear that, 'specially about their cat, but your cat, he adapts to it just fine. I'll leave ya this pamphlet we got on it." Wayne pulls a crumpled and stained publication from his back pocket, which document His Lordship accepts with his fingernails. "Anyways, we're gonna have to charge ya for pickup and delivery."

"Pickup and delivery? But surely it would have cost you more to keep him at the shelter," the judge says, reaching for the carrier.

"We take Visa," Wayne replies, his humid mitt gripping the carrier's handle, his muddy size twelves planted firmly on the Italian marble tiles next to Penny Mariner's lovely potted laurel.

"Of course," the judge says. And despite his grudging welcome, I am moved that he does not deny his guilt in the matter, or even protest the summary fine levied by Wayne, never mind that the charges against Justice Mariner are not quite accurate.

No, he hasn't let me roam at large, exactly. Indeed, he has gone to considerable trouble to prevent that eventuality. It's a case of no criminal intent at all, on his part. *My client is innocent, me Lud, more or less.* But he does not bother to inform Wayne that my presence "roaming at large" at the Kennedy subway station was not so much a matter of letting the cat out of the bag as what the criminal law bar hereabouts calls "escape lawful custody."

∾ᘓᘔᘓ∾

As regular readers of my memoirs will recall, I have shared much of what passes for my domestic life these days with Justice Mariner, formerly an esteemed member of the criminal defence bar and now a judge of the Ontario Court of Appeal, the highest court in the province and arguably the most influential court in the country, save the Supreme Court. No, we are not a gay couple, or a particularly cheerful one, as you already will have noted. He is *Homo allegedly sapiens* — an H.A.S. or Has-being, as my kind put it, for short. Of the quadrupedal bar of *felis sylvestris*, I am dubbed by my companion Has-beings Amicus, from the lawyers' Latin *amicus curiae*, "friend of the court." Taken in as a stray at the library of Osgoode Hall, the downtown Toronto home of the province's law society and highest courts, I had my vagrancy pardoned there by His Lordship, who more or less took my case on Legal Aid, with well-disguised enthusiasm. He looked the other way when the law librarians put me up in their workplace. However, the Chief Librarian soon evicted me without notice, on grounds of cat dander and allergens. Similar complaint kept me from rehabilitation at 1415 Elysian Fields North. So the upshot was, no room at the inn: I had nowhere to go but back to Her Majesty's Doghouse, the shelter on River Street, where I was at risk of being declared a long-term offender incapable of salvation and subject to capital punishment by gas chamber or lethal injection. For reasons that will soon be clear, the judge was unable to secrete me in his chambers at Osgoode Hall, where sometimes he had stowed me in the past.

And though I have only just arrived back "home," it seems I am condemned to the natural nomadism of my species, however reluctant I might be to acknowledge the gypsy in me. Generous in deed if not word, His Lordship opens a can of flaked white tuna — packed in water, of course, given our mutual middle-aged tendencies to store calories for the long winter — and he sets out said nosh for me on his teacup's saucer, next to the desk in his study. Then he sits himself back down, recollects his thoughts, and recommences delivery of judgment:

. . . the presumption that a trial in our law courts is simply the search for truth.

Indeed, this appeal puts one heartily in mind of Sir Francis Bacon's essay of Elizabethan times, "Of Truth," particularly where the future Lord Chancellor remarks, "But it is not only the difficulty and labour which men take in finding out of truth . . . that doth bring lies in favour; but a natural though corrupt love of the lie itself."

Lies. "The love of the lie itself." The heart of the matter, as this case shows, is

At this point, Penny Mariner enters smartly, nose crinkled, without knocking or similar by-your-leave. "What the . . .?" says she allusively.

We look up sheepishly at the Porlockian Penny, me from my tuna *sur soucoupe*, His Lordship from *R. v. Pasties*, shrugging in a pantomime of helplessness. *Ya got us bang to rights, guv'nor.*

"He ran away from Herskowitz's. The Humane Society brought him back here."

"I *thought* I smelled my best tuna."

"The poor little guy was starving."

"He's not staying here, Ted."

So opens the case for the prosecution.

"I know. You said already. I'll deal with it."

"I mean he's not staying here another minute."

"But Pen . . ."

"I told you before: I can see it snowballing. A minute'll become a day, and that'll become six months. He can stay in the garden shed, until you make arrangements."

"Arrangements? The shed? But Pen . . ."

"He'll be all right there. When I was a girl on the farm, we had cats in the barn, and they did just fine."

"The barn? The farm? But, Pen . . ."

Mrs. Mariner has gone back about her business. Case closed. Guilty as charged. *Take 'im down, bailiff.*

⋙⟨∾⟩⋘

Once she has given judgment, Penny Mariner is not prone to sustain objections or to over-rule her own convictions. As detailed in *Murder's Out of Tune,** that seminal document in Anglo-American legal history (and coincidentally the previous volume of my memoirs), only a few months back Penny had evicted His Lordship himself from 1415 Elysian Fields North. A little matter of Ted's choice of a particularly attractive law student to be his clerk for the year. So both he and I were homeless for some time. Turfed, as it were. And once the Mariners were reconciled, well, the Chief

---

*ECW Press, 2005.

Justice felt unready to welcome Ted *or* me back at work in chambers at the Court of Appeal until, as the CJ put it in the vernacular, "Time and tide take the pecker off your peccadilloes, Ted."

And you couldn't blame the CJ, really.

During Justice Mariner's estrangement from Penny and the matrimonial home, well, to give you the summary-judgment version, His Lordship was lunching with an old girlfriend. It was all quite innocent really, like a high school reunion, as Justice Mariner tried to explain to Penny . . . after he had encountered Penny herself lunching in the same establishment, at the same time, and *not* with an old college pal or the Volunteer Committee of the Canadian Opera Company. Rather, *Mrs.* Mariner's luncheon companion had been Hernando Cactus, justice of the Ontario Court (since promoted) and eligible widower about town. A somewhat alcohol-injected donnybrook ensued between the two ageing lion-judges, fighting over middle-aged Penny and compelling the proprietors to evict Justice Mariner from said upscale diner, in the middle of a work day, hard by the law courts. Not the sort of news Her Majesty likes to read about her higher court justices as she sits down to her fried bread, sausages, and beans of a morning.

Worse, Mr. Justice Cactus lodged a formal complaint with the Canadian Judicial Council, and while the council was at it, they decided to have a sniff around whether His Lordship was in fact canoodling with his lissom articling student. An embarrassing sort of "trial" ensued, resulting, of course, in an acquittal for Justice Mariner on all counts. *Sir, you are free to go.* Well, more or less.

I refer you to *Tune* for the gory details. Suffice it to say that the stigma remained. And so, the Chief Justice resorted to what is known here, north of the forty-ninth degree of latitude, as stick-handling. In other (non-hockey) words, the Chief Justice offered Ted Mariner and his nearly thirty years of legal experience at the bar on short-term loan to the Mervin Goldfarb and Estelle Holstein-Goldfarb School of Law at Scarborough University — the Farb, as it is known to familiars who want to save their breath for retirement. "A little six-month sabbatical for you, Ted," the CJ explained, "to allow time and tide to soften the pecker on your recent peccadilloes. A nice break from the quotidian stress and strain, as it were. You'll make a fine law teacher, I'm sure." Here the Chief Justice patted old Ted on the shoulder, like a cow he was sending out to pasture. "Call it your semester abroad."

Exile, is what His Lordship called it, actually. Banishment to the 'burbs. Outlawry in the original sense of a bad boy condemned to life literally beyond the law's protection. Anyone could take a pot-shot at you and turn your hide in for the reward. That's what outlaws were, originally, you know. Truly hors la loi. Out(side the)law. Talk about giving a dog a bad name.

And in the end I had to agree with Ted Mariner's assessment of the situation — Exile — just as I was about to be consigned to the garden shed at 1415 Elysian Fields North. Solitary confinement. Outlawry. Exile.

CHAPTER 2

A mixture of a lie doth ever add pleasure . . . but it is not the
lie that passeth through the mind, but the lie that sinketh in,
and settleth in it, that doth the hurt.
Francis Bacon, *Essays*, "Of Truth"

THE FACTS

*Nathalie Robicheaux is Canadian blueblood on at least her father's
side. She grew up in Annapolis Royal, Nova Scotia, very near to where
the Europeans first settled in Canada during 1604. Her mother is a
Dutch immigrant, but Dad traces his roots back to those first Euro-
pean settlers, pioneer immigrants from France who believed that in
the New World they had found the Promised Land. Thus, in those
days was Canada called Acadia — from the Latin for "earthly paradise,"* Arcadia. *Eden.*

*But as often occurs, not until Nathalie had children of her own
did she pay much attention to her family history. As her son Omer
and her daughter Willy grew and studied history in school, they began
to ask difficult questions about their Acadian background. Why was
it that so few people in Nova Scotia and the other maritime provinces
spoke French any more? Why did their French ancestors join with
Indian bands and the Americans to fight the British, who anyway
became the principal power in what we now call Canada? Why did
the British governors so despise the Acadians that they expelled them*

from the country, forcing them to seek refuge in the United States and even Britain? And why did some people still hate French-Canadians so vehemently today?

These historical complexities and Nathalie Robicheaux's embarrassing ignorance of her own heritage energized her. By nature "a doer," she became an activist for the preservation and promotion of Acadian culture. She helped establish cultural awareness events and French-language training for members of her community who were interested in such things. And her neighbours mostly responded with enthusiasm. The renewed focus on their region's interesting history as the birthplace of modern, multi-cultural Canada became a wellspring, they believed, of community pride and heritage, and also a source of tourism and other economic resources. So it was with some surprise that Nathalie opened her e-mail one day to find t

It seems that even in the garden shed, Justice Mariner is to find no peace to write the court's decision in *R. v. Pasties*. His bark being worse than his bite, he has donned an old cardigan and his baseball cap of many colours (blinding yellow, with **Port Hope Jazz Festival** printed in various hues: you can't miss him in a crowd or at a distance), and he keeps me company while I "settle into the little old shed." He has plugged his laptop computer into the outlet that runs the pump in his garden pond, six feet or so from the shed's open barn-style doors. "Not to worry, old son," he has said, patting my head as he sits on a decrepit stool he keeps here for taking refuge from the household hurly-burly. "It's not winter quite yet." Then, observing that "Besides, George Bernard Shaw wrote some of his better plays, you know, in a garden shed," he smiles and taps away at his reasons for judgment.

I take the opportunity to catch my breath, at last, and survey the prospect from the doorway, where we have taken shelter. Eight or ten feet to the left of us sits the more official doghouse — the real one, that is, the one meant to lodge the Mariners' idiot golden retriever, Stong,* though generally he manages to con his way into the main house of an evening. Still, the shed is not at all uncomfortable, particularly when one dosses down in the old laundry basket the judge keeps there, piled high with the burlap, old potato sacks, and the plastic sheeting he uses to protect his plants from frost. Though several years old, the shed has the lovely aroma of fresh-cut lumber — the bouquet, somehow, of freedom, of forests, of rain. Set on four inches of pea gravel and inch-thick paving stones, and fitted by the judge himself from a prefab unit he bought at Home Depot, the little outbuilding is dry and cozy. It even has a couple of mullioned windows on either side of its double doors. Avid gardener that he is, His Lordship keeps the interior clean and tidy, his lawn mower, spades, hoes, and rakes arranged along the walls or on hooks near the ceiling, his gardening pots, trowels, and gloves carefully stacked on shelves, the paving-stone floor regularly swept free of leaves and earth. You could eat off it, and often I do. We are more than a little relieved to be here.

But then Penny lets the idiot Stong out the sliding doors at the deck, and he comes bounding at us, whining and slavering like the

---

*You will recall that Stong is so named on the advice of James Thurber (another favourite writer of His Lordship) in his essay, "How to Name a Dog." One day, Thurber explains, he visited a dog-owner who sheepishly admitted naming his hound Thurber. The dog-owner's name (you guessed it) rhymed with pong, Stong Mariner's being unusually ripe, given his inexplicable fondness for swimming in mucky streams and lakes.

illiterate frat boy he'll always be. "Pen, I'm trying to work here," His Lordship whines. But the sliding doors have long since slammed shut. Try saying that three times fast, and you'll get some idea what Stong's enthusiasm does to our thoughtful composition on the subject of judicial notice.

Fortunately, His Lordship keeps handy in the shed some rawhide chews, which might explain Stong's enthusiasm on seeing the doors flung wide, with the judge seated near the shelf which holds the coffee tin of leather stewed in cattle or pork renderings. Fobbed off with faux flesh (yes, three times fast and all that), Stong trots back up to the deck with his booty, and we get back to chewing up and spitting out Mr. Ian Luther Pasties.

Nathalie opened her e-mail one day to find the following message:

THE BIG LIE!!!
Ever asked yourself this: If the Acadians were "expelled" in 1659, why are they as common as welfare cheques in what used to be Acadia and the rest of Canada? Is their [sic] really any hard evidence for the so-called "expulsion"? Or could it be politically-correct folklore, the foundation of the grander French separatist scheme, to continually hold the rest of North America hostage to special-interest demands for bilingualism, tax breaks, pork-barrel projects in francophone ridings, and MONEY MONEY MONEY??!!!
(Our TAX money!!!)
Is it really just coincidence that four of Canada's last five prime minister's [sic] are from Quebec?
The francophones already have their own country —
OURS!

To find out more about this historical on-going conspiracy, and to join us in doing something about it, visit our website at . . .

Horrified, yet intrigued, Nathalie Robicheaux followed the link in the e-mail to the website. There she

"Ted!" Penny stands on the patio in her house slippers and apron, holding the cordless phone. "It's Sandy!" That would be Sandy Pargeter, His Lordship's secretary at the Court of Appeal. "She wants to know if Sid Fierstein's articling students* can use your office. The new clerks. As they're hard up for space and you won't be around the place for awhile."

"Bad news travels fast, eh boy?" the judge asks me. I blink assent. Then again, his past marital problems would have been old hat to his colleagues on the bench, not to mention half the country's legal profession. To Penny he yells, "Do they have to?"

"Ted!" Penny is highly successful at pantomiming extreme irritation. Then she hisses, presumably because the trees have ears: "How the hell should I know?"

"Well, okay, I guess, if they don't touch anything."

There is a suspenseful pause as Mrs. Mariner listens to Sandy. Then:

"Sandy says should she put your judicial robes in mothballs?"

"Bloody hell," His Lordship mutters. "*Et tu*, Sandy."

At this rate, it seems we won't get through even the basic facts

---

*In Canada and other Commonwealth countries, law students must serve an apprenticeship — in the jargon, work as articled clerks or articling students — and pass examinations administered by the provincial law society before being called to practise at the bar of that province.

of *R. v. Pasties.* I shall cut to the chase for you, courtesy of the final, edited version as it will eventually appear in *Ontario Reports:*

Nathalie Robicheaux discovered that this nasty article Pasties was not just your garden variety racist. He was on a mission. "Frog-bashing" was his life's work. Robicheaux managed to get him charged with spreading false news (*Criminal Code* section 181), but the trial judge ruled that the offence was unconstitutional as an unreasonable limit on free expression: Pasties had the right to express his anti-French views, no matter how repellent. On that basis, the trial judge acquitted Pasties, and the Crown appealed the ruling to the Ontario Court of Appeal — which is how, you will now understand, His Lordship ended up trying to write the appeal court's reasons for judgment.

Yet to get full and fair disclosure of THE FACTS and my role on the case as junior counsel, you still need to know how and why I escaped lawful custody and came to be arrested by the perspiration-challenged Wayne, animal control officer by special appointment to Her Majesty. Re-enter Penny Mariner, to provide us all a bit of highly relevant evidence to that purpose:

"Ted!" There she is on the deck again, some fifty yards away, frowning, waving the portable phone. "Now it's Mack Herskowitz. He says he's done his best but your bloody cat's run off again somewhere, electronic monitoring device and all."

His Lordship and I exchange bemused gazes as he leans over to remove said device from my chafing neck.

Home, more or less sweet, home.

CHAPTER 3

I will endeavour to explain to you why I am called wise and
have such an evil fame.

Plato's *Apology*

Who in tarnation, you reasonably ask, is this arch-servant of injustice, gaoler to the wrongfully convicted, this Maccabeus, a.k.a. Mack, Herskowitz?

The short answer is that he is a professor of law at said newfangled Farb, built by the Mervin Goldfarbs out of the vast proceeds of Merv's enterprises in strip-mall and "affordable" condominium development, a.k.a. post-Aztec cliff dwellings. As with most of said properties in the Goldfarb empire, the university is set like a space station in the suburbs, just east of Toronto proper in a quasi-wasteland — all the drearier in its quasitude than were it a complete and utter Nowhere, a no-person's land of windburnt asphalt, dust-blasted strip malls, and the occasional oil refinery wafting its malignant air over public gardening allotments scattered as consolation prizes to Mother Nature. The Gulag, as Justice Mariner has taken to calling it in his exile there from the Court of Appeal. And that it had become for the both of us, orthodox urbanites banished like outlaws to the Far Territories, not unlike Robin Hood and his not-so-merry men, sore-footed and dusty exiles, literally outside the law's protection.

But why me? you naturally ask again, impatiently, as Your Roving Correspondent has asked about himself many times in the past days. Well, after reconciling with Penny and discovering I was not welcome as an adoptee in the matrimonial home, His Lordship did the decent thing, really, checking around for potential official guardians to Amicus, Q.C., for Quixotic Customer (and Questing Cat). He approached another of his former law clerks, for instance, Leland Gaunt, known to my regular readers as defence counsel in the murder prosecutions of Katrina Slovenskaya (see the first volume of my memoirs, *Murder at Osgoode Hall*) and of the great jazz musician, Des Cheshire, of the aforementioned *Murder's Out of Tune*. Leland pleaded allergies, himself — and if you know him, you will accept the plea as pathetically credible. But, desirous of remaining in His Lordship's good books, he promised to ask around at the law school.

"That would work out nicely," Justice Mariner replied. "I'm teaching there next term, you know, Lee. We'll be colleagues again."

"Oh, yeah, Judge? Super. What will you teach?"

"Oh, a bit of this and that, I guess. They've put me down so far for Legal Profession — you know, the lawyer in society and history, legal ethics, law and morality, the nature of legal education, that sort of thing."

Gaunt nodded, clicking his double-jointed jaw. "Mack Herskowitz's baby."

"That's it. He's giving it up for the term so I can take it on, and he'll concentrate on his institute. That Wrongfully Acquitted Institute of his, or whatever he calls it."

The two men made wry faces. "Well, why don't I ask him

about little Amicus Curious?" Gaunt said, trying to pat me as I
deked sveltely to avoid it. "Ever since Mack's divorce, he's lived in
the student housing, in one of those towers they built right across
from the law school. It would be perfect. The penthouse. You
could visit little Amicus every school day."

"Thanks, Lee. That'd be super. And at your earliest conven-
ience, if you wouldn't mind. Penny's not an Amicus fan, you
know. And the options are limited, if you see what I mean. Mark
file 'Urgent.'"

Sure enough, the Farb Gulag is where Professor Maccabeus
Theodor Herskowitz runs, wouldn't you know it, his Institute for
the Wrongly Acquitted Criminal, IWAC for short, pronounced,
emphatically, I-WHACK. I kid you not — although, to be fair, the
institution is not as bizarre as it sounds. Mack, as he is known to
his familiars (Jerk-O-Twit, Jerk-O-Snits, and, particularly at exam-
time, Jerk-O-Shits to some of his more puerile students), founded
the centre as the crime victim's response to those organizations for
the wrongfully convicted, several of which are based, indeed, at law
schools. Having set up IWAC after that jury in California acquitted
sports celebrity O.J. Simpson of the slasher-murder of his wife and
her male friend, Herskowitz declares IWAC's unofficial motto to be
"Giving new life to dead cases."

Like mine, I suppose. And possibly, as you shall see, his own.

∿◦◦∿

So, His Lordship was anyway making the trek to Scarberia (as
Scarborough is semi-affectionately known to downtowners) to visit
Herskowitz in his penthouse at the Farb and discuss the transfer of

power re: Legal Profession to the judge as visiting professor. On the principle that you can't go home again, or at least your cat can't, Justice Mariner schlepped Yours Unwanted along in the Humpty Dumpty potato chip box that, accessorized with a worn army surplus blanket and a layer of my own fine black hair, generally serves as my bed.

Being a bit of a *bon vivant* and portly with it, Herskowitz transacted business with the judge over white port and unpasteurized Sicilian cacciocavello (at sixty-five bucks a kilo, a particular redolent favourite of Your Quadripedal Gourmand). "They order it in for me specially," he explained, "at La Salumeria on Yonge Street." As the wine and cheese became a mauzy memory, and over La Salumeria's biscotti and Swiss chocolate with hazelnuts, it was arranged that Justice Mariner was to feature as a guest of honour at Mack's upcoming High Table, the dinner Herskowitz throws *chez lui* for law school faculty and students at the beginning of each term. Then, as Herskowitz licked the last biscotti crumbs from his fingers, His Lordship cleared his throat.

"I hate to mention it, Mack, and I'm embarrassed to abuse your splendid hospitality, but there's just one more thing."

"Mm?" Herskowitz replied, his mouth crammed full.

"About my, uh, cat, here. I was wondering if you were, well, expecting him, as it were."

His Lordship went on to explain that when he said his cat he didn't really mean *his* cat, it was more like this sort of problem he'd inherited, little Amicus Curiae, so-called, friend of the court but if you looked under both mischief and nuisance in *Black's Law Dictionary*, you'd see his picture there — Amicus adversarius, really. Oh, but, you know, don't get him wrong (the judge hastened, you couldn't help noticing, to add), he didn't mean to say that I was really any trouble. It was the *responsibility*, he meant, of taking care of a pet and all that. His daughter's and granddaughter's allergies, when they visited — which was fairly often, even though the grand-kids lived in Calgary. Actually, I was quite a little helper, and pretty damn smart, to boot. Here the judge sipped at the caffe latte Herskowitz had made in his own espresso machine, smacked his lips, and added, "For a cat, anyway." He just meant, didn't Herskowitz see, that his wife wouldn't have little Amicus, nor would they allow him back in the Great Library at Osgoode downtown, where the staff originally had taken him in as a sort of homeless case. Allergies, the smell, and all that again. Well, not the smell really (here, His Lordship engaged in a bit of nervous, not to say girlish, giggling) — wasn't that bad — just, you know, regulations, public buildings . . . But mostly it was because people had allergies, that was all. Same went for his former student and clerk, now Herskowitz's colleague teaching Criminal Law I, etc., Leland Gaunt, who might have mentioned the matter to Herskowitz . . .

Herskowitz didn't bat an eye. "How does the mischievous nuisance feel about penthouse apartments?" he asked. He poked at me with a cheesy finger as I sniffed from my box, stretching suggestively toward the crumbs on the otherwise cheese-bereft plate. The professor waggled a dirty nail at me, offering beggar-all refreshment to this other house guest.

How did *I* feel about his penthouse, not that he really cared? Life at the top is not my idea of any life at all, particularly the top of an exurban apartment tower. The Gulag. As a lifetime street scholar and boulevardier — a true *clochard* — I could not rest from travel.

For always roaming with a hungry heart
Much have I seen and known . . .
Translation: *Hiss and piss and piss and shit on Jerk-O-Twit's favourite Persian carpet.*

༄

Yes, hiss and piss, piss and shit! Conditional sentence. That's what the *Criminal Code* calls it. *Hiss and piss, piss and shit!* Lately Her Majesty has decided that Her Household Budget no longer runs to enrolling every drunkard and five-finger-discount artist in her finishing schools for the professional criminal, a.k.a. the state correctional facilities lately styled as "institutions." (Mustn't bruise the sensibilities of Her loyal rapists and murderers by banging them up in anything called a jail or penitentiary.) Also, She seems to have concluded that rehabilitation is best achieved by letting many customers serve their sentences "in the community" — at home, in other words. In return for such mild indulgence, the convict must "report to a supervisor," *Code* section 742.1 says, "keep the peace and be of good behaviour," and anything else the judge dreams up in a conniption fit of social engineering. Like making one wear that so-called monitoring device, a.k.a. electronic bracelet, for instance. *Hiss and piss, piss and shit.* That's why they call it a *conditional* sentence: if you mess up, you go straight to Her Majesty's Doghouse, do not pass Go, do not serve your time in your own La-Z-Boy in front of the idiot box, with your ankle bracelet up on the built-in hassock. But of course "conditional sentence" is just house arrest by a five-dollar name.

So hiss and spit and piss and shit on Jerk-O-Snit's favourite

Persian carpet, the tea-washed one in the living room — his beloved, highly expensive, one-of-a-kind novelty tapestry bedecked with red urns and golden blooms and cornflower blue curlicue what's-its, and, look, look, don't you see?, fornicating couples, too, look, look, can you see them, poker-faced Indians going at it like rabbits who've read the *Kama Sutra*? He's on the edge of his seat waiting for you to spot them and, of course, for you to react when you do . . .

And His Orneriness didn't take kindly to coitus interruptus by shredding as I claw-raked these gymnastic lovers *in flagrante delicto*, though they didn't seem really to be enjoying themselves, anyway. It was arguable (as we say over at the Court of Appeal) that one could enliven the proceedings by doing the old S&M manicure number on their emotionless sex-manual exertions. But of course, that — my private prosecution of the lovers for public indecency — was all part of my Great Escape Plan, my scheme to piss off old Professor Herskowitz royally, so that he swore off me and life as my parole officer.

And it worked quickly, after a fashion. During my house arrest with him I had essayed more direct stratagems, of course, such as my daring high-wire performance on the railing of his balcony fourteen stories in the air. This succeeded as a quintessentially feline reconnaissance mission, assuring me that the balcony was not a feasible escape route, never mind those human rumours that so-called cat burglars climb from one to the other of such structures on skyscrapers. In all other respects, my circus maneuver failed miserably. I was snatched up with a cry of horror (a sort of duet from both Herskowitz and Yours Foiled Again), then banged up in solitary confinement, which is to say the well-appointed interior of the Jerk-O-Twit's penthouse. (Imagine, if you will, being trapped in a sort of *art nouveau* time warp, leather furniture on the fine imported Persians, Indians, Afghanis, whatever — Herskowitz is a collector, you see, of silk Tabriz and Qum, Isfahan, Nain, Sarough, Bidjar, Kashan, Nain, Mashad . . . hand-woven, no doubt, by enslaved six-year-olds. Then there's the French abstract art on the walls, Charlie Mingus on the stereo — all in all, his apartment's best described as early Hugh Hefner meets late Sigmund Freud.) "You end up like Sylvester splattered all over the pavement," he had scolded, whisky-and-herring- breathed, as he frequently is, "your judge is going to send me straight to the cala-boose." Prescient, that. Anyway, I was banned thereafter from parading on the little concrete cliff which had served as my only exercise yard.

But because the professor frequently receives business parcels, the UPS man provided an Escape Plan B that nearly succeeded. I began making it my habit to greet the couriers effusively, wan-dering innocently into the hallway to rub around their legs in cheery welcome. Soon it was no trick at all to follow one of them to the elevator. That was how I ended up wearing an electronic monitoring collar. Herskowitz cadged a spare one off a cop he knew through his Institute for the Wrongfully Acquitted — a peace officer only too pleased to assist "the rare lawyer who's on the good guys' side." "Can't afford to piss off a judge at the Court of Appeal, can we, your friend there?" the cop agreed with Her-skowitz, fixing the cursed device around my poor balding neck.

So I was well and truly under house arrest, left with nothing but shredding the tony King Street furniture and collectors' car-pets. I mean, seriously: Your Urbane Boulevardier, banged up day and night, night and day, in a penthouse apartment at a student housing complex in the suburban tundra! Outlawed. Exiled.

∾ꔮ∾

As I say, this last, and admittedly most unimaginative, tactic (the hissing and spitting and shitting and shredding, I mean) proved some greater success. It at least got me out on day parole, because it heartily discouraged Herskowitz from leaving me on my own in his well-appointed digs. Instead, he began schlepping me around in a Canadian Tire pet carrier, and I spent the workday with him in his office and classrooms, for some continuing legal education on such subjects as Corporation Law, Torts, and Maccabeus Herskowitz himself. It was thanks to Torts,* in fact, where I shared MW 9-11 a.m. (as the timetable put it) with some thirty-five other miserable inmates, that I at last enjoyed liberation from "false imprisonment" (pages 118-136 in the course casebook) via my "trespass to chattels" (pages 22-60 suggest that vandalizing the bejesus out of somebody's home furnishings qualifies under this heading). It was like this:

There is the professor in full flight, talking, in fact, about trespass to chattels and using Yours Wrongfully Convicted as a teaching aid. The innocent enslaved yet again in service to humankind. "Mr. Fergus." As is his wont, and in the Socratic tradition,

---

*Torts, from the French for "wrongs," is the broad area of private liability that impels humans to purchase insurance. Because it covers a wide spectrum of intentional harm, accidents, and negligence (from assaults to car accidents to medical malpractice), law students call it "everything Mom warned you about."

Herskowitz chooses a student not quite at random, settling on the poor sod who seems least likely to know the answer. "My cat, here."

His cat?

"*Ferae naturae* would you say, Mr. Fergus? Hmm?"

We have been discussing how, in times past, the law regarded the skin of a dead dog as private property, but the live dog itself usually was *ferae naturae*, a free-roaming beast incapable of human ownership. The upshot for tort law was, unless Fido regularly herded your sheep, you'd have a bloody time of it showing ownership or that you'd suffered any money damages when some neighbour filled him full of lead shot.

I peer out of my carrier at wide-eyed Dougal Fergus, awaiting his callow verdict from where he sits in the back row of the stadium-seating classroom, unsuccessfully trying to hide behind his laptop computer. He prevaricates. "Well, I guess he doesn't seem very free-roaming right now, anyways, does he?"

General laughter at one's caged expense.

"You guess that, do you? And I'll ask the questions. Of Ms. Hnatyshyn, for instance. Ms. Hnatyshyn, do you have an equally-pathetic, totally non-lawyerly guess about the property-law status of this overfed vermin?"

"Well, sort of. I mean, today he'd be like personal property, wouldn't he?" Seated just two rows from Herskowitz's desk, Hnatyshyn glances over her shoulder at Fergus, commiserating. "As somebody's pet, like? He belongs to you, sort of. So taking him would be a theft, like?"

"Who sort of said anything about, like, sort of criminal charges?" Herskowitz erupts, going all red in the face. "Like. Sort of look at your timetable, Ms. Hnatyshyn, hmm? I believe it says something about torts."

Anthony "Tony" Albinoni does not raise his hand. He simply calls out, "Well, like, let's sort of put it this way. You say he's your cat, but we all know that he can't be associating with you by choice."

Nervous general tittering. I lift my left upper lip to signify my shackled agreement.

"So he's, whaddayacall, fairly domesticus, or whatever it is."

"Domitae ferae," Herskowitz corrects, glaring at Albinoni. Generally, Herskowitz's Socratic method is of the strictest purity, all questions, no responses, the answers supposedly being inherent in his questions, although most of the students despair of sorting it out, until by exam time at the end of term they achieve hysterical panic, coupled with unremitting hatred of Herskowitz. Or so I have heard. And he loves it, no doubt. Apparently his inevitable response when they complain to him, and ultimately to the dean of the law school, will be: "The only answer in law is 'it depends.' That is no answer at all, but it is the law's answer. The law's answer is a question. Always roaming with a hungry heart, the law provides no final answers. In law, there is no final truth."

The students find this supremely irritating, of course, all the more because he delivers it like Elizabeth I coldly ordering that they be hanged and pulled into quartered segments by the royal horses, after which their bloody heads are to be mounted on pikestaffs outside Newgate Prison. Yet when Herskowitz can use the old declarative sentence as a weapon, he goes for the jugular, all in the name of training young advocates. *"Domitae ferae,* tamed beasts, much like the majority of you so-called law students. And, judging by your performance today, 'tamed' is a gross exaggeration." Then he scoffs, almost spitting on the floor, "'Fairly domesticus!'" Herskowitz shouts, making several students jump: *Domitae ferae! Domitae ferae!*"

"Whatever." Albinoni tosses his greasy black hair, flicking away the Latin as irrelevant, never mind his own heritage. He wears a dress shirt and slacks, but of discount store sheen. His face is greasy, hawkish, and proud, but overall he has the look, not uncommon among feral cats (*sylvestri naturae*, as we barristers put it), that humans call lean and hungry — or skinny and disgruntled, in his case. "It's demonstrable that you've forced your will on the poor little kitty and therefore you have domesticated him. So he's personal property."

"So you say — on the bald assumption, apparently, that my will has anything to do with how the law classifies property." Herskowitz sneers, projecting skepticism in his tone, while I do the same in my squint through the bars of my cell.

"Yes, I do say, in fact. And I think if somebody stole him or let him out or whatever, *you* would get damages for trespass, justice being mostly a parlour trick by and for the benefit of the legal profession and their richest clients. But see, to me it's the cat who *deserves* damages, for having to put up with you like we do, involuntarily . . . "

As much as I might agree with the cheeky sentiment, I present this scene by way of painting the broader tableau. You perhaps have detected from the interchange that, like Socrates, Mack Herskowitz is one of those messianic types you find among teachers — confident, ebullient, bright, persuasive, but also highly opinionated, extravagantly arrogant, a plausible bully. Like messiahs and the philosopher-teacher Socrates (executed via a tea infused

with the poison hemlock, you will recall, for blasphemy and misleading the youth of Athens), Herskowitz makes a lot of disciples,
but also many vocal and dangerous enemies. Tony Albinoni, for
one, does not seem especially enamoured of the Socratic method
of legal education.

∾ᴏᴇ∾

Which is why some find it passing strange that he works as a
research assistant to Herskowitz, helping the professor with his
biography of Francis Bacon, now in its seventh year of production.
When asked about the seeming disconnect, Albinoni shrugs, by all
accounts, and replies, "Actually, it's a match made in Heaven. I
need the money, he needs my grunt work. Also, law's become so
cut-throat, I need his cred. In that respect, everybody wants to
work with Mack Herskowitz, even all those guys writing 'Hemlock for Herskowitz!' in the law school's toilet stalls. I mean, this
dude's well connected, you know."

Which was irrefutable. Herskowitz had deliberately modelled
himself on his Elizabethan mentor, Sir Francis, a serious man of
letters, of course (some say he wrote the plays generally attributed
to Shakespeare), but Bacon's claustrophobia in the ivory tower
drove him to become a mover and shaker at the highest levels, a
personal acquaintance of the king and queen, a man of action and
of letters. Like the calculating Bacon, Herskowitz had all the same
bases covered.

First, of course, his institute was enormously popular among
those of a certain political class which had the means to endow
their favourite right-of-centre, law-and-order causes. Herskowitz

had married and divorced well, too, with and from none other than Becky Holstein-Goldfarb, princess-daughter of strip-mall/cliff-dweller royalty Mervin and Estelle, prime founders of the Farb law school. Becky had begun life in a grotty walk-up flat off lower Spadina Avenue, where her mother borrowed gardening books from the local library and mooned over a golden future in a suburban castle. One by one she made sure her three daughters personified her dream. Instead of Rosemary, Marigold, and Susie, Estelle named the girls Rosemarinus, Calendula, and Rudbeckia (for "Black-Eyed Susan"), on the theory that the airy bouquet of the Latin botanicals would lend an upwardly mobile trend to their lives and the family's general fortune. It worked, perhaps, although Mervin and Estelle became rich with such sudden, dizzying force that Estelle was left as breathless as an overnight duchess (at the first million dollars, she was not yet queen, quite). She forswore the actual landscaping at her new stately home in suburban Rich-mond Hill and expediently hired a crew from Sheridan Nurseries. Inevitably the girls had long since become Rosie, Cal, and Becky, and every one of them loathed the outdoors, let alone household gardening (all that dirt, all those bugs and animals). They fancied the landscapers from Sheridan Nurseries well enough, though, one of them being Mack Herskowitz on summer break from his stu-dent days at Osgoode Hall Law School.

Mack and Becky married while Herskowitz served as a clerk to a particularly dyspeptic justice at the Supreme Court of Canada. Not long thereafter, the Herskowitzes had two sons, Hillel and Aaron, now teenagers who attended the best private schools and still lived with Becky in Richmond Hill. Like their mother, maternal grandparents, and just about everybody else, the boys blamed Mack for the breakdown of the marriage, but happily accepted the many gifts and holidays he lavished on them — which generosity was of course seen by them and everybody else as symptomatic of paternal guilt, something to exploit to the maximum: Nobody, it seemed, really liked Mack Herskowitz, not even the fruit of his loins. Still, out of the division of family property, Mack took a condo at Harbourfront, which the boys and their friends sometimes used, managing to suppress their bitter feelings toward their father while Mack lived on campus at the Farb — paternal guilt, conceivably, preventing him from renting out the condo to actual paying tenants.

∾෴෴∾

Anyway, I have wandered, as is my feline habit. Of course you are impatient still and again to hear about The Great Escape. Well, I had an accessory, what Canuck law calls a party to the offence — and it was rather a laugh for us all. Picture it:

It is ten o'clock and time for the break in Torts, Herskowitz, MW 9-11 a.m. His Jerk-O-liness is off like a shot, to call his broker or carpet repair-person or divorce lawyer-person, no doubt. Several students come up to poke at and mewl over Yours Subject to Torture. Albinoni picks up my carrier and heads toward the door.

"Tony, what're you doing?" Hnatyshyn asks, aghast.

"Well, the implication is he's fair-eyed naturally, right?, a beast of the wilds who belongs to no-o-o-body?"

General tittering.

"Fairly naturely," Hnatyshyn corrects, scowling fairly schoolmarmishly.

"Whatever."

The Farb's front door being only about thirty yards from the classroom, Albinoni transports me there, places my carrier on the pavement, and sets me loose on the grounds.

Free at last, thank Tony almighty, we are free at last!

Apparently Albinoni then closed the carrier door and took the Canadian Tire rig back into the classroom such that Herskowitz didn't discover it was a case of *felis absconditus* (in the vernacular: the cat didn't come back) until he went to lift the thing after class, at eleven o'clock. Staggering backward with the lack of counter-balancing weight, he would have noticed that the students had absconded quickly themselves, leaving the Jerk-O-Snit alone, I imagine, and palely marvelling at my Houdiniliness. I can't say for sure, because I had trotted off at high tail, following the bus-stop markers along Midland Avenue until the Kennedy bus wheezed up at last and I was able to scoot aboard, unnoticed at the feet of a scrum of Scarborough U. students. Which is the how and why of my encounter with sweaty Wayne S., Animal Control Officer, at the Kennedy subway station, the bus terminus. *Home, James!* And thus is the first mystery solved.

CHAPTER 4

Certainly it is heaven upon earth to have a man's
mind move in charity, rest in providence, and
turn upon the poles of truth.
Francis Bacon, *Essays*, "Of Truth"

THE LAW

"Publishing or spreading false news" is a form of defamation. It has similarities to other rabble-rousing offences against public order, such as sedition and hate-mongering. It is rooted in the Statute of Westminster, 1275, which called the crime scandalum magnatum. *On something of the reasoning of sharia law practised in some Muslim cultures, the Elizabethans lopped off the ears of scolds — those who scandalized over the fence and in taverns — and the hands of scribbling libellers.*

It is a brisker fall day. Yellow leaves from the Japanese katsura and a nearby beech tree blow about the back yard, among the more numerous and striking red maple discards. It is raining cold fire, you might say. From the shed's open doorway, I can see among the leaves that the pond has a mysterious white cast to its surface, a premonition of imminent frost. Having cut the fingers out of his gardening gloves, the judge sits on his little stool, tapping at his laptop as I watch from the pile of burlap and such in the old laundry basket.

The offence came to us via Sir James Fitzjames Stephen's British Digest of the Criminal Law, 1877 . . .

There is a shadow in the doorway. It is Penny, with Stong gambolling at her side, angling for rawhide. "This looks fun," says Mrs. Mariner, handing the judge a note on raggedy-arsed paper:

Your attendance is required
At Mid-Term High Table

Where:
The Penthouse, Lo-Karb-Kola™ Towers
The Mervin Goldfarb and Estelle Holstein-Goldfarb School of Law
at Scarborough University

When:
All Hallow's Eve (Oct. 31),
seven-thirty p.m. for eight

Attire:
Academic/barristerial (tabs, waistcoat, gown),
business or costume dress for civilians

R.S.V.P.
Prof. Maccabeus T. Herskowitz
416-555-0486

Politics and self-proclaimed messianism have made Mack Herskowitz many enemies, but of course his ability to box clever is also the secret of his success. Twice a year, fall mid-term and at spring finals, he more or less redeems himself within and without the Farb when he throws his "High Table Gourmet Nights." His Jerk-O-liness invites as many as two dozen guests to his on-campus penthouse, prepares the more or less haute cuisine himself, and serves up the finest wines and spirits from his own cellar — a wine refrigerator in a lock-up. in the parking garage, the lock-up being situated next to the building's laundry room and meant for student trunks and bicycles. (Herskowitz was able to appropriate the area by terrifying the superintendent with his Socratic-Baconian manner.) He's not much out of pocket, gossip says, dipping instead — in the name of "advertising and promotion" as the income tax authorities call it — into the trust account held by his Institute for the Wrongly Acquitted Criminal for its operating funds. Whether he means these uxorious evenings to make amends for his habitual arrogance — as a sort of Serf Appreciation Day — or he uses the dinners as part of his usual game of keeping everyone else off balance, I will leave it to you, patient reader, to decide as the ultimate trier of fact. However you rule, you will see that the fall mid-term affair was to be his Last Such Supper.

How do I know this juicy tidbit? The fall has been mild enough that my banishment remains half-hearted. I accompany His Lordship on his daily commute to and from the Farb, and on our return *chez* Mariner each afternoon or evening, outlawed from the matrimonial home, I spend the night in the domesticated wilds of Forest Hill — nightly rounds of the garbage bins at the chi-chi coffee shops on Spadina Road; a nosey through the back alleys toward Upper Canada College (which likes to think of itself as Canada's Eton); and finally a stroll of the school's grounds, topped off with a midnight snack in the skips outside the cafeteria before I head home to the garden shed of 1415 Elysian Fields

North. So that I may allegedly spend the wee hours indoors, albeit without heat, the judge lately has installed a little cat flap in the shed's double doors. Then, as His Lordship skims the *Globe and Mail* with his morning coffee and toasted whole wheat bagel, for me it's Friskie's Gourmet Turkey in Chunks in said shed (Turkey and Pâté Tuesday, Thursday, Sunday) before the new day's commute to the Farb. This particular morning, we have no classes. So it's a spot of *al fresco* decision-rendering (the gentler maple-tree variety of our confederation, not the derided "palm-tree justice" of so-called banana republics) while the mind is clear, then we'll clean the windows and eavestroughs before winter sets in good and proper.

"Yes, absolutely," the judge says to Penny, handing back Herskowitz's invitation. "We'll go. I think I have to."

"I think you do," Penny says, "as the so-called guest of honour." And she heads back to the house with the idiot mutt.

In 1987 this court had occasion to consider the constitutionality of the scandalizing offence. In that case, the trial court convicted a German immigrant of spreading false news after he published booklets attacking generally-accepted views on the persecution and murder of Jews by the Nazis. The historical revisionist appealed, arguing that the Charter of Rights and Freedoms *guaranteed his right of free speech in such matters. A five-judge appeal panel unanimously concluded that the "spreading false news" law was constitutional as a reasonable limitation on free expression. However, the panel also ruled that the trial judge erred in accepting without any evidence that the Holocaust was an historical event. That is, this court stated that the trial judge could not simply take "judicial notice" of the Holocaust as a factual event. Given that the actuality of the Holocaust was directly in issue in the trial, the trial judge was obliged (this court said) to hear evidence on the truth (or not) of the Holocaust.*

In this case, we have some striking similarities. Mr. Pasties seeks to deny the historical truth of the expulsion of the Acadians from Canada by the British colonizers. The trial judge ruled that he did not need to hear evidence on the expulsion, because it was "so notorious as a fact of Canadian history as to be beyond dispute." He said he was able to take judicial notice of the expulsion without hearing proof. Mr. Pasties disagrees. He says his case is the same as that of the Holocaust revisionist.

CHAPTER 5

He that dies in an earnest pursuit is like one that is wounded
in hot blood, who for the time scarce feels the hurt.
Francis Bacon, *History of Life and Death*

Because we are not heading straight home this particular Hallowe'en, I end up crashing Herskowitz's Hallowe'en High Table
shindig. His Lordship and I are in formal court apparel for the
grand occasion (our robes remaining unmothballed, despite our
outlawry; mind you, nature has determined that I habitually wear
a gown of barristerial black and white stripes down my chest posi-
tioned very much like barristers' tabs), with Penny (who has
driven the new Subaru Forester out here to meet us) looking very
elegant in a gown she bought a couple of years back for the
Mariners' thirtieth wedding anniversary rave (well, party,
anyhow), in a private room at Canoe. I must say, however, that I
kick up something of a ruckus, scrabbling in my carrier as though
that will cause it to go where I want as we relentlessly enter the
elevator at the LoKarb-Kola™ Tower — flashbacks and all that,
post-traumatic stress disorder, they call it in personal injury law.
And truly I have been personally injured in the environs of the
Penthouse Suite. I feel as though I am about to be banged up in
the Herskowitz Maximum Security Institution all over again. If I
had a metal slop cup, I'd scrape it along the bars of my cell.

It must be said, though, that the bouquet of seared meats and steamed vegetables now wafting from the Jerk-O-Twit's suite has the quality of the most sumptuous burnt offerings humans have made to their gods, including cats, anciently. It certainly sets the stomach to rumbling, anyhow, after a gag-making day amid the flat, old-gravy pong that smogs constantly out of the Farb's dining rooms, including the faculty lounge. If you remember junior high school, no doubt you will recall that sad and nauseating perfume. But Herskowitz truly has outdone himself tonight, having rented restaurant-style steam tables and a battalion of servers, students kitted out like annoyed penguins, grim-faced against Mack's marching orders, deking and bustling and trying desperately not to look like they're this close to staging a peasants' revolt. As it is, they have flung off their black velveteen masks after one of their number crashed into a wall with a tray of just-filled champagne flutes. There goes the damage deposit.

That particular disaster cleared away, we are met at the door by the self-appointed greeter, Professor Reginald I. Holdsworth, transplanted from Sheffield, England, and the Farb's most effusive left-wing *provocateur* on the subject of corporate crime and "unethics," as Holdsworth puts it. Among the students he is particularly notorious for his dramatic lecture style, his Business Associations (a.k.a. Corporation Law) class being known in the local argot as The Hush and Holler Hour ("Hush" being whispered, "Holler" shouted, and all aitches pronounced — *hush and HOLLER how-wer*), a description reflecting its roots in Haydn's *Surprise Symphony*, although I don't imagine most of the students have a clue about that. During his classes, "Red Reg" — who vociferously admits to studying corporate law for the sole purpose of keeping his enemies closer than his friends (just as Herskowitz keeps Reg Holdsworth very close, no doubt) — will bow his head over the casebook and whisper, "Let us now read together in our hymnals." Then he will deliver, *sotto voce*, a derisive recitation of the facts of the particular case, camouflaging his foxhole for the coming howl of outrage over what the court decided, generally on the side of corporate greed and social depredation. In short, if you attempt to use Reg Holdsworth's Business Associations class to catch up on your sleep, you quickly learn that you are better off staying in bed. Between a Holdsworth and a very hard Herskowitz, the Farb's genuine business law keeners are driven to sign up for the Jerk-O-Twit's version of Bus. Ass. (as the students dub the course), and settle for a C, if they're lucky.

Amid the background clatter of dishes and scurrying, unmasked penguins, Holdsworth grabs my carrier from Justice Mariner's grip. As I stagger back and forth in the thing like a drunk on a runaway train, Red Reg steers his freight of breathless Mariners to the drinks table, where a haggard-looking young man in fool's motley hands out dry sherries. He toots at us, off-key, on a plastic recorder, then throws us a skew-whiff smile as he clumsily shoves the not very musical instrument into a leather pouch tied to his cord belt. The fool is none other than Tony Albinoni of Holdsworth's Tort Law 101, his coxcomb hat bobbing drunkenly with his pallid head, darkly accented by the smirk on his long, thin mouth. Looking even more dissolute and bitter than usual — *louche*, I believe is the *mot juste*, but perhaps he simply has been pulling those so-called all-nighters (as if being nocturnal were something exotic!), boning up for mid-term examinations — he advises that, although the sherry is South African, the pre-dinner wines are of inferior local vintage. He would recommend holding out for the Barolo that Herskowitz is reserving to go with the meat course. He winks at us, showing some of his blue teeth. Sherry in hand, Holdsworth stows me at the other end of the table, next to the arugula-and-goat-cheese puff pastries and the stuffed manzanilla olives the size of robins' eggs (driving me even wilder with hunger), as he whispers to Justice Mariner, "Sniffy little squirt, what?" He seems to mean young Albinoni, not Yours Incarcerated For Life. Then he bellows at Herskowitz, who stands some distance away with a group of guests, "For shame, Herky. The lad advises that you intend to inflict on us the Canada goose-piss that passes for Ontario wine."

"Always nice to see you, too, Reg." Herskowitz comes over and puts his hand on Albinoni's shoulder. As per, his breath stinks of expensive Scotch whisky. "You've met young Anthony, in his first and probably last year at our esteemed faculty?"

"Know him, and his prospects, well." Holdsworth nods at Albinoni as the judge shakes the student's hand. With my feline acuteness, I can hear Red Reg mutter sideways to His Lordship, "As will you, too, squire, any day now. Bit of a rabble-rouser is our Tony."

Justice Mariner introduces Penny, and without bothering to greet or even actually look at Mrs. Mariner, Herskowitz impatiently signals to a young woman across the room that her presence is required. "I want you to meet someone," he mouths at said *jeune femme*, squinting and gesticulating frenetically. To his guests, he says, "I've got the meal to see to, folks, but I want you to meet Zippy and the boys."

Zippy, they are about to learn, is Herskowitz's live-out girlfriend, law student Zipporah Kyriakos. She is dressed, she says, as

"Anne Boleyn, before she literally lost her head," second wife to Henry VIII and mother of Queen Elizabeth I. And she is truly comely, a bird-like, highly-freckled queen of about twenty-three, with long wiry hair the colour of hay, a confident manner, and an easy intelligence. Mack had met her (I've heard him tell Justice Mariner) while pursuing one of those so-called wrongly acquitted criminals of his. Summarily (as we say over at the Court of Appeal), she was girlfriend to a lawyer named Merdnyk who had committed a gigantic fraud, encompassing his clients, staff, friends, and eventually Kyriakos's mother and grandmother. Although the Crown had been unable to put Merdnyk away (even with Kyriakos's enthusiastic assistance), Mack had pretty well bankrupted him with civil actions, landing both him and Kyriakos in the street. A student of philosophy part-time who danced in strip bars the rest of the time, Zippy had possessed few resources of her own, besides her native ones of beauty, intelligence, and backbone. Now, a few months later, she is assistant director of Mack's institute, a first-year law student (thanks to Mack's championing her cause to the admissions office), and ex-wife Becky Goldfarb-Herskowitz's main excuse for keeping Mack's access to his sons at the bare minimum.

I can report these latter facts with confidence, by the way, as I heard the nasty phone calls when I was resident in the Herskowitz penthouse. In any event, Zippy introduces the Mariners and Red Reg to the host's two sons, fourteen-year-old Hillel, and Aaron, "Hillie's" junior by two years, both of them clad in white dress shirts and black bowties. While they look more like a down-on-their-luck comedy team than a serious brother act — Hillie is gawky, smirky, and tall, while Ari is squat, morose, and swarthy, a miniature Mack Herskowitz — they apparently share a strong mutual desire not to be there, although, or perhaps because, they are in the care of their father's unusually fetching young lover.

At table, which is decorated with fiercely scowling jack-o'-lanterns sitting in phony cobwebs at each end, Holdsworth sits next to the Mariners, preparing to feast on Your Choice Of prime rib or salmon, with mash or granular Basmati rice, tons of veg, pumpkin mousse with maple ice cream, chocolate-almond biscotti, over-boiled coffee, and a Niagara Bench Riesling icewine. As they take their places hard by the drinks table ("He fits in nicely with the All Hallow's theme," Holdsworth insists on remarking of my presence there), I can see that Red Reg is rendered into a particularly favourable mood when a tall, young steward — blonde, female — brings a bottle of Bordeaux to the table, compliments of Herskowitz's private cellar, and presents the label. "That'll do nicely," Holdsworth ways, smacking his lips after the ceremonial foretaste. "Well played, Herky!" he shouts into the steward's bosom, compelling her to spill the Bordeaux on the virgin tablecloth. "All is forgiven!" Clearly Holdsworth is a champagne socialist. And his predilections oil the conversation nicely.

I doze for much of the subsequent festivities (it's that or go mad), but whenever I surface it seems that the meal is taken up with Farb gossip, naturally, and discussion of how work progresses on Herskowitz's endless Francis Bacon biography project. By the time the port arrives, Reg Holdsworth is congratulating the chef. He stands at his place, unsteadily, and tapping at his nose, he says, "You're right to do the cooking yourself, Herky. With your reputation, there's no telling what your many, well, adversaries, might slip into the feed." He lifts his glass, sweeps the gaping sleeve of his barrister's robe to the side, and proposes a toast: "Ladies and gents, charge your glasses to salute our favourite Socratic-Baconian host and his cellar of lovely vintage hemlock, funded by the government and other wealthy donors."

"You're pissed, Holdsworth," Herskowitz yells, calling the kettle black. To his right, son Hillel cracks a malicious smile. Young Ari, portside, just looks miserable.

"What is hemlock, anyway?" The Porlockian inquisitor is lanky and middle-aged, something like Mr. Justice Mariner, his high, pink brow in a permanent furrow. He projects a sort of aggressive good cheer as though through chronic pain, and in this case he gets away with it because he is the Farb's dean of law, Howard Seward Pilchard. "I mean, it's a tea isn't it, made of some kind of poisonous plant?"

"Conium maculatum," Holdsworth growls, his port still at half-mast and mid-toast. "A.k.a. spotted cowbane, spotted parsley, muskrat weed bunk. Looks like a bloody carrot, smells like rotting garlic." He drinks, and the assembled company hubbubs "To our host," "To Mac," "To Professor Herskowitz," "To Jerk-O-Witless" and such-like. "And it's not a tea, Howard, you juvenile delinquent, it's a plant that you can make into a poisonous brew. Go sit in the corner, dunce. And no afters for you, just broccoli, boiled to mush. Mack, no dessert for Howard."

"You're pissed, Reg," Herskowitz repeats. "Never mind him, Howie. He's pissed as a bloody newt." Herskowitz looks even more irascible and red-faced than usual — quite agitated, in fact, never mind that generally he enjoys a good insult. "One drink, and that's it," he hisses at son Hillel. "And wine only!"

"Actually, Professor Holdsworth, it's not the plant, *per se,* that you make into the poison, it's the fruit of the plant." Sure enough, it's Albinoni, showing off again, even while tiddly and more than ordinarily sniffy-dismissive. He has made an extravagant display of helping to clear the main course glassware, drinking down what is left in each wine glass he collects, remarking with a shrug that the alcohol would have killed any communicable diseases he might otherwise contract. "In fact, it's the dried, *unripe* fruit of the hemlock plant, and in lower dosages it works rather well as a sedative and anodyne." He surveys the assembled diners. "You know, a painkiller. Which some of us could use right now."

"See, there, Herky," Holdsworth says. "Just as I was warning you. The lad's been boning up on poisons. *Et tu, Albinoni?* Beware the thirty-first of October, Herky! Watch your back, and front!"

"And that would be a novelty for me?" Herskowitz asks, unsmiling. *"Et tu, Reggie."*

"I read it in a pharmacology text, is all," Albinoni sniffs, drinking his own port, now, and refilling the glass from the decanter on the table. "At the clinic where Deena works."

Deena Topo — a woman a year or so younger than Albinoni, petite, rail thin like him, dark and silent, giving herself the air of almost brutish stupidity — is Albinoni's wife. She is also a family physician's receptionist, it seems. And she has stuck glumly (and silently) this evening to mineral water and green salad, daring to look up from her mesclun with goat cheese in raspberry vinaigrette only to watch her husband drain the sundry glassware down his gullet.

"You're loaded, Red Reg," Herskowitz mutters. "Stinko as a pinko. Drunk as a bloody commie shkunk."

"That would be the coniine," someone else says in all seriousness to Albinoni. It is Vern Gander, I believe, one of Herskowitz's former students, now Assistant Deputy Minister of Justice in Ottawa, which explains why he gets to sit next to the Chief Justice while we three Mariners are exiled to the end of the table with the effusive and mildly terrifying Red Reg. Outlaws we remain, beyond the Queen's protection, although the CJ nodded in our general direction when first we sat at table. Having flown in especially for the dinner on Her Majesty's tab, Gander's probably drunk, too, like just about everyone else (including the CJ, a couple of the servers, and the lissom blonde sommelier: a real Greco-Roman debauch is shaping up here), but he is determined to hide it. "The sedative aspect of hemlock," he says, not quite as sober as my judge. "Relaxes your muscles, like curare. And actually, Tony, the whole plant is toxic."

"That's not what I've read, Vern." Student and former student are on a first-name basis, apparently, and arguing pedantically, in the great academic high table — not to mention lawyerly and Socratic — traditions.* Maybe they compete for their host-mentor's affections. "Anyway, it's not as uncommon as you might think for people to die of hemlock poisoning. You eat a game bird that's grazed on the fruit, boom, predator becomes prey."

"Revenge of the food-chain, *per se*." Holdsworth sneers extravagantly at Albinoni, then leans into the Mariners' table space and complains in a wine-breath undertone that isn't nearly "under" enough, "Didn't I tell you he was a know-all, ungodly little pain.

---

*Recall that, in England, the homeland for our legal system, to qualify as a barrister you must eat a set number of dinners at your Inn of Court. And of course you must always be prepared to argue about anything and everything, twenty-four/seven, as *Homos allegedly sapiens* like to say.

Gadfly to the gadfly. Mack's bloody pest-in-training." He's tapping at his nose again, and then at Justice Mariner's. "That's why they hate each other's guts, you know, Judge."

"Well, how do you know so much about poison yourself?" His Lordship asks, pulling away in genuine irritation, no doubt thinking, himself, of black pots and kettles. And in his outlaw position, he can hardly be seen to conspire with the local Robin Hood. I mean, with the Chief Justice sitting across the table and all . . .

"Don't get him shtarted, Judgsh," Herskowitz says, as if to emphasize the point. "He'll turn you into a fucking commie, you don't watch out, having you give up your seat at the trough for the waiter. Anyway, I thought we were in mid-toasht to y-yours ho . . . ho . . . hostingly."

"Actually, it seems to be Mack's unique view that Socrates *committed suicide* with the cup of hemlock," Holdsworth says. "'Pride as Suicide in the Socratic Dialogues' or some such, eh, Mack?"

"He's talking about our latest paper, Judge, published this month in *The Osgoode Hall Law Journal*. It's causing quite a stir, we're pleased to say." This new and more pulchritudinous speaker is Herskowitz's *conjointe*, Anne Boleyn, alias Zipporah Kyriakos, sitting across from Penny at table. Never mind her youth, beauty, and pleasant manner, Herskowitz bellows at her, actually seeming to foam at the mouth, bringing the high table to a new low: "What's this '*our* latest paper,' white woman?"

Kyriakos turns vermilion, or at least burgundy, and it isn't from the Hospices de Beaune, vintage 1983. "I did seventy-five percent of the goddamn work on that paper, Mack, and Tony did the other twenty-five — while you went to lunch with all your cronies and donors. Vern can back me up, even if Tony's too drunk to know his ass from his elbow just now. Vern was at half those lunches with Mack, weren't you, Vern? You can back me up."

Vern is backing up, all right. He stands, asks to be excused, and summarily leaves the dinner table.

"Never mind your 'I would like to thank my research assistants' bullshit, Mack, in a little footnote on the first fucking page," Kyriakos continues. "It was my fucking idea."

"You're lucky I didn't acknowledge there what you really did for me, Zippy. Speaking of fucking."

Hillel flushes, but seems at last to find the evening entertaining. The younger Ari hides his face in his hands and says, "Oh, Jesus."

Her face set with anger, Kyriakos addresses the Mariners, who are looking decidedly dyspeptic at this late stage of the gourmet night. "He did manage to sweat out the title, so why shouldn't he get all the credit? Which, by the way, was 'Socratic Method in His Madness: Pride as Suicide in the *Apology*, *Crito*, and *Phaedo*. '"

"And *that*, actually," Albinoni says, eyes glazed, raising his glass, "was my fucking idea."

"In Europe, they call hemlock 'fool's parsley.'" Holdsworth taps at his reddened nose again, smiling gaily, trying to haul the party back onto the festive rails. "And its effects are rather less dramatic than people think. Death is quite slow, actually, as the *Crito* shows" — here, he nods at la Kyriakos — "with Socrates babbling on and on for hours as the stuff does its work on the poor sod." He slurps at his port. "You don't just drink it and fall over into your grave, you know."

It is precisely at that point that Herskowitz falls over into his moussey dessert stuff, face first, spilling his lovely port all over his prize handwoven carpet, where all those lovers disport themselves obliviously, already drunk — with lust, maybe, but more likely abject boredom, *in medias Kama Sutra.*

∾∽ℴ∾

Even as the professor sinks into his pudding, Deena Topo pulls out her cell phone and waves it distractedly at her husband. "Here, Tony. Call nine one one." She is not exactly jumping out of her skin, but otherwise gives every appearance of being alive, after all, albeit only marginally more social than before. Her face remains blank and miserable, her voice subdued, but perhaps it is simply chronic fear.

Albinoni stands with a silly grin on his face, and calls around the table, "Nine one one. Nine one one. Anybody got bingo yet?"

"Hang on," Kyriakos says, and in no particular hurry, walks to Herskowitz's side of the table. She pulls him by the shoulders from the mousse and shakes him a few times for good measure. When this does nothing more than fling pudding on the silk tablecloth and nearby guests in all their finery, Zippy shrugs and mutters: "Shit. Here we go again. He's probably just lost another battle with the fermented grape. He'd sucked back most of a bottle of the Barolo before anyone even arrived." She tries the Heimlich maneuver, digging her clasped hands into the soft belly of her aged lover, who responds something like an overfed rag doll — which is to say he doesn't respond at all beyond sort of lolling about heavily in his mistress's long, slender arms.

"Shit!" Hillie says, pulling back from the comatose spectacle of his bellicose father.

"Oh, Jesus," Ari says, standing and backing up, invigorated

with mingled disgust and terror.

"Yeah, okay," Kyriakos agrees at last, "maybe we'd better call for help." Now Herskowitz is crumpled against the back of his chair. His head hangs obtusely, and the blood has drained from his face and hands, although he seems to be panting through his flared nostrils. Then again, as Albinoni points out, maybe they're just plugged with aerated egg white.

"How lovely to suffocate on *soufflé*," he says, nodding at Topo but addressing himself, as usual, to the crowd. "It's French, you know, for 'puffed.' 'Aerated.' 'Blowed.' 'Breathed-into.' Jerk-O-Shit's soufflé has collapsed. Blowed up real good. Literally *à bout du souffle*. Right outta puff."

"Jesus, Tony," Topo says, stabbing her bitten-down nails at her phone. "Get a grip."

Albinoni the jester laughs. "Help, help," he says, barely audible, then giggles. "Give me something to grip on . . . or gripe on. Or, better yet, grope on. Just like old Mack. Old goat Mack, the horny groper."

While Albinoni waggles his eyebrows Groucho Marxistly at Kyriakos, his wife apparently reaches Emergency Services and asks around the dinner table, the phone still at her ear, "Where are we? On-campus or off?"

"Oh, Jesus," Ari says.

Albinoni giggles once more and says, "How can you be in two places at once when you're really nowhere at all? Truth falls in the gap." He takes the recorder from its pouch, dislodging a key fob from same, so that it falls from his hip to the table.

"Hey!" Kyriakos says, from her lookout over mine slumped-over host. "Those are Mack's keys. The keys to his Sebring."

Albinoni dangles the fob before the dumbfounded party, still giggling. "Not any more, they're not."

"Tony! On campus or off?" Albinoni's wife shouts, flushing, but still, oddly, barely animated.

Holdsworth takes the phone and shouts into it that the LoKarb-Kola™ Towers are at the periphery of the campus. "Just as you come in off Midland. And step on it. We've got a man unconscious here." Then he holds the phone away from his face to glare at it, muttering, "They seem to've rung off already. Christ, and Mack's turning blue."

"Oh, that," Albinoni says, dismissing Holdsworth's anxiety with a fey wave at Herskowitz. "Dead cat bounce, I'd wager. Right, Vern? Not what he seems, old Mack." He raises his port glass again, and, giggling, repeats, "Help, help," so softly he is hardly audible. Then, he collapses into the drinks table, pulling the tablecloth and several bottles of "inferior" Ontario wine with him to the floor.

CHAPTER 6

There is rarely any rising but by a commixture
of good and evil arts.
Francis Bacon, *Essays*, "Of Great Place"

"Well, obviously somebody poisoned him."

"Why 'obviously'?"

"Duh! You don't just stop breathing and pass out at the dinner table."

"You do if you choke on your feed."

"He didn't choke. I was there, remember? And not so coincidentally, the table-talk was all about hemlock and Socrates."

"Maybe it was an aneurysm. Maybe he had a heart attack. Maybe he drank himself comatose. Everyone was drunk, you said."

"He stopped *breathing*, Josh. The paramedics were asking us did he take tranquilizers or sleeping pills."

"Well, there you go."

"Come on, Josh. If Mack was taking tranquilizers, they weren't exactly working. He was manic. Agitated. Florid. That was him. Manic Mad Red-Faced Mack."

"Well, okay. So it was hemlock for Herskowitz, you say, just like the graffiti has it all over the law school toilets. But who, exactly, would have slipped him the poisoned chalice?"

"Who, *exactly*, wouldn't have?"

"Some of his students quite liked him."

"A lot more of them quite despised him. Not unlike Socrates, as it happens. Over time, he's made a lot of enemies, in and out of the law school."

"He insisted he was 'a Baconian,' actually, Megan, not a Socratic at all — combining a life of politics and action with the life of the mind. Francis Bacon was his model, an intellectual power broker and the true Renaissance man. Not Socrates."

"Meaning that, like Francis Bacon, he was well-connected — well greased and political. So people were jealous, envious. And he was aggressive. He broke eggs to make his omelettes. He made enemies."

"He had friends, though, he really did. Just like Bacon — and Socrates. I mean, it's implicit in what you're saying. He had powerful friends, in high places."

"Powerful, maybe. Friends? High places? It's all relative. Just as, yeah, okay, as with Francis Bacon — can we say we have friends in high places when we sell our souls to the devil to get ahead in life? Only on twisted logic. Wasn't it Bacon, in fact, who said, 'All rising to a great place is by a winding stair'?"

"Actually, Bacon had a lot of those quotes about rising high in the world, and how it took its toll on a guy. He was obsessed with it. Making it while making wry observations about making it."

"That's what I'm saying. So was Mack obsessed with making it. Power. Influence. Moolah."

"Yes, well, and speaking of climbing spiral staircases, Mack liked to say, 'In the long run, it's useful to have friends in high places. But for immediate effect, friends in low places are best.'"

"Case closed. He would have known about that, mind you — friends in low places."

"How do you mean?"

"Well, his institute, for one thing. He dealt with a lot of lowlifes, on both sides of the law. People looking for payback. I mean, think of the Merdnyk case, the corrupt lawyer. Mack bankrupted him and stole his girlfriend, for cripe's sake, that calculating little girl, what's her name?"

"Zipporah. Zipporah Kryiakos."

"And Mack was always on the make, always playing politics, always looking for the advantage, even if in the long run he gained nothing by it. He climbed the spiral staircase by stepping on those he found under his feet. He pissed off students. He pissed off his colleagues. He pissed off the dean. He pissed off his clients. He pissed off his wife. He pissed off his girlfriend. He pissed off his kids . . ."

These damp pleasantries are interrupted by the entry of Dean Pilchard. We are, in fact, in a faculty meeting the day after the Last Supper — or, more precisely, we are early arrivals for the "Extraordinary Meeting of Faculty and Staff," as Dean Pilchard had put it in his memo regarding same. Unable to keep me at home, and taking a page from the Book of Mack Herskowitz, His Lordship has brought me along in my Canadian Tire carrier. He has set me on the table next to the coffee urn and bran muffins, hard by the long boardroom table: (Yes, formerly a Ulyssean adventurer, always roaming with a hungry heart, I am become mere decoration on the office drinks table, for peckish employees. Also available for dinner parties, receptions, retreats, and Hallowe'en disasters.) We sit mute as Assistant Professor Megan Skaldpedar (Family Law, Feminist Legal Studies, and Labour Relations) prepares herself some herbal tea while giving Associate Professor Josh Peacock (formerly, in his

Old Left grandfather's day, Pinkoff — Criminal Law II; Sex, Drugs, and Public Morality; Introduction to Legal Research) an eyewitness account of the doings at Herskowitz's fatal Gourmet Night. But now comes our fearless leader . . .

"You'll all be pleased to hear," the dean says, convening the meeting, "that Mack's going to be okay. I talked to the hospital and the police this morning."

The news is met with widespread gasping and a sort of academic, low-roar hubbub — and, possibly, some disappointment: "Not everyone will be that pleased," Reg Holdsworth mutters to no one in particular, casting a glance at Skaldpedar and Peacock.

"He came to, actually, at his own apartment," Justice Mariner interjects, masticating a muffin, "while they were working on the student. After you left, Megan. I mean, he was out of it, but he was conscious. Babbling, even. Something about gadflies at the orgy."

"In fact," Holdsworth says, "the first paramedics didn't even bother with him at all. They just spirited Albinoni, the student, off to the hospital. In quite a panic, I guess."

"Well, yes . . .," the dean begins.

"Funny thing about that," Holdsworth adds. "The first two medic types, they brought a back-board up to the penthouse. Said they couldn't get their actual gurney — the collapsible stretcher they use in ambulances — they said they couldn't get it in the elevator. So, you know, they strapped Albinoni onto the board and just carried him out, by hand. Made a bit of a hash of it, besides. He was lolling half way off the thing, and the ambulance guys weren't exactly models of efficiency in maneuvering it, either. But — and here's the really odd bit — the ones who came later, the medics who took Mack off with them, they had a gurney up there, right in the hallway outside the penthouse. They looked perplexed when I asked about it. They said there was no problem getting in."

"Lucky thing, too," Peacock says. "Mack weighed at least twice what the kid did."

"Yes, okay, but what I mean is," Holdsworth impatiently replies, "how'd they get the bloody gurney up there?"

The dean shrugs. "Maybe they used a service elevator or something. Maybe the first guys used the regular elevators and they were smaller. Anyway, please — the sadder news is, never mind how fast they got the student out of Mack's apartment, I'm afraid he didn't make it."

"No!" Holdsworth says.

Everyone has stopped chewing and shuffling and slurping. Justice Mariner puts his muffin on a napkin and shoves it away. "My God," he says. "The poor kid."

Dean Pilchard shrugs helplessly. "His wife called this morning. Eureka spoke to her. Apparently he died on the way to the hospital." The dean nods at Eureka Hoover, the Farb's Administrator of Student Affairs, whose accustomed scowl seems more than usually appropriate. "Apparently Mack is just shattered about it — it's holding up his recovery, the doctor says, I'm told. Mack keeps saying it should've been him."

"And Mack is right," Peacock mutters to Skaldpedar.

"So we're bringing in grief counsellors from the social work faculty," the dean continues. "And we're going to cancel classes for today. We'll conduct a memorial service of some kind next week, once we can get it organized. Have some students and profs who knew the student give eulogies, remembrances. That sort of thing. I'll put it up on the website, invite the press. Eureka's arranging flowers and a card."

"And you'll need to drop by the front office to sign it," Hoover immediately adds in her gravelly voice (though she has never touched a cigarette in her long life), moving her unblinking gaze from pedagogue to pedagogue. A generation earlier, it would have been said of her that she was married to her job. Six years past eligibility for retirement with full benefits, she is the Queen Victoria of student affairs — wrinkled and grey as old library paste, but pure grit and gristle. Everyone present is well aware, by virtue of Hoover's comportment alone, that she has been with the law school for thirty-five years, from when it was still run by the law society downtown and Mervin Goldfarb was schlepping around samples as a junior salesman in his father-in-law's schmata business — Radwanski's of Spadina, Fine Casual and Formal Wear. So Eureka Hoover doesn't need any jumped-up kid of a personnel director to tell her to take ownership of her job. Hell, she owns the entire bloody law faculty. "I can't chase you people down all over the school and back."

PART II

Spreading False News

Spreading False News

Every one who wilfully publishes a statement,
tale or news that he knows is false and that
causes or is likely to cause injury or mischief to a
public interest is guilty of an indictable offence
and liable to imprisonment for a term not
exceeding two years.

Criminal Code of Canada, section 181 (as of 1992)

CHAPTER 1

All colours will agree in the dark.
Francis Bacon, "Of Unity in Religion"

Applying the Law to This Case

We noted earlier that Nathalie Robicheaux confronted the respondent Paisley at one of his public meetings. During the question period after the respondent had perpetrated his diatribe, Ms. Robicheaux pointedly asked him, "Mr. Paisley, have you never heard of the French fact in Canada? That is a common phrase, is it not? The French fact?"

"Certainly, madam," the respondent replied. "And the French fact in Canada is that the French have done nothing but extort money and power from the taxpayer on the strength of persecution myths and manufactured wrongs. The French fact, as you call it, would be no fact at all if they had been expelled beginning in 1659. They wouldn't be here, would they?"

"Well, sir, you say 'myths' and manufactured wrongs,'" Ms. Robicheaux then remarked, "but here you yourself persecute and perpetrate wrong against our community. Anyway, sir, as the descendant of Acadian settlers in this country, I will tell you what is the French fact in this country. I, sir, je suis le fait français, I am the French fact, Mr. Pasties — je suis le fait français, the very concrete French fact you are going to have to deal with from now on." Ms. Robicheaux was

shouted down, and pelted with foam coffee cups and half-eaten butter tarts. Someone in the room yelled, "Speak white!" The next day, Ms. Robicheaux brought a private prosecution against Mr. Pasties — in Jolieville, Ontario, where Mr. Pasties lives and the venue of this particular meeting — for spreading false news. Upon reviewing the file the Attorney General of the province took the prosecution over from her. At trial, the respondent Pasties successfully argued that the charge of spreading false news infringed his constitutional right of free expression. The Attorney General is here appealing that ruling. On behalf of Her Majesty, the Attorney General argues that the anti-false news law is a reasonable limit on free expression, and the abuse against Ms. Robicheaux at the public meeting demonstrates that, in certain cases, there is a clear and present danger that, like the perpetration of hate propaganda, the spreading of false information can lead to violence — that disseminating lies is a trespass, in the old phrase, vi et armis, *with force and arms against the Queen's peace.*

The question before us then is, in fact, what exactly is the French fact in this country? And is it open to the court to take notice of that fact without hearing evidence from scholars or historians to support it? In other words, is it open to this court to take judicial notice of the expulsion of the Acadians? Can we . . .

A man stands at our office door in the faculty wing at the Farb. He is about thirty-five, tall, pale, and bespectacled. He wears a blue business suit and a sort of regimental tie, striped a vibrant red and blue. His clean-shaven face is pinched, but that seems his habitual demeanour. Constipation. From my perspective atop the desk as Justice Mariner types on his notebook computer, the man is all razor-burned Adam's apple. He swallows.

It bobs.

He knocks tentatively.

It bobs.

He is Vernon Gander, assistant deputy to the Minister of Justice in Ottawa and former student to Mack Herskowitz at the Farb. He looks as though he's still hung over from Herskowitz's Hallowe'en dinner from hell. "Mr. Justice Mariner," the rashy constipated apple says.

The judge looks up from his reasons for judgment. "Mr. Gander. Come in, come in."

The very civil servant Gander continues to stand in the doorway. "I was wondering if you could spare a few minutes. It's important, I think."

"Well, I have a class in about twenty minutes. But until then, I'm all yours." His Lordship smiles a welcome.

Gander steps into the office and turns to close the door behind him. We watch, a little unsettled. Not to put too fine a point on it, I decide that my participation in this particular tutorial will take place under the desk.

"It might take longer than that, to explain. But I think I'd better at least give you the main points." Gander looms over the desk like the Ghost of Christmas Present. It's coming on for the winter holidays, after all. He wears faded, brown penny-loafers with his blue suit, and argyle socks.

"Sounds serious." The judge smiles, nodding at the guest chair, on whose edge Gander perches, leaning intensely toward His Lordship.

"It is," he says quietly. "It's about Tony Albinoni. The student who died."

"Yes, a terrible misadventure. They're thinking a heart attack, probably." The judge shakes his head. "At his age! I guess kids are under incredible stress these days. And he liked the fast lane, I hear. Lived on the edge. But can you imagine? At his age!"

"Well, that's just it, Judge. I think there's more to it than that."

"How do you mean, Vern?"

"Well, when I was here at the law school, my experience was something like Tony's."

Eyebrows up. "You were a bit of a hellion, you mean?"

"No, not that." Gander looks offended on top of his worry, then grimaces, then sniffs with what he means to be irony. "Actually, I tend to be one of those Goody Two-Shoes types, for all the good it does me."

You do surprise me, old goosey Gander.

"I'd say Assistant Deputy Justice Minister is not doing all that badly."

Gander scowls. "That's me. Toady. Your black-letter play-by-the-rules boy. Conscientious. Do my homework. The type who finishes last. I love a parade, as long as I'm at the back, on clean-up duty."

The judge's smile begins to look a little plastered. "Well, yes, I thought I detected the earnest mien of the nice guy."

"What I mean is, I bought into the Herskowitz cult, myself."

"Cult, Vernon? It must be a pretty small one, from what I hear."

"I believed that, with all his tough-minded Socratic business, he really wanted to make good lawyers of us. It stimulated the over-achiever in me. So I worked really hard in his first-year torts class, put up with his sarcasm and bullying, and I became one of his little — yes, it was quite small, that was part of the attraction, see? — his little coterie of disciples. It was like *The Paper Chase* or something, you know, sort of challenging, romantic. I was going to beat Mack Herskowitz at his own game, like whathisname and Professor Kingsfield, the Socratic Contracts prof, in that movie. And, like Tony Albinoni, apparently. Just like him, when we got an elective in second term, I signed up for Mack's Legal Profession course. I was going to prove I was worthy of the challenge."

"Yes, I'm covering that off for Mack this term, Legal Profession. But I wasn't aware that Tony was to be in it next semester."

Gander is uninterested in hearing about the judge. "At one of the receptions for Mack's institute, Tony mentioned the course to me, asked what I thought." Gander has grown more anxious, and is almost panting. "I told him that I took it, and became Mack's research assistant."

"As Tony already had." The judge makes a chin-rest of his thumbs and elbows.

"Like Tony. And that's when it started."

"Started?"

"I don't know how to put it." Gander looks as though he might weep. "Forgive me, judge, but Mack. Well, he came on to me."

"You mean, he wanted to be personal friends with you?" We know better, of course. We're just hoping he doesn't mean what he seems to mean. "Invited you to his high table dinners? He's quite a socializer, for someone who pretends to be anti-social. Mixes business with pleasure. To him, it's all one, as far as I can tell."

Gander shakes his head. "I wouldn't say he pretends, Judge, about being anti-social. He wanted to do things with me. You know, sexually. There was nothing friendly about it at all, I can assure you. The pleasure was meant to be all his."

A soft "Oh" is all the judge seems to manage at first. Then: "I had a feeling that's where you were heading."

"It gets worse."

"Are you sure you want to tell me this?" I see the judge sneak a peek at his watch, but Gander is staring at the edge of the desk in a sort of trance. The real question, of course, is does the judge want to hear this?

"He insinuated he would trade me high marks for, you know, friendship. Intimate friendship. I mean, what he said, actually, was that we could help each other get what we wanted, get where we wanted. I should have had them anyway — the good marks, I mean. I earned them in most of my other courses. But I was a, what do they call it . . .?"

"A keener?" The judge looks dubious. "As you've already intimated . . ."

"Yes, but I mean I was also really anxious about my future. I was determined to do well. And in the end, sure enough, I got to clerk for Chief Justice Laskin at the Supreme Court."

"Well done."

"No, you don't understand. I mean, I think I would have managed it anyway. But I sort of went along." Gander swallows and the fruit of the Forbidden Tree bobs at his collar. "More or less. To Herskowitz's indecent proposal, I mean. His illegal contract."

"Yes. That it would be, Vern, if in fact a professor, uh, wanted some quid pro quo from you while he was a person in a position of influence over you. At the very least, that could be undue influence or duress, I would imagine. *If,* and I don't have all sides of the story here, *if* he was in fact, you know, seeking something from you in return for marks or whatever."

"Mack did want a quid pro quo, Judge, and he was in a position of very great influence, as you know. And I'm still paying for it. I'll always be paying for it."

"I'm sure it's hard. But you can move on from it, can't you? I mean, as I say, look at your success so far. And maybe — I mean, as I say, I don't know — but maybe there was some miscommunication, misunderstanding . . ."

"No, Judge. You don't understand." He is still staring at the desk.

"Well, I'm trying, Vern. I mean, this is a lot to take in, as you can appreciate. I mean, Mack is a friend. I'm sure it's still shocking for you, too. Did you tell any of this to Tony? That Mack was abusing you?"

Gander swallows, and, yes, it really, really bobs. "I wanted to. But I couldn't. I'll regret that forever."

The judge makes his face as sympathetic as possible, and I'm sure he means it. "Look, Vern. I have to go, but let's talk about this some more. If you want to, I mean. Will you still be in Toronto later today?"

"The thing is, Judge, I think Tony was less obedient and scared than I was. You know, he was more, how do you say, in your face, rebellious. A hellion, as you put it. Didn't play by the Establishment rules." Gander and his Adam's apple take a beat. "I think that's why he killed him." Gander finally aims the high beam of his unfocussed glare at Justice Mariner's face. "I think that's why Mack Herskowitz killed him."

CHAPTER 2

The Death that is most without Paine, hath beene noted to
be, upon the Taking of the Potion of Hemlock . . .
Francis Bacon, *Natural History*

I take it that on his way back to the office from teaching Legal
Profession, His Lordship runs into rumpled Reg Holdsworth, who
accosts him with, "Feel like a drink or three?" I deduce this from
the facts that (1) after the judge spends another anxious half hour
in his office with Gander, before Vern flies home to Ottawa, we
are off to the student pub in the Farb's basement, and (2) the day
has been unusually thirsty work. Given the speed at which we make
for the local watering hole, I might as well have been at the Canada's
Wonderland amusement park, swinging in my carrier at the end of
Holdsworth's overly enthusiastic arm as it pumps its way to ye not
very olde Wig & Gown (Law Students' Semi-Public House), the
judge being encumbered with his laptop and briefcase.

Stationary at last amid the video games, foosball, and lager fumes
at the Wig (as the students call their pub), I try to recover my equi-
librium as the judge stick-handles Gander's explosive confidences:
"Reg, I wanted to ask you something about Mack Herskowitz."

"Just one sec," Holdsworth says, and makes a beeline to the bar
for a couple of draughts. As he returns bearing said pint-sized
gifts, and after slurping the head off the one in his right mitt, he

says, "Fire away, Judge. Mack Herskowitz."

"Actually, I'm interested in his girlfriend, what's her name, Kyriakos."

"You wouldn't be a red-blooded male otherwise, old darling." Holdsworth sits, quaffs, wipes his mouth on the back of his hand. "Zippy's quite, uh" — Groucho Marxist waggling of eyebrows — "zippy."

"Well, that's sort of where I'm going."

"You wish."

"Seriously. Between you and me, Reg, does Mack, well, does he tend to fraternize with his students?"

Panting, pedantic Holdsworth takes another pull at his lager, then shrugs. "Or 'sororitize' in this case, what? Well, he has his little pets. As for la Kyriakos, to be fair, she became a student *because* of the fraternizing. I mean, they were already an item, you see, before she was a student. Mack supported her application to get into the Farb, but she doesn't take classes from him. And he would be expected to declare a conflict of interest if, I don't know, if he was on a faculty committee, say, dealing with her performance at the law school. Like if she appealed her marks or something. But she's a smart cookie. She deserves to be here. It's kosher — kosher enough for faculty politics, anyhoo." Holdsworth shrugs. "She deserves to be here."

"Was Vern Gander one of Mack's little pets?"

"Oh, yes. Gander was his research assistant for the whole three years he attended the Farb. Summers, too, if I remember correctly. Mack tends to adopt certain students, disciples, you might say, and to become their champion and referee when they apply for jobs. He calls it his legacy. Creaming off the cream, then indoctrinating them. Mao's Cultural Revolution in reverse. Why?"

The judge shrugs. "Just curious. But you wouldn't have called Albinoni one of his pets or disciples?"

Holdsworth laughs. "I'd say nemesis, more like. As I said before, gadfly to the gadfly. They went at it like an old married couple."

"Um." The judge nods over the foam of his pint. "But Albinoni seems to have been working on this paper with Kyriakos. The one they were fighting about at the dinner, she and Mack."

"Yes, well, Tony and Kyriakos are both quite bright. Mack does tend to cultivate that sort of student, as I say, for his own ends. But you have to remember, Albinoni was only in first year. He'd only just arrived at the law faculty, really."

The judge looks quizzically at the law professor, but for a moment says nothing. "I'd like to ask her about that. Kyriakos, that is. I mean, between you and me, there are some rumours going around."

"You don't say?" Holdsworth asks, leaning forward with a beery leer.

"I can't really divulge anything else about it just now. But do you know where I can find her?"

"Zippy? She uses the IWAC office a lot. She's the director of Mack's little institute, you know."

"Yes, I guess I could try her there. I'd rather speak to her more privately, though. It's a bit sensitive."

"Well, she lives here on campus. Just across the way, in the same building that Herskowitz lives in. The LoKarb. You know, separate retreats and all that. I'll take you over there."

"Really? That would be great, Reg, thanks." The judge finishes the last half of his pint in one go, just like he's back in law school himself and bussing tables part-time at the Chicken Alley Bar and Nightclub downtown. "Let's make tracks."

"Whoa, old son. Pace yourself. The night is young. Let's finish our business here first."

"But my wife will be waiting dinner."

Holdsworth tilts his head at His Lordship, launching the sort of body-language bunker-bomb that pierces a man's soul, nuclear-tipped with the sentiment: SHAME!

"All right, then," the judge says, pretending to be abashed. "Just a couple more. But I'd better give the old girl reasonable notice."

I happen to know beyond a doubt that His Lordship would never call Penny Mariner any sort of girl to her face, never mind an old one. In any event, communicating with her at all promises to be a challenge. He reaches into his briefcase and retrieves a cell-phone, which he waves around like it's radioactive. "You know, the Chief Justice gave me this damned thing, as a sort of consolation prize in my exile to the suburbs, I guess. Supposed to make me feel like I'm still able to keep in touch. The trouble is, Reg, do you have any idea how this damn thingamajig works?"

❦

Perhaps it's because, as we confess, Zipporah Kyriakos is not expecting us; or perhaps it's because His Lordship and the pro-fessor have lost track of time at the pub and are giggling like drunken schoolgirls after their last exam of the term. For some reason, anyway, the porter (or is it concierge these days?) at the

LoKarb-Kola™ Towers — "Joyce," her name-tag professes — is not anxious to disturb Ms. Kyriakos on our behalf. Holdsworth does not help matters appreciably by informing Joyce lubriciously, "Madam, I had understood that you were the guardian of this venerable redoubt, but now I understand you to be the redoubtable gargoyle menacing the env-en-venirons. Environens. The env . . . The joint. No doubt."

Joyce looks up grimly from a stack of papers through which she has been sifting, occasionally licking her fingers to separate the pages. For this reason, when she glares at us over her spectacles (pushed halfway down her nose) her tongue hangs straight down her chin, gargoyle-like, or, actually, like the Rolling Stones' "sticky fingers" logo much in vogue during His Lordship's university days.

The men giggle at this for a moment, before the judge recovers and says, "He doesn't mean it, Joyce. We've just come from the pub and we're in sort of high spirits, is all." This causes my companion *Homos allegedly sapiens* to break up again, but Justice Mariner soon resumes his apology. "Sorry, sorry. We really don't mean to be pu-puerile." His choice of word catapults the two human visitors into another fit of hilarity. "We had some very nice ale, you see, spilled a little, too, as maybe you noticed on my learned colleague's shirtfront, and it occurred to him, to Professor Holdsworth here, that as professors at the law school, you see, like us, I mean, professors, so it occurred to us that maybe we could talk briefly, just very briefly, with Ms. Kyriakos about some important law school matters. She knows me. Us." Silence. "And we're not drunk, really, just happy. And I'm a judge."

Holdsworth finds this last bit side-splitting as Joyce retracts her tongue. "Come back when you're sad . . . Your, uh . . ." She pauses to look the ancient Mariner up and down, says, "Honour," and returns to her papers.

～eco～

It is just gone five p.m., so Holdsworth suggests, rubbing his hands, his breath frosty in the fall air: "The old gargoyle's bound to clock off, soon. We can see the office from my car in the lot. Let's go sit there and wait 'til she scarpers."

"I don't know, Reg. It's getting late. And cold. And I'm not sure we should be seen playing private eye near the law school, let alone sitting in a car with beer-breath."

"Might as well be hanged for a sheep as a lamb," Holdsworth advises.

The judge rubs at his left temple. "Speaking of which, I don't think she liked us," he says, reducing himself and the professor into another prolonged fit of hilarity.

Through tears, Holdsworth sputters, "'We're not drunk, really, Joyce. And I'm a judge!'"

"Jesus. Don't remind me. That's probably earned me another year of exile here in Scarberia. The Judicial Council's already got their pub police on it, no doubt."

Apparently the encounter with Joyce has begun to sober the both of them.

About an hour later, the night porter — an old scarecrow of about seventy in a mock-police uniform — finds them perfectly so, and sad enough to pass muster. He phones Zipporah Kyriakos, who agrees to come down to the office. Holdsworth asks for the phone and persuades Herskowitz's young mistress to allow us to speak to her in private.

The scarecrow shows us to suite B-310, where Kyriakos rents a single. It must be one of the more expensive dorm rooms available insofar as it has a small balcony and is probably a few square feet larger than the typical rooms. Otherwise, though it's not bad for a bankrupt stripper, it resembles any other student digs — a bed in one corner, a cluttered desk in the other, clothing and books on the floor. You can tell a female student is resident, inasmuch as the clothing and books and papers are arranged in piles at one end of the room rather than strewn randomly as litter. And Zippy seems to be a more than usually ardent student: against a pile lays not one but two bookbags, the kind you carry on your back. Spilling from each of them are (*inter alia*, as we like to say over at the Court of Appeal, when what we really mean is "among other stuff") what appear to be identical copies of Hogg's *Constitutional Law of Canada*. Well, you've got your regular copy, I guess, and then you have your copy for constitutional emergencies, which seem to be unhappily common in this country.

"You know, I'm beginning to wonder whether I need to talk to a lawyer," Kyriakos remarks. She looks tired now, hollow-eyed and betrayed in her terrycloth bathrobe, but beautiful, still, more waif than a princess.

"You're talking to two, actually," Holdsworth assures her, rather defensively through the haze of stale lager, apparently unaware that the young woman might have intended irony. When this fails to impress, he asks, "Anyway, why would you wonder that?" He squints hard at her.

"All these questions. Where's it leading? I've had the police here twice today. What do I know about any of it?"

The judge shrugs. "Sometimes one knows more than one realizes until one's memory is jogged," he says. "Anyway, there's nothing to worry yourself about. We're not the police."

Kyriakos sighs and sits on her bed, crossing her slim legs, most of which are no longer under the robe. "And that shouldn't worry me?" The judge tries not to look as she adds, "Poor Tony."

"Quite so," Holdsworth agrees, staring quite openly.

"You were explaining at the dinner," the judge says, "that you and Tony co-authored the Socrates paper."

"I don't care what Mack says, Judge. That was *my* publication. With help from Tony, such as it was."

"Publish or perish, so to speak. Publish and perish, in this case." Holdsworth is the only one who laughs at his joke.

"I was just curious about two things, really," the judge says. "First, do you know if Mack has ever dated any of his other students?"

Kyriakos shrugs, and the robe springs open, exposing her lacy black brassiere and making Holdsworth catch his breath. "You'll have to ask him, Judge. Not my business. Not yours, either, I wouldn't think. Not to be rude or anything." She opens her eyes wide at His Lordship. "Sorry."

"No, no, you're quite right." He stares back, carefully, at her face. "As I say, I was just curious. I didn't mean to be rude, either, and I do intend to ask him, the very next time I see him."

"I'm sorry to be blunt. It's just that so much has been going on, and I really don't know anything about all this."

"Of course."

"I can tell you that he always had a group of students he socialized with, to a certain extent. Took them out for the occasional drink or meal, had them over to his place, like at the gourmet night. Typically they included the students who worked with him as research associates. The bright lights. But we were together — he and I, I mean — we were seeing each other before I became a student."

"So I'm told. The other thing, just out of curiosity. About that paper: Did either you or Tony or Mack make any notes about the poisoned chalice? The hemlock business in the Socratic dialogues?"

"I certainly didn't. I mean, I don't know if you've read our paper, Judge."

"I have, as it happens. Read it just this afternoon, in the library at the Farb. And it doesn't address my question."

"Well, that's because — as you must know, if you read it — that's because it was about what killed Socrates, but not literally. Whether it was hemlock or falling on a dagger or jumping off a cliff wasn't the point. It was about how he had, like, a messianic complex, he was on a mission from the gods, holier-than-thou, a 'gadfly' who was pretty well asking for it. As a matter of principle."

"The pride that goeth before a fall," the judge says, nodding.

"Not unlike our dear old Mack," Holdsworth insists on pointing out as he idly examines a razor on Zipporah's desk.

"That's as may be," Kyriakos continues. "But the point of the thing was that the Socrates of the Platonic dialogues, well he prefigures Christ, as a sort of sacrificial man-god, self-proclaimed — sacrificing himself for our sins, as it were. He offers himself up in a sort of martyrdom, and also to secure his own reputation — a sort of immortality. He dies and rises in a purer form. He's resurrected as an immortal philosopher and an example to his students, of the uncompromising intellect."

"My own view, Judge," Holdsworth interrupts, snuffling in the overheated, dry air, "is that this argument is more than a little obvious, and not particularly worthy of publication."

Bad tactic, offending the witness, I muse, and the judge ignores Red Reg again. "But do you know if Tony or Professor Herskowitz made any notes, on the cause, I mean, literally, the cause of Socrates' death?"

It is Kyriakos's turn to shrug, so that her robe falls rather farther open. Poor Holdsworth is nearing cardiac arrest. Maybe the girl is a cunning murderer, indeed — committing the perfect crime, in this case. Death by titillation. "I can show you what I've got in the file." She regathers the robe then bends over one of the piles on the floor and extracts an off-white file folder from somewhere near the middle. More floor show, as the judge looks at the ceiling and Holdsworth goes back to examining the razor. Kyriakos leafs through the pile cursorily, then brandishes a few sheets.

"That's it?" Holdsworth asks, snorting and turning from the student's personal belongings on her desk. "Just three pages? Why am I not surprised?"

The young scholar shrugs again. "I told you: I did all the work. That's the sum total of Mack's notes on file." She hands the pages to the judge, then does up her robe more tightly and folds her arms, remarking, "Good luck. Mack's handwriting's impossible. Tony's isn't much better. *Wasn't* much better." She begins to weep silently, and neither man seems capable of deciding if it is appropriate to comfort her.

The judge glances from the blurry-faced young woman to the notes and back again. "Zipporah," he finally says. "I noticed there's a photocopier in the warden's office. Would you mind if I took copies of these notes?"

∾◦ᢍ◦∾

At first, Zipporah Kyriakos resists the request to copy Herskowitz's scrawls: the notes aren't really hers, she doesn't know what's the right thing. "What about copyright?" she asks, and without having the first clue, or so it seems to me, the judge babbles on about fair use. Usually, he has the submissions of at least two lawyers to help him decide such things. Cutting short this judicial bafflegab, Holdsworth asks Zippy what's the difference, given that they have already read the notes. "They're hardly secret or publishable," he points out.

Kyriakos purses her lips, shakes her head, and says, "I don't know. Go ahead. But if anybody complains, I'm not responsible."

"The slogan of the new millennium," Holdsworth mutters.

During this colloquy, I can see the pages fanned out on the desk. On one, there are notes about narcotics, including hemlock:

conium maculatum
spotted hemlock, parsley, kill cow
sedative, anti-spasmodic, pain-killer
30 minutes

Morphine = form of opium — Percodan, Oxycontin . . . Slows heart, breath. $\frac{1}{2}$ hour react x, but up to 12 hrs lead-x?
Naloxone = antidote. Booze speeds uptake

The second page seems to comprise only three lines:

Turkington, K. Poisons and Antidotes
Penguin Med. Encyc. Wingate
West on Toxicology

What I can see of the third page reads:

Apology: false modesty, pre-Christian. Socrates: "God chose me, but for the sake of humankind. If you kill me, I will still enjoy immortality as a righteous and thoughtful man, you eternal damnation. I am willing to sacrifice myself for your sins . . ." Disciples (e.g., Plato, Crito . . .) Like the phoenix (Dodd's theory about Bacon, also), I will die and rise the same, out of my own ashes.

Bacon: "He that dies in an earnest pursuit is like one that is wounded in hot blood, who for the time scarce feels the hurt."

Downstairs, the scarecrow copies the sheets for us, smiling vaguely and muttering something about hieroglyphics. The judge pats his papery, liver-spotted hand and says that just like hieroglyphics they will reveal the secrets of time and tide.

"And you were there," Holdsworth tells the aged night porter gravely, "Xeroxing for anthropology." *Like the old bag of bones you are, sirrah,* he adds *sotto voce* so that only Zipporah and the judge (and Yours Redundantly) can hear, nodding politely and waving with the papers as we bow out.

"Good night sweet prince," Holdsworth says aloud.

CHAPTER 3

For these winding and crooked courses are the
goings of the serpent, which goeth basely upon
the belly, and not upon the feet. There is no vice
that doth so cover a man with shame as to be
found false and perfidious.
Francis Bacon, *Essays*, "Of Truth"

My morning patrol of the faculty wing ends at the closed door of
Mack Herskowitz's office, lately occupied (according to the com-
puter-printed letterhead that serves as a temporary door-plate) by
Justice T. E. Mariner. At the moment, however, I can hear that
both men are inside. On the off-chance, I stretch my forelegs
toward the knob and let my weight fall against the hollow-core
door. As it is not quite latched, it gives a little, leaving the door
just sufficiently ajar that I can slither back down it and through
the gap.

"Well, Mack," the judge is saying, "I'm going to have to tell
him he should go to the police."

"I'm not convinced of that, Judge. I'm trying to explain to you
that, no matter what anyone thinks of me, I don't see how they
would say I'm capable of murder. Not even my many detractors go
that far."

"Well, but that's not the whole story he's telling is it? If it was
just that, you know, idle suspicions about somebody doing in
mouthy little Albinoni, I might be able to let it lie. I mean, the
police are already looking into that. Arguably, one can assume

they're investigating all the angles." The judge grimaces and sighs.
"But he's accused you of all that other business. I know the atmos-
phere in schools is fraught these days, Mack, with these sorts of
allegations amid the raging hormones. Particularly this sexual
harassment business. A student or a co-worker can accuse you of
it for the most innocuous little off-hand comment or friendly gesture. I know that. I, well, you know, I've been on the end of it
myself — which is partly why we're having this conversation in
this particular place today. It's why I'm here, really. And I've seen
it from the bench. But whatever the truth of Gander's allegations,
Mack, well, as a judge, I can't just ignore it. You know that. As
lawyers, none of us can ignore it. From what you've told me yourself, we really have to move on to the investigation stage — leave
it up to the investigators, I mean, whether they want to pursue it.
If they decide this is all miscommunication and misinterpretation,
or an ex-student bitter about his time here, well, it'll end there. I
don't have to tell you any of this. You're the expert, and a celebrated supporter of the police and prosecutors. As a judicial
officer, I can't just sit mum. I'm involved, never mind that I didn't
ask to be and I don't want to be. I mean, obviously, it's the last
thing I need just now."

"The last thing *you* need? Cry me a river."

"The Chief Justice will go ballistic on me, Mack."

"Yes, well, so why don't you let me talk to Gander first, Ted, to
try to sort it out, get all our chestnuts out of the fire? That's all I'm
asking."

"I can't stop you talking to him, Mack, although it could just
as easily make matters worse for all of us. But I think the better
thing would be for you to phone a lawyer — defence counsel, I

mean. Because what I'm trying to convey is that, no matter what you do next, I have to phone Gander. I've thought about it, and I've decided. I have to tell him that if he's serious about any of this, well, you know, he should speak with the police. So the best thing for you is probably that you should avoid talking about it with anybody and everybody, including me, at least until you retain counsel. Don't dig yourself in any deeper." The judge looks put upon and a little pitiful. "I know you've been through a lot, lately, but I'm giving you my best advice. I mean, come on, Mack. You're the professional ethics expert. What would you do in my shoes?"

"I wouldn't be in your shoes, judge." Herskowitz stands abruptly and virtually flies out of his own office.

"He wouldn't be in my shoes." Justice Mariner frowns at the empty doorway, then at Yours Breaking and Entering. "Is that sympathy, do you suppose, or is that a threat?"

Suspecting it's the latter, on little cat feet I trot toward my hidey-hole under the desk. Sighing, exiled, alone, His Lordship telephones Vern Gander.

CHAPTER 4

A wise man shall make more opportunities than he finds.
Francis Bacon, "Of Ceremonies and Respects"

"Hellwo dare, chubby-wubby wittle bwack kitty! Wha'soo doin',
huh, you pwetty wittle boy? Wif dose wittle white stwipes down
your chesty-westy, just wike a wittle Bay Stweet witigator, isn'
choo?! A weguwar barrwistuh lawyer. Dey wook jus' wike wittle
tabs, don't dey, duh wittle white tabs dat barrwistuhs wear in duh
court? Doing the bookie-wookies for us, is we, you woly-poly
wittle wascal, you?"

I believe the appropriate adult English response to this frivolous,
vexatious, and scandalous cross-examination is, "Gag me with a
spoon." Anyway, I don't give Zipporah Kyriakos the satisfaction of
a sideways glance, all the better to obscure the fact that she has
caught me red-handed, or inkstain-pawed, scraping my way
through the accounting ledger in the broom-closet headquarters of
the Institute for the Wrongfully Acquitted Criminal. Zippy has
come back untimely to her little IWAC bailiwick — hemmed in as it
is (like her semi-messy apartment) by bankers' boxes, higgledy-
piggledy piles of paper, old law school casebooks, and grey-
skinned computer equipment of sundry vintages — just down the
hall from Herskowitz's faculty digs. She carries a mug of herbal tea

(mango-passion fruit, if my nose does not deceive me, the favourite blend of Claire Mariner when she comes from Calgary to visit parents Ted and Penny). Redolent of some more subtle bath oil, Kyriakos sets down her mug on a box to scoop me off her desk, but not before I have one last goggle at October–November/07:

Hallowe'en Dinner pledges

Source	Re
Justice & Mrs. Mariner	donation, $350, send rcpt
Prof. Nairvnek	donation, $20 (cash), rcpt
Sam Fitz-Niblick, Q.C.	donation, $100, rcpt
R. Nobb, Q.C.	donation, $75, rcpt
Ministry of Justice	$10,000 (grant, no rcpt, tax slip to come)
Dean Pilchard & Mrs. (Booleem-Pilchard)	donation, $50, rcpt
Chief Justice	donation, $100 (cash), rcpt
Vern Gander	"dead cat bounce," $1,000 (cash), no rcpt
Prof. Holdsworth	book donation, to come?, rcpt for?
Dovvy Weissmann	book donation (to come), rcpt for $1,500
Atty Gen. (Ont.)	contact his deputy re funding application; deadline Feb. '08
V. Gander	dead cat . . . $500 (re Aug.), no rcpt

Expns against same: as per ledger 1, caterer, wine, servers, cabs, invitations, postage, cleaners, steam tables, decorators, Tony A., etc.

After further nauseating monologue about how sneaky-weaky I have been to "wunned off from your poor ol' judgy-wudgy," cutesy-wutesy Zippy walks down the hall, carrying me toward Herskowitz's office. In the interests of energy conservation, I allow myself to be transported; as with an outlaw shipped to Van Diemen's Land of old, resistance is useless. We arrive to find two uniformed police officers standing on either side of His Lordship, who is perusing a fan of documents as the officers look on.

"I hope no one's phoned nine one one just because this wascally wittle cat went missing." Zipporah flirts with the younger of the officers, a constable in full regalia, including a bullet-proof vest and a belt larded with pepper spray, service revolver, cuffs, radio, and T-bone nightstick.

Justice Mariner glances up at her. "I'm afraid it's a little more serious than that, Zippy. These gentlemen have search warrants, and they seem to be in order."

"Why, judge," Zipporah says, in a sort of Blanche Dubois, *Streetcar Named Desire* voice, "what have you done now?"

I imagine it's the "now" that makes His Lordship wince. He takes a beat and replies, "Actually, it's regarding Mack."

"Mack?"

"They want to search this office, your office up the way, the penthouse, and his condo." His Lordship fixes the young woman with a challenging stare.

She seems unfazed, though still on planet Tennessee Williams. "But whatever for?"

Before the judge can reply, the older officer, a detective constable, says, "I take it you're Ms . . ." — he looks at the papers in Justice Mariner's hands — "Ms. Kyriakos."

"That's right. And this is sneaky wittle woly-poly Amicus."

"In which case, I'm going to have to ask you to come with me to the office of your, um, centre, ma'am." He consults the papers again. "This Institution for the Wrongfully Acquitted Criminal. I'm afraid I'm going to have to secure it."

"Don't be afraid, officer," Kyriakos replies. I wonder if they can arrest her while they're at it, for animal cruelty — or cwoo-ellty. "But just so you know, nobody goes in there but me and Mack. That's it. And it's full of documents subject to lawyer-client privilege. Confidential stuff." Kyriakos is distracted now from how pwetty and wascally one is, and in fact returns one to the floor more suddenly and from a greater height than one quite anticipated. But she is smiling still, and recalls herself. "No one has access but Mack and me. Except the occasional wascally cat. I mean, it's secure already. Just let me know when you want to do your search. I'll point out the privileged documents."

"You heard the judge, ma'am." Zipporah smirks at the TV cop-show honorific, and the judge has to struggle with the pretty contagion of her mirth. "We're going to have to secure that office. We have a warrant. You can call your lawyer, if you want."

"No problem, officer, but can't I just clean up in there a little, first? I mean, that would make your job a lot easier. The judge can vouch for it. It's a terrible mess in there. Not very organized. Embarrassing, really."

"I'm going to ask you not to touch anything, miss. I'm going to send Constable Rumble with you, and we're going to secure that location forthwith."

And forthwith it is. "Just let me get my personal things first," Zipporah says, turning and walking brusquely back toward the office — with Constable Rumble in hot pursuit like another of her ardent admirers in the legal community, the armoury on his belt keeping a jaunty beat by way of accompaniment.

⁘⁘⁘

After Legal Profession that morning, we are back at the LoKarb-Kola™ Towers with a fruit-and-nut basket to express our condolences to Deena Topo, Tony Albinoni's wife. Joan the porter casts a suspicious glance at my carrier on her desk, then at the fruit basket before she advises, "She's not in." After another pause pregnant with sarcasm she adds, "Judge." Smirking, she goes back to her word processing.

"Do you have any idea when she'll be back, . . . Joan?"

"I'm not her mother, . . . My Lord." She does not look up from her work, but a little smile cracks the gargoyle facade.

"Yes, of course not, . . . Porter. I don't mean to trouble you. I just thought she might have said, in the circumstances." The judge chuckles as Joan's smile broadens. "And actually, it's Your Honour, these egalitarian days, not My Lord. The Chief Justice sent around a practice notice about it in the law reports. Didn't you get it?"

"He consulted me about it first." Joan sighs and puts her hands behind her head, throwing herself against the back of her leather desk chair. "I told him you lot were just too full of yourself. Even when you're also full of fire-water." Pursing her lips and chuffing through here nose, she considers the tall, lean, likable man standing before her. The two of them are, after all, of an age. "Look. You could check back here around five-thirty. That's when Deena's usually home."

"Usually?"

"From work."

"She's back at work already?"

Joan shrugs. "People cope with these things in their own way, Judge. She's a receptionist for Dr. Schuss on St. Clair West. Maybe she finds it helps her to cope, to be in that care-giving environment, or whatever. Being near a medical man and someone she sees almost every day. Distracted by the contact with the patients." Joan shrugs again. "It's probably comforting. Help yourself by helping others and all that."

"Maybe so. Schuss, you say, like in the giant slalom?"

Joan's sense of humour fades back to default as she impatiently consults a phonebook, which she soon flips around so that the judge can read it. "It's pronounced *shush*," she says, "like" — she gazes up at the judge — "shut your face." Under her carefully manicured and blood-red nail we can see that Dr. Lester Schuss's office is conveniently located in upper Forest Hill Village, just north of 1415 Elysian Fields.

⚬∾⚬

In fact, Schuss's offices are in an old Forest Hill house just up the street from the Spadina streetcar stop on St. Clair West. We disembark into a warm autumn afternoon almost blinding with the yellow and red leaves on the pavement and the sun low on the horizon. Inside, Deena Topo sits mostly obscured behind a reception divider cluttered with several calendars, a little brass plate that says "Deena," and piles of medical files. Two middle-aged men sit facing her and the divider, which slopes away from them at about twenty degrees and is plastered with brochures and posters for their edification: "Erectile Dysfunction and You"; "Multi-Vitamins: Miracle or Myth?"; "Getting Acquainted With Your Colon: What You Don't Know Can Hurt You!"; "Fat Chance: Good Cholesterol vs. Bad." "Don't let your *prostate* make you prostrate *in the end.* " Justice Mariner sets my carrier between a couple of stacks of files and stands expectantly as Topo sits rocking and vigorously chewing a wad of gum, her head bent over what I assume is office work.

"You'd better be careful there or you might accidentally prescribe the wrong drug," the judge says.

Topo looks up sharply, eyes wide, face flushed. "What? Whaddayou mean? What are you saying? I can't . . ." The rocking and chewing have stopped.

His Lordship smiles, proffering the fruit basket. "Doodling away on the doc's prescription pad like that. You might accidentally give it out and the pharmacist will fill it, with God knows what."

Perhaps because of her untimely loss, she doesn't see the joke. In fact, I believe I see the hint of a sneer set briefly around her swarthy maw. "He wouldn't." She quickly flips the pad into a drawer. "Anyways, I was just fooling around. You know, passing the time. It wasn't a prescription."

"No, of course not. I was only teasing." The judge holds out his hand. "I'm Ted Mariner. Perhaps you remember me from the other night, at Mack Herskowitz's?"

Topo shakes hands limply. "Oh, yeah. Yeah. I thought you looked sort of familiar, and I didn't think Dr. Schuss had any more patients in his book for today. You're the judge, right? Yeah." She nods and rocks and chews. "I remember."

"That's right. I've come to say how sorry I am for your loss."

Topo maintains her accustomed demeanour, what psychiatrists call a flat affect, I believe. And it looks even flatter, clothed as she is a starchy white smock. "Oh," she says. "Okay. Yeah. Thanks."

"So, will there be a memorial service?"

Chewing away bovinely, Topo considers the query. "Well, we're gonna do the cremation as soon as the, um," *chew, chew,* "wha-dayacall," *chew, chew,* "coroner, as soon as he releases the body. Yeah. But, you know, it's just for, you know, the family. Private. But, yeah, uh, memorial service. We're working with the school, the grief counsellors and all that. There's going to be like a memorial service next week, probably in the moot court at the law school. Yeah." *Chew, chew.*

"It was so sudden," the judge says. "And he was so young."

"Yeah, I know." She nods and clacks her gum, looking at her desk. "Is that a cat in there?" She taps with a dirty, bitten-down fingernail on my portable gaol.

"Yeah, that's Amicus. Say hello, Ammy. Maybe he wasn't used to drinking. Tony, I mean. I mean, did he drink much?"
Topo shrugs, looking down again at the desk. "No more, no less than the average couch-potato student. You probably shouldn't have a cat in here. It's no sweat off my nose-ring, except some people have, like, allergies and that. The doctor wouldn't like it."

"Oh, we're just about on our way. Just came to drop off the fruit basket."

"Yep."

"I was just curious. Tony and Mack Herskowitz seemed to have had sort of a love-hate relationship."

The young woman snorts and looks up at the judge. "Hate-hate, more like it." The thought of love makes her head jerk and her mouth stretch in a spasmodic grin, all rictus.

"So why did Tony work for him? Why was he planning to take Legal Profession from him? And Business Associations, too, I believe."

"To be honest, I don't really feel like talking about this stuff. Sorry, but I'm trying not to think about it for now. But yeah, just so you understand, we needed Mack, you know? I mean, we're living on just my crappy little salary from this place." She lowers her voice. "It's peanuts. So, like, Tony needed the research jobs, and also, like, the help Mack could give him with, you know, getting law jobs. Mack knows a lot of Bay Street lawyers, see, and a lot of judges, too, like you." She widens her eyes, to make sure His Lordship gets the point. "Tony says — said — you need allies, but that doesn't mean you have to like them, or even agree with them on most things." She clacks. She shrugs.

At that juncture, Dr. Schuss emerges from his consulting room with a patient and hands Topo a couple of documents, referral letters, they must be. She stands and turns from us wordlessly toward the fax machine. He scopes us out briefly over his spectacles, then takes a chart from the pile on the desk and calls his next patient, throwing Topo a sideways frown. Our visit of mercy is over.

CHAPTER 5

" ' . . . they put him into a good bed warmed with a pan,
but it was a damp bed that had not been lain-in in about
a year before, which gave him such a cold that in two or three
days . . . he died of suffocation.' "

John Aubrey, recounting what the philosopher John Hobbes
described as Francis Bacon's final illness.

I am in attendance at the memorial service for Tony Albinoni, given that it is slated to start at three p.m. and His Lordship intends to leave for home after the speeches. Dean Pilchard is speaking when we arrive. Behind him, on folding chairs placed in front of the three-judge dais in the Farb's moot court (or, as it is formally known on the gold plate above the main doors, the Wyedangle Sexton Tosspottant Moot Court and Webcasting Auditorium, in honour of a large cheque from the eponymous Bay Street law firm), sit Deena Topo, Albinoni's friend Betsy Hnatyshyn, and Mack Herskowitz. This is my first time in the room, one of the most comfortable spaces in the school — windowless and bristling with the latest electronic gewgaws, but pleasantly in-the-round like a coliseum, warmly lighted, with tiered seating in the court's well at sweepingly curved tables. Given that it also serves as the school's main assembly and largest examination room, the dais sits on a stage. While the dean introduces Herskowitz as the first speaker, the judge manages to get Lee Gaunt to scooch over so His Lordship can sit on the aisle and place me on the step there, facing the stage-dais area.

Looking fully recovered from his fainting fit — which is to say, looking pugnacious as ever — Herskowitz speaks of the bright future stolen from Tony Albinoni. Tony Albinoni was the type of student he always looked for, Herskowitz says, a student who used the law school experience to its fullest, a student who wasn't interested simply in toeing the line to secure a position on Bay Street, but one who pushed the envelope, challenging conventional wisdom and preconceptions in the way of a good apprentice lawyer. In fact, Tony had been indispensable, Herskowitz went so far as to say (and for him it was very far, indeed), in assisting him with his biography of Sir Francis Bacon, another lawyer who achieved great things by pushing the envelope. Tony's assistance had been so valuable, in fact, that it looked like the work of a lifetime was actually going to see publication in Herskowitz's lifetime — maybe even within the year. And it would serve as a lasting tribute to Tony.

Perhaps because it was self-serving and not entirely suited to the occasion, this observation stimulates the judge to whisper to Gaunt, his own researcher as was, "Speaking of which, what do you know about Francis Bacon, Lee?"

Gaunt shrugs. "Two things. One, that they turfed him out as lord chancellor for taking bribes. Two, that he supposedly died when he caught pneumonia or something after stuffing a chicken with snow."

"Yeah. The famous refrigeration experiment, wasn't it?"

"Yes. Supposedly he was out on a coach ride or something" — here, Megan Skaldpedar turns from one row forward to glare at Gaunt, who nods and smiles at her obliviously — "and he saw this farm-woman out among her chickens. She slaughtered a hen for

Sir Francis on the spot, and supposedly they stuffed it together. With the snow."

"Can't see the Chief Justice of Canada doing that, myself."

"Anyway, supposedly Bacon caught cold out there in the frigid weather, then he got pneumonia, then he died."

Josh Peacock, seated next to Skaldpedar, throws the judge an over-the-shoulder glance of disapproval. At the same time, Reg Holdsworth, seated in front of Justice Mariner and ear-wigging as usual, turns to advise, in not much of a whisper at all:

"Apparently Mack had the kid following up an old canard about that — how Bacon didn't really die at all, you know."

"Show some respect!" Skaldpedar says, fully *viva voce* in her public outrage, making half the assemblage jump in their pews and effectively ending the conversation until the reception following, in the student union.

"It was on April Fool's Day, you see." Holdsworth accosts us, spraying crumbs while masticating one of the two muffins in his paws, as he balances a paper cup of hot coffee against one of them.

"What was?" the judge asks.

"The supposed refrigeration experiment. The day Bacon was supposed to have died. There's a theory that this was a clue. April fool's, you know. April fish, as the French say, only in this case it was a chicken."

"A clue to what?" Gaunt asks.

"Well, that Bacon didn't really get sick. Or die. That, in fact, it was all a ruse so that in his disgrace in getting thrown off the Woolsack, you know, fired as lord chancellor, he could make a new beginning. I mean he was down forty thousand pounds, remember. That was what they fined him for the bribe business.

And he was without regular work, with an aristocrat's household to run."

"How did stuffing a chicken fix that?" the judge asks. "Unless he made soup out of it for his cold."

"Well, actually, the chicken was incidental. As an amateur scientist, Bacon was genuinely interested in food preservation methods. So there's something to that. But he was driving around in that carriage with his physician, who also happened to be the king's physician. And the theory goes the doc shot him up with a dose of opium or whatever, so that Bacon went comatose. Again, sort of experimentally. In the interests of science."

"But he didn't die." Gaunt nods.

"Supposedly he fled to France." Holdsworth shrugs again, spitting muffin.

"To be reborn as Shakespeare, of course," the judge scoffs.

"Well," Holdsworth allows, "they do say he actually wrote the Bard's plays."

"Not if they've actually read Bacon's essays, they don't."

"Anyway, the story goes that he was buried on Easter Sunday — reinforcing the resurrection joke."

"Sort of like the messianic theme Mack's paper identifies in Socrates, too. In your death, living on like a demigod. In your afterlife, you are more powerful than ever. A martyr."

"April fools," Holdsworth says, wide-eyed, and moves off to mingle.

CHAPTER 6

One of the Seven [wise men of Greece] was wont to say:
"That laws were like cobwebs; where the small flies were
caught, and the great brake through."
Francis Bacon, *Apothegms*

ONTARIO COURT OF APPEAL

BROSSARD, MARINER, and FIERSTEIN, Justices of Appeal

B E T W E E N:

HER MAJESTY THE QUEEN

Appellant

- and -

MARTIN LUTHER PASTIES

Respondent

The judgment of the court was delivered by:
MARINER, Justice of Appeal

The philosopher Wittgenstein once postulated that it was impossible to know if a hippopotamus had entered the room — that, in other words, objective truth was a fantasy. At least in terms of human expression, truth, he said, was a matter of linguistic perspective semantics, grammar and the like. What we mean when we say

I love a parade — not. We are sitting quietly — thoughtfully, would not be an exaggeration — in our sedate office at the Farb, our anyway temporarily sedate office on loan from Mack Herskowitz, mooning yet again over the introductory bit to our reasons in *R. v. Pasties*, when said parade materializes on the immediate horizon. At its head is a middle-aged woman, tiny, wiry, tanned, freckled, well-preserved, lightly made up, neatly groomed in a pink cotton pantsuit. She marches straight into the room with a proprietary air, followed by two teenaged Has-beings, both of them in wool dress pants and carefully-pressed, long-sleeve cotton dress shirts. The first we recognize vaguely, tall for his years, lanky, pale, his over-sized, hatchet-shaped head resplendent with curly reddish-brown hair. The other boy is perhaps two years younger, swarthy, considerably shorter, pudgy, smeary-faced, breathing over what must be a deviated septum. His shirt, although otherwise newly laundered, has a big chocolate stain over the pocket and third button. He looks and sounds, yes, like Mack Herskowitz in miniature. I don't know about hippopotamuses, but it is impossible not to know that Becky Goldfarb-Herskowitz and her brood have occupied the premises. As I take cover again under the desk, Becky says, "You must be Ted."

Roused from his philosophy, His Lordship seems to be in some doubt about this, but ultimately he cannot deny it. Becky thrusts her tiny, freckled, heavily jewelled hand at him, introducing herself. "I hear we're neighbours."

Still bewildered, the judge essays, "You teach here, do you?"

Becky looks irritated. "No, no, no. God forbid. I mean neighbours in Forest Hill. I live on Dunvegan. You're on Elysian Fields, I'm told."

"That's right. North," His Lordship confesses, signifying he's on the other side of the tracks from the mansions of the Lower Village.

"This is Hillel," says Becky of the older child, who overcomes the inertia of puberty long enough to emit an extravagantly insincere "Hi." Then he takes up residence on the edge of His Lordship's desk, swinging his leg in my face, back and forth, back and forth. "And that's Aaron." Aaron has already occupied a seat opposite the desk and without acknowledging his mother or anyone else begins playing with some portable video game.

"Oh, yes, of course. We've met." His Lordship nods uselessly at the bored children. Before he can say anything else, Becky advises, "We've had a visit from the police this morning."

"The police?"

"About Mack." Though she's probably not a hair (expertly dyed dirty blonde) over five feet tall, she stands intimidatingly against the prow of His Lordship's desk. "That's why we're here."

"Oh. I see."

"Do you, Ted? I was hoping so. I mean, that's why we've driven all the way out here in very heavy traffic. What the heck's going on?"

"Well, I can't really say, Mrs. Herskowitz."

"Can't or won't?"

"I mean, I think you should ask Mack. I mean, if it's about him."

"Ask Mack? You must be joking." The expression on Becky's face suggests that she's never heard anything quite so stupid. "You know what they wanted to know, the cops? They wanted to know if he'd ever touched up the boys. You know, *touched* Hillie and Ari."

"Yes, I'm pretty sure I get your drift." If the boys do, they aren't revealing anything. Hillie gazes at the judge with that lazy smirk, his intelligent black eyes taking in the scene with a sort of bored sadism not uncommon considering his age, stage, and species. Ari just keeps at his video game.

"They were also asking about his students. Did we ever have them to the house. Did Mack socialize 'or fraternize' with them."

"Sounds like you already know much more about this than I, Mrs. Herskowitz."

"I think they think Dad's a bum fucker," Ari explains sombrely, without interrupting play.

Hillie makes a noise in the back of his throat meant to express derisive amusement. "Or maybe a kiddie diddler," he says, his leg swinging forward and back, forward and back. His socks are an expensive wool and nylon blend. Forward and back, forward and back.

"Okay, guys," Becky says, "we've got the picture. Judge, you can tell him for me that he's not coming near the boys any more. Not even for a tenth of a second. He can take me to court if he wants. I'll get a no-contact order. And you can tell him to stay away from the condo, too. The boys are using it. I'm applying for a possession order."

His Lordship buzzes his lips and cantilevers his brow. "I don't see much of Mack these days. And, again, this is between you and him, no?"

"I can see you're protecting him. Normally, I could understand that, but we're talking about child abuse, sir."

"Alleged," His Lordship says, with a grim smile.

"Kiddie diddling," Ari says, smirking at his older brother.

"I think it's all crap," the latter says, perhaps demonstrating, if crudely, why he is named after the first-century rabbi who headed the Sanhedrin, Jerusalem's highest court. His shoes are kangaroo leather stained a lustrous maroony-brown. Forward and back, forward and back.

"I think Dad's actually a mind fucker," the younger boy says.

"Ari," Becky scolds reflexively, smiling at her son with pride. Ari giggles at his game.

"I think it's all crap," Hillie says. "He's crap. This law school's crap. It's all crap."

As the young critic is distracted with all the excreta in the universe, it seems the moment to pounce on his well-clad ankle. He howls. "Ow! Shit! Ow!" I give his ankle bone a good nip, then let go and retreat. "Crap!" Obviously, his sense of humour is not as developed as he imagines.

The judge, however, laughs, ducking his head under the desk to hide it. "Amicus! Bad boy! I'm sorry, Mrs. Herskowitz. My pesky little cat down there can be a bit of a nuisance. He likes the attention. Felt left out, I guess."

"He's crap," Hillie says, his smartass face scrunched up like a baby's, like he's about to cry. "He's a piece of shit." He kicks at Yours Mischievously, merely succeeding in banging his knee on the desk edge. "Shit!" he repeats, albeit with new emphasis, doing a little hornpipe, jiggling his doubly-insulted leg hither and yon. No doubt he has acquired this magnificent vocabulary at the country's finest private schools. I believe, in fact, that Mack Her-skowitz has mentioned rather bitterly the fees related to Upper Canada College, not to mention a bar mitzvah in Jerusalem, anciently home of the Sanhedrin.

"Mrs. Herskowitz," the judge contributes to the general out-break of free expression, "why would I protect Mack from such a serious allegation?"

"Because you're buddies?"

"I've only just met him, for goodness' sake. I've only just arrived here, as a sessional instructor. Temporarily. I'm not even full-time faculty. I mean, we're friendly, but . . ."

"You lawyers all stick together. Everybody knows that. And I've been on the inside, married to him for fourteen years."

"Come on, now, you know that's not true. How would the law society ever discipline anybody if that were the case? You're put-ting me in a very tight spot here, Mrs. H. I *can* tell you from experience that these allegations get thrown around in the heat of the moment. Particularly in an academic environment, or any-where there are raging hormones and high emotions. Where things, careers, are at stake. Even among law clerks, articling stu-dents, I can tell you, Mrs. Herskowitz. People have become extremely touchy, and I don't mean touchy-feely. And of course, with divorced couples, well, the acrimony that develops, the accu-sations flying hither and yon . . ."

Now she's getting mad. "You're forgetting one thing, Ted. The police came to me. I didn't go to them. This has nothing to do with the divorce. I'm just looking for answers."

"To be honest, Mrs. Herskowitz, so am I. That's my job. And I'm afraid that very often the truth is not exactly what it seems. In

fact I was just writing here about how the philosopher Wittgenstein . . ." Taking this more conciliatory tack, His Lordship looks
at the screen on his laptop computer, then taps away at the key-
board distractedly, "the philosopher Wittgenstein . . . Oh, crap —
uh, heck! What've I done here? Damn! Oh, jeez! What've I done,
now? Sh . . . Crap! I think in all this excitement I deleted the file.
Damn! I'm not very good at this new technology, I'm afraid. I bet
your boys are though, aren't you, guys? Oh, jeez! In chambers, I
have my assistant Sandy, of course. Damn! Well . . . Anyway, right
before you came in I was . . . Crap!, to coin a phrase, . . ."

His Lordship looks up, seeking eye contact to make his point.
But like Bacon's Pontius Pilate, Becky Herskowitz has asked
"What is truth?" and will not stay for an answer.

⌒∽⌒

ONTARIO COURT OF APPEAL

BROSSARD, MARINER, and FIERSTEIN,
Justices of Appeal

B E T W E E N :

HER MAJESTY THE QUEEN

Appellant

- and -

MARTIN LUTHER PASTIES

Respondent

The judgment of the ~~coots~~ court was delivered by:
MARINERA, Justice of ~~Apples~~ Appeal

*What is ~~turth~~ truth? The philosopher Wittgenstein once ~~pustu~~
postulated that it was logically, or at least grammatically, ~~impiss~~
impossible to know if a hippopqqatumus had entered the ~~rim~~ room.
This was not mere fancy. His point was that a given ~~fart~~ fact ~~pr~~ or
~~turth~~ truth was a matter of linguistic preespective. What do we meann
by "~~hippi~~ "hippopotamus" and "entered the rom"? Could it include a
drawing of a hippo hanging on the wall, or perhaps a very large,
"waterhorse" sort of man who was is crowding us at a cocktaiil party?
~~Hooweever~~ Whaateverr the philosopohical answwer, in this ~~casse~~*

Although the afternoon is bright once more, it is late November
— a cold day to be sitting in a garden shed with the doors open,
seeking refuge from Porlockian interlopers, tapping away at one's
laptop. Justice Mariner wears his custom-crafted fingerless gardening gloves for the purpose, and blows on his hands every three
words or so, but the going is rocky re: revising his reasons in *R. v.
Pasties* with the index finger of each stiff hand.

*There are certain ~~mutters~~ matters on which reasonable ~~pimple~~
people are in general consensus. If every ~~fart~~ fact of ~~hyster~~ history were
debartable, civilization would be paralyzezed. In that*

In the environs of His Lordship's right haunch, a merry, if

static and high-pitched melody plays. *Dee deedee dee dee dee dee dee dee!dee!dee!deeee!* . . . It is, in fact, "Merrily We Roll Along," an historical fact which I have plenty of time to verify as the judge fishes his cellphone from his jacket pocket and tries to figure out how to answer it. By the time he accomplishes this feat — having fruitlessly pressed the Send button many times — the calling party has rung off. Soon, however, Penny Mariner is on the deck again with the portable house phone, bare-legged and blowing smoke, or at least the cold air makes it seem so.

"Ted! It's Mack Herskowitz. Can you talk to him? It's urgent, he says. He says he's been trying to get you for the past half hour. And I'm bloody freezing out here!"

"Tell him I'll call him right back on my cellphone." Not to be bested by modern communications, His Lordship waves the thing nonchalantly, as though he'd invented it.

Several aeons later, we manage to find the Send button again and connect with Herskowitz, who clearly is in some lather. I can hear, well, something of what he says, or shouts, as His Lordship is obliged to hold the verbal assault of it away from his shocked earhole.

"[inaudible] police [inaudible] charged [inaudible]."

"No, Mack. It can't be. I mean, as I said to you . . ."

"[inaudible] . . . represent . . . [inaudible.]"

"Look, Mack, I don't know about that. I mean, I suppose I could, in the circumstances. But let's slow down, eh? First things first. Where are you?"

"[Inaudible.]"

"Bloody hell. Okay, look, I'll be right there. Just hang on. I won't be long. I had your ex-wife around to the office, by the way . . ."

Flipping his phone shut, the judge looks at me and says, "Well, bud, I guess you've had the last laugh. They've arrested your foster-father-as-was for murder. And they've banged him up in Her Majesty's Meanest Doghouse, a.k.a. the Metro West Detention Centre. No way he's going to hightail it out of there à la Amicus the cat. Not exactly a humane society down there, either, I can assure you, old son. More like Her Majesty's House of Horrors."

But I am too distracted to take any sadistic pleasure in such news. I am busy contemplating how, of all the species one has encountered in this life, only *Homo allegedly sapiens* is incapable of realizing when a hippopotamus has entered its living room.

PART III

Murder on the Rebound

dead-cat bounce *noun* [from the facetious notion that even a dead cat would bounce slightly if dropped from a sufficient height] (1985) : a brief and insignificant recovery (as of stock prices) after a steep decline.
Merriam-Webster Collegiate Dictionary,
11th ed.

CHAPTER 1

A man must make his opportunity as oft as find it.
Francis Bacon, *The Advancement of Learning*

It was Herskowitz himself who suggested the Crown should conduct his preliminary hearing in the moot courtroom at the Farb.
"That way I'll really get a jury of my peers," he explained, defiantly.

"Or a real peering at," Justice Mariner replied. "With fury and
jeers. I mean, this is your own doorstep, Mack. And some of the
residents have been sharpening their knives over you for years."

"But that's the point, Ted, isn't it?"

"Well, to begin with, there is no jury in a preliminary inquiry,
old son."

"Okay, my refresher course on criminal procedure is just
beginning, but you know what I mean. I can vindicate my name
where it matters. And how can they argue against it? It would be
very educational for the students. For a change, they'd get to see
the practical application of what they're learning. Of course, the
weird sisters like Skaldpedar and Peacock will fight it."

The grief counsellors, however — professors and students from
U of Scarborough's sociology department — seconded the motion,
on the argument that it would provide the law faculty "closure,"
whatever that might be, while being of practical instruction, as

Herskowitz said. In most cases, after all, the preliminary inquiry is a formality. Its purpose is to decide whether there is enough evidence to send the case to a full trial. Usually there is enough evidence to clear this low hurdle. For that reason, the accused person can waive the inquiry and go straight to trial, preventing the Crown from getting a dress rehearsal for that main event. But some still choose the prelim, on the off-chance that they will be discharged, or because the inquiry provides a free look at the Crown's case and witnesses, giving the defence a chance to sharpen its tactical plans for the trial. The *Criminal Code* gives the presiding judge the power to "change the place of hearing, where it appears desirable to do so . . . for any other sufficient reason." And the thinking in Herskowitz's case was that, as a justice of the Court of Appeal, Ted Mariner could make it all happen at the Farb.

"I can?" he asks Herskowitz, over the speaker phone in the professor's law school office. Also present are Leland Gaunt and Dean Pilchard, at whom His Lordship directs a look of incredulity.

"You're my lawyer, aren't you?" Herskowitz asks, over the migraine-inducing din of the Metro West Detention Centre, where he does bed and breakfast these days.

"I am? Well, I mean, I have been to this point, Mack, *de facto*, I guess. But you might want to retain someone who actually, you know, practises criminal all the time these days. I mean, this is getting serious, here. You need folks who know what they're doing with the law. I'm just a judge."

"You and Lee have been working on the case for weeks now, Ted. For God's sake, you practised criminal for nearly thirty years, wasn't it? And you sit on criminal appeals all the time. I want you to do it."

"I don't know, Mack. I've been more of a spectator than glad-
iator of late." The judge asks his listeners at large: "Do we even
know what the kid died of yet?"

"Ah," Gaunt says. "Bit of a hold-up there, apparently. They
seem to have misplaced the body."

"You're kidding," the judge says.

"They took him to Scarborough General, I guess," Dean
Pilchard says, "and it's a huge, busy place, you know. So he got lost
in the shuffle. It happens, they say. Poor kid. Even dead he's s.o.l."

"So the coroner hasn't had his way with him yet," Gaunt adds.

"Holy crow," the judge says. "Well, I guess that's more or less
to our advantage. The Crown has no proof it wasn't just misadventure. I mean, no body, no cause of death, no crime."

"They'll find him," Herskowitz says. "But my immediate
problem is, I'm still in the hellhole here, Ted. I take it as you're
saying 'to *our* advantage,' you'll represent me?"

His Lordship again looks for help from his colleagues in the
room.

"Up to you, Judge," Gaunt says.

"Gee, thanks, Lee. Who's presiding at the preliminary inquiry,
guys?"

"Ah. Another bit of a curveball, Judge," Gaunt advises. "Apparently they wanted a more senior judge on the case, in the
circumstances. It's got a lot of press, of course, you know, a scandal
in the legal community. So they wanted a firm hand and all that.
I hate to tell you this, but they've got Hernando Cactus down for
the prelim. The last thing he'll do before his promotion to the
Superior Court. They think he's got the experience and gravamen
to pull it off, having sat in the lower courts for so long."

Justice Mariner emits a loud vocalization somewhere between a howl and a monosyllabic laugh. "Then you don't want me representing you, Mack. I'm the last guy you'd want. Cactus and I have wrestled before, you know, and I ain't talkin' intellectually. And, well, let's put it this way. I didn't win. That's why you're speaking to me now, in fact, as I sit in your office."

"I don't agree at all, Ted. Cactus dropped his complaint against you. The judicial council never proceeded with it. You're still a leading light in the profession, known for your ethics, fairness, and basic humanity."

"That's true," the judge generously agrees. "But why would you want to take the chance, Mack? The cream of the criminal defence bar — well, you know them all. The cream. You could have your pick."

"Or lick," Gaunt mumbles, winking at me and rubbing my head. He looks up at the dean. "You know, cream, lick . . ."

"You're forgetting my institute, Ted, and especially the Merdnyk case. He was an icon to the criminal defence bar in this town. I'm not flavour of the month with them these days. 'Who among us is next?' they're asking. And you're a judge of the highest court in the province," Herskowitz says. "Talk about cream. That will add super credibility to my case." There is some greater commotion on the line — a muffled but deafening scuffle sound, and shouting, as from a big sewer culvert — before Herskowitz goes on. "Look, I'm going to have to hang up, guys. Some of the other fellows are waiting to use the phone, and it's not Marquis of Queensbury Rules around here, if you get my drift." Herskowitz attempts a hoarse whisper. "Also, they've pretty well stuck me in protective custody, guys — or what passes for it here. Because of the institute — I'm not exactly up for a People's Choice award hereabouts, either."

Dean Pilchard makes a half-hearted attempt to cover the transmitter on the phone and whispers hoarsely, looking around our borrowed office with an earnest air he might adopt for divulging state secrets, "He's not exactly Miss Congeniality here at the law school, at the best of times."

Oblivious, Herskowitz has resumed his normal arrogant tone: "As I said, you're best placed to put the plan to Cactus, Judge, and the trial office or whatever. I'm counting on you."

After Herskowitz has hung up, abruptly, the judge says to Gaunt and the dean: "I feel queasy about holding the prelim here, guys. He's got enemies on every side, and all the attention we'd get could work against us."

"Well, but on the other hand, Judge," Gaunt allows, "it's the *locus in quo*, the scene of the events. It's the community where it happened, as well as the community to which the victim and the accused both belong. I mean, it's a unique chance to put our legal system in historical context. For the students, I mean, but also for the general public. It's good PR."

"Well, yes, I suppose it really would make clear the vested interest of the community in the rule of law — before our cities grew so big that it all got disconnected, I guess, eh? Keeping the Queen's peace and all used to carry a more community-based message," the judge muses in his new role as professional pedant. "We could score some points by restoring the connection. And it would provide excellent fodder for my Legal Profession class. A field trip right in our own back yard."

"Besides, it would put you in a good light downtown, I would think, a judge of the Court of Appeal using his tenure here to bring the courtroom to the law faculty. Making the course work relevant. I mean, not that I don't think it's our privilege and honour to have you, you know, on, well, on, uh, on loan, Judge. But doing the prelim here, well, it might contribute to your, your . . ."

"My rehabilitation?"

"Well, I mean, uh . . ."

"We'd certainly look on it favourably," the dean interjects, rescuing Gaunt but also no doubt thinking of the prestige that holding such an unusual event would bring to the school, not to mention the funds it could attract to its coffers as a celebrity law school in all the papers and newscasts. Yet more gold plaques on yet more classroom doorways from yet more law partnerships whose generosity is limited only by what they can charge their clients for it . . .

"I can see that," Justice Mariner agrees. "It's just that the last time I argued before Justice Cactus, well, we were practically rolling around in the pasta fagioli."

CHAPTER 2

Pyrrhus, when his friends congratulated to him
his victory over the Romans . . ., but with great
slaughter of his own side, said to them again; "Yes, but
if we have such another victory, we are undone."

Francis Bacon, *Apothegms*

Justice Cactus is one consideration, certainly. And then there is Paul Frederick Katz, representing Her Majesty in *The Queen against Maccabeus Theodor Herskowitz.*

Despite being counsel to the sovereign, Katz is rather more of a Maus, if you get my drift (hence his nickname "Fraidy" among criminal defence counsel), a sandy-haired, pasty-faced, chronically harassed-looking, eternally snivelling, red-nose-blowing, allergy-afflicted hypochondriacal nebbish who puts you in mind of that old joke, What has four legs and chases cats? Answer: Mrs. Katz and her lawyer.

True enough, it doesn't work on paper, exactly, but you get the idea: Fraidy Katz's peaked demeanour is chased, and chaste (which works *only* on paper). His general manner is not so much driven as pursued, preyed upon. He is all of five-foot-four and seems to try to compensate for his short, pasty stature, or to use it to best advantage, Napoleon Bonaparte-style, in a restless, all-elbows-and-sniffles assault on daily life, including lunch. You never know which way he is likely to swing in proactive defensiveness, and if you guess wrong you can get blood on your freshly laundered white court shirt and wind-flapped tabs. Your own blood, that is.

And Fraidy Katz is not keen to move the preliminary inquiry from Old City Hall, his accustomed stomping grounds near my former haunt at Osgoode Hall, into the Scarberian wilds. This means that we must bring a formal motion for a change of venue, and Leland Gaunt is deputed to City Hall on that mission. As he describes it to Justice Mariner when he returns that afternoon, never mind last year's donnybrook at Pasta La Vista, Justice Cactus had some problems persuading his voice stenographer to make the commute out to Scarberia every day. His clerk, however, was only too happy to oblige, as she lives a four-minute drive from the Farb. And Justice Cactus, Dean Pilchard, and Justice Mariner are of the same mind as far as making the trial something of a showcase. To prosecutor Katz's objections about inconvenience in the Attorney General's office and among court staff, Justice Cactus replied, "What's a little drive into the suburbs, Mr. Katz, compared to Professor Herskowitz's right to a fair hearing in a forum where it is likely to be in the widest public interest? I take it Her Majesty pays you enough to run a car? Plus travel expenses in said vehicle?"

In fact, Gaunt informs us, Fraidy Katz runs a bicycle, and an ancient, banged-up Radio Flyer, single-gear, with a wicker basket on the handlebars, at that. Straight out of *Anne of Green Gables*.

"For the reasons put forward by Mr. Gaunt, namely, the interests of all parties, the educational benefits to the students and faculty at the law school, and thereby to the public at large and the administration of justice, I order that the preliminary inquiry be held in the moot courtroom at the Goldfarb School of Law. It is the job of the courts to promote access to justice and public legal education. This is truly an exemplary way to do that."

"Well, that sounds pretty enough," Justice Mariner says in congratulating Gaunt for his success on the motion. "But from the point of view of 'legal realism,' as we discuss it in my Legal Profession class, I suspect there's something in it for His Honour, personally. I mean he's already high on his coming promotion to the Superior Court, and looking at the big picture from his seat on the bench, generally — well, he can up his public service profile yet another notch by moving the venue out here. It could be big brownie points. 'Judge Brings the Real World Courtroom to Law Students.' And he can use the PR later to maybe get bumped up to my court — hell, maybe he's got his eye on my seat while I'm in Her Majesty's disfavour."

"Also," Gaunt adds, a little too enthusiastically, "if he pulls this off, he can get himself appointed to some juicy government commissions and public inquiries."

"Exactly. And the cherry on it all is, if I act as defence counsel, he can beat the merry hell out of me while he's at it. Just desserts after Pasta, as it were. Sweet revenge."

"Ah, but you got the girl in the end, Judge. So he'll never best you in the main contest."

"Is that what's known as a Pyrrhic victory, Lee?"

"You don't mean that, Judge. Penny's lovely. Anyway, you always used to tell me that Cactus is one of the least prickly judges on the bench. Keeps a firm hand on the rudder and all that."

"Generally speaking, yes, Hernando's fair, balanced, keeps a firm hand on the *tiller*. (Your hand's on the rudder, Lee, when you're sinking, which I know from personal experience these days.) He fancies himself a bit of boulevardier — urbane and what-not. But part of that conceit is this gentlemen's honour thing

— pistols at dawn or whatever. And as a peace-and-quiet sort of guy, well, I'm not much of a shot these days, am I?"

⁂

Dean Pilchard doesn't want to funk a chance in the limelight, either. Before court begins on the appointed day, with every seat and all the aisles filled, he takes the stage in front of the dais in the moot courtroom to advise the law students what a rare privilege they are about to be granted. In that light, the students should remember to refrain from treating the proceedings as a broadcast in their living rooms of "Texas Justice" or "The People's Court." For the duration, there is nothing moot about the law school's courtroom. They are not to eat, drink, study, or read newspapers, please, during the hearing. And no baseball caps, worn forwards or backwards. (Much to Justice Mariner's despair, the school has no such prohibitions during lectures, which often resemble hockey night at the sports bar.) They may take notes for their own use and consult their *Criminal Code*, but they are not to use any recording devices or cameras.

Presumably, no pets are allowed either. But as homeless junior counsel, Your Court Reporter enjoys his accustomed seat on the aisle, front row, albeit banged up in the bloody carrier, next to leading counsel for the defence.

Justice Cactus enters, bows to the not-very-learned assemblage, takes his seat on high, and proves more than a little conscious, himself, of the Socratic nature of the occasion. "For the benefit of the students assembled here today," he begins, "I would like to point out that, should he wish it, the accused, Mr. Herskowitz, has the right to demand a ban on publication of the evidence in this hearing. You will find this in section 539 of your *Criminal Code*, which I trust you have all brought along with you today." These words instigate the din of conspicuous scholarship — a susurrus of backpack rifling, banging of bindings on tables, and the riffling of pages in Her Majesty's hymnal. His Honour waits patiently for the delicate cacophony to subside, then addresses the defence. "But I believe, Mr. Mariner, that in this case we've already established there is considerable value in keeping the matter public. Particularly, students, as the public seems to believe that we lawyers are prone to hide our indiscretions from them as much as possible. So this is an opportunity to show our good faith. To be completely public, as it were."

Justice Mariner stands, buttoning his suit jacket, inadvertently kicking my carrier at his feet, so that I can view the bench only through the side vents. I can see quite clearly, though, that because the matter is before a lowly provincial court judge (if only a *pro tempore* one on his way up), no counsel is robed. "Thank you, Your Honour. In fact, we are making a section 539 application for a publication ban. As well, I would ask that witnesses be excluded from the room until they have testified."

"I see," Justice Cactus says, pushing his lips out skeptically to convey that he doesn't really see at all. "I see."

"Also, with respect, Your Honour, I would submit that, as my client has the right to be presumed innocent and he has not been so much as arraigned yet, there is no evidence that anyone committed any indiscretion."

Justice Cactus looks like he has been pole-axed, then waxes forgiving and a little sad, leaning toward the well of the room. "Of

course not, Mr. Mariner. Students, for the purposes of this proceeding, Justice Mariner is a mister, as he is counsel in the cause.
I, in this case, am the judge." His Honour nods a little glary-eyed,
I'd say, at Justice Mariner. "And *Mr.* Mariner would be the first to
tell you that it is one thing to bring on your defence, and quite
another to be defensive from the get-go. Being defensive, ladies
and gentleman, being reactionary, as it were, too anxious to object,
well, it can quite hurt your case, isn't that so, Mr. Mariner? It can
make it look, indeed, like one has something to hide. Isn't that so,
Mr. Mariner?"

"Absolutely, Your Honour. But of course Your Honour is
widely celebrated as a beacon of justice and fair play. And in
keeping with that well-deserved reputation, well, I just didn't want
to start things off with any premature adjudication, as Rumpole of
the Bailey calls it."

Justice Cactus shows his teeth, but only after the hilarity in the
rest of the room dies out. Studiously ignoring counsel for the
defence, he says, "Well, for better or worse, Mr. Rumpole is not
with us today. When I mentioned indiscretions in our profession,
students, I of course was speaking generally, about the general
public's unfortunate — and, in fact, prejudicial — view that we
lawyers, generally speaking, can be shifty. They forget all the good
we do for them in society, such as" — His Honour nods at Justice
Mariner without looking at him — "defending and promoting
civil rights, taking cases for free or on legal aid and contingency,
representing societal outcasts, the so-called outlaw, that sort of
thing. I mean, it is lawyers, students, isn't it?, who ended segrega-
tion in the United States, brought abortion out of the back alleys,
who staff our human rights commissions?" His Honour smiles

down at the assembled students, fifty-six percent of whom would be female if they are a representative sampling of Eureka Hoover's official statistics for the entire law school. "Lawyers who helped women get the vote. As to the publication ban, well I had understood that we were dispensing with it in this case. However, students, it is mandatory if Mr. Mariner requests it, so I must instruct everyone in the room that they are not to publish or broadcast the evidence in this hearing until Professor Herskowitz is either discharged or his trial, *if ordered*," — His Honour cambers his eyebrows at Justice Mariner — "is ended. If there is any person in the room who is to testify in this hearing, please remove yourself and someone will show you where to wait until you are called. Dean Pilchard, could you see to that, please, sir? Meanwhile, witnesses, please do not discuss your evidence with anyone. The reason for all this, students, is to ensure that the testimony of one witness will not influence that of any other witness. All right, then. Madam clerk, would you please arraign the accused?"

Althea Thornicroft, Justice Cactus's clerk, stands and recites: "Maccabeus Theodor Herskowitz, you stand charged that on or about the thirty-first day of October, 2006, in the City of Toronto, you did cause the death of Antonio Albinoni and thereby did commit murder in the first degree, contrary to section 235(1) of the *Criminal Code of Canada*."

"You will notice, students," Socrates-Cactus instructs, painstakingly demonstrating yet again that he is fairer than fair, "that we do not ask the accused man how he pleads. This is because the whole point of the exercise is to determine if there is to be a trial at all. We ask for a plea only at the start of the trial" (he turns his wooden grin on Justice Mariner) "*if, if* the case ever gets there.

Now Mr. Katz — this is the Crown prosecutor, students, Mr. Frai . . . Mr. P. Frederick Katz — at this point, Mr. Katz will begin his attempt to send us down that road."

Fraidy jumps to his feet, and opens his mouth, only to be immediately squelched by the presiding pedant. His Honour surveys the room in his best judicious manner, before glaring at Justice Mariner as he says, "And can anyone tell us the test the Crown must meet to send the case on to trial? What Mr. Katz must show before anyone can say anyone committed any indiscretion let alone crime?"

Only one student raises her hand. It is Betsy Hnatyshyn, and she is sitting in the second row, centre, just behind Mack Herskowitz. (For the unusual occasion, Justice Cactus has dispensed with the prisoner's dock.) "Yes?"

"I think it's section 548, right?" Betsy reads from her *Criminal Code*. "Mr. Katz has to give you 'sufficient evidence to put the accused on trial for the offence charged or any other indictable offence in respect of the same transaction'?"

"That's correct as far as it goes," Justice Cactus says, immediately giving poor Hnatyshyn the cold shoulder, gazing around the large room. "But there is a specific test in the case law. Anybody?"

There is a voice behind me, faint enough as to come from the very back of the room, anonymous and shadowy. "'The Crown must put forward evidence upon which a reasonable jury, properly instructed, could return a verdict of guilty.'"

The voice belongs to Zipporah Kyriakos.

CHAPTER 3

One of the fathers saith . . . that old men go to
death, and death comes to young men.
Francis Bacon, *Apothegms*

Some say that, after Einstein, we live in the age of pure relativity. Everything is relative, shifting, contextual, evanescent: nothing is absolute. Nothing is ever for certain. This view has infected even our moral universe. But the truth is not a matter of perspective. Truth is always absolute. That is its nature. Consider the following story:

A psychiatrist develops a simplified Rorschach test of three figures. He draws a triangle and asks his patient, "What do you see?"

"I see a tent. Inside, a couple is making love."

The psychiatrist draws a rectangle and asks, "Now what do you see?"

"A big bed. Two couples are making love in it."

The psychiatrist draws a circle.

"That's an arena. A dozen couples are making love there."

The psychiatrist remarks, "You seem to have sex on your mind."

"But doctor," the patient replies, "You drew the pictures."

The truth of what the man sees is subjective: he sees what he sees, through the lens of his own being and experience. That is his truth — a relative truth. But the objective truth remains: a triangle, a rectangle, and a circle. In the end, truth is not relative.

I have one, M'lord. I have one: Two laboratory rats are talking. One asks the other, "How's it going with the scientist?" "It's great," the second replies. "I've got him so well trained, every time I push that lever he brings me food." And that is the rat's relative truth. But it is only the rat's . . .

Mental derangement takes many forms and warped perspectives, including racial prejudice. Some among us close their eyes to the objective truth. That is what we find in the views of the respondent, Mr. Pasties. He asks what is truth, but will not stay for an answer. He asks . . .

Interrupting our deliberations in *R. v. Pasties*, the Crown begins *R. v. Herskowitz* with witnesses Reg Holdsworth and Dougal Fergus, chiefly to show that Herskowitz is a square peg in a round hole. His perspective is not the conventional one at the law school. The students complain about him regularly, the Crown establishes, and he often butts heads with the law school's administration. He's antagonistic by nature.

"Mack can be uncompromising," Holdsworth admits.

In cross-examination (and having stored *R. v. Pasties* in its proper file), Justice Mariner asks Holdsworth only four questions:

"You respect Professor Herskowitz as a teacher, do you not, Professor Holdsworth?"

"I do."

"And when you say he's uncompromising, well, as another professor in the faculty you're pretty firm on certain matters of law and philosophy yourself, isn't that so?"

"Well, in my own view I'm a man of supreme reason, Judge.

You know that."

"So what some people call uncompromising, many of us might call principled?"

"Yes. I would say Mack is a man of principle. Not always my principles . . ."

"But, your principles, Professor, or my principles, or His Honour's principles are not in issue, correct? And you would still say Mack is a man of principle. As far as you know, one of his principles is that teaching law is not a popularity contest, but requires only that the teacher do his best to turn sometimes shall we say reluctant students into competent lawyers, people who deal with the most serious problems in our lives?"

"Oh, I'm sure of that, Judge. Mack has very high pedagogical standards. And the students don't always appreciate it. That's the whole point of being a so-called Socratic. It's not a popularity contest. It's a matter of teaching them the subject. And he mentors some of our best students."

After Red Reg gives his scrupulously supportive evidence, he takes a seat in the front row of the auditorium, just behind the counsel tables, to listen to the Crown's next witness, Megan Skaldpedar.

The Crown has called the assistant professor largely to say that many modern law teachers view the Socratic method as past its best-before date. "In fact, many people now think it's abusive," she testifies, "that it puts the professor at the top of a paternalistic hierarchy, talking down to the students. We view this as bad, professionally, because it sets up a hierarchical system of bullying and entitlement that persists when they join law firms as junior associates. It's indoctrination along traditional paternalistic lines, with the students and junior lawyers as serfs, and the senior partners as lords of the manor. The great slave masters. It just perpetuates hierarchy and sexism."

Immediately this inspires Holdsworth to trot over to our table and whisper hoarsely into Justice Mariner's ear, "That's codswallop, Ted. Call her on it! Mind you, I'm not surprised, coming from that one. Remember what George Orwell said about socialists? 'All that dreary tribe of high-minded women and sandal-wearers and bearded fruit-juice drinkers, who come flocking toward the smell of "progress" like bluebottles to a dead cat'?"

Apparently Skaldpedar's not red enough for Red Reg, the comrade in the grey flannel suit who quotes repulsive dead-mammal metaphors.

"I'm not sure old Cactus reads Orwell, Reg. My guess is Andrea Dworkin or Catherine MacKinnon is more up her dead-cat alley."

Holdsworth cups his ear. "Sirens of the mind, both of them. Or is that just the thought police I hear rushing to the scene?"

"But I'll certainly cross her on the point."

Well, in fact we manage to establish that reasonable law professors can differ on the appropriate methods of instruction. And there's this, as the official transcript has it:

Mr. Mariner: I believe Socrates was lecturing and teaching about five hundred years before Christ, is that correct, Ms. Skaldpedar?

Witness: I'd have to take your word on that, Justice Mariner. I'm not up on my classical philosophers, or at least not on their dates.

Mr. Mariner: In fact, you're rather young and new to law teaching, are you not?

Witness: This is my second year at the Farb.

Mr. Mariner: And your specialties in law are labour, feminism, civil rights?

Witness: That's correct.

Mr. Mariner: Sort of anti-Establishment, left-leaning — critical legal theory and all that modernist sort of thing? Out with the old, in with the new, especially if the old's a bunch of white males who oppressed women and minorities? And "the new" is young and more often female?

[*And high-minded sandal-wearers,* His Lordship resists the temptation to add.]

Witness: Maybe from your point of view. Maybe from Mack's point of view.

Mr. Mariner: Oh, really. Am I misstating your point of view?

Witness: Maybe oversimplifying it.

Discussion off the record regarding conduct of the proceedings. Which is to say (according to the official Amicus, Q.C., transcript):

"Right on!" Unrecorded on the official transcript, a hoarse woman's voice rings from the tiered seating.

"Hey, ancient Mariner! Bullies never prosper!" someone else hollers, eliciting some nervous laughter.

"Students." Justice Cactus looks not so much annoyed as saddened. "If we want to continue in this forum, you must conduct yourselves like professionals, not like members of Parliament. I remind you: This is a courtroom."

Dean Pilchard stands at his seat in the front row, actually wringing his long, white, and probably wet hands. "Students, these outbursts are not a credit to you or the law school. Justice Cactus would be thoroughly within his rights to demand that you explain why he should not hold you in contempt of court." His voice is shrill with anxiety. "I will warn you once that the law school takes this matter very seriously."

The Court: Mr. Mariner. You were asking Professor Skaldpedar about her view of Professor Herskowitz, professionally.

Mr. Mariner: Thank you, Your Honour. The point is, Ms. Skaldpedar, you've never really approved of Professor Herskowitz, have you, never really cared for him as a live, white male?

Witness: Well, it's none of my business really what his opinions are. As you said, different profs have different views. I don't sleep with him. I just work with him.

The Court: Students, please, despite certain appearances, this is not a situation comedy.

Mr. Mariner: You might not be intimate with Professor Herskowitz, but that doesn't mean you find his views tolerable, does it, Ms. Skaldpedar? As a teaching colleague, you don't really approve of how he teaches, or of his professional and personal views, his institute, all that sort of traditional — that perhaps Establishment or patriarchal, in your view — all that baggage. You think he's a bit of a dinosaur, don't you, and one with teeth, at that? One of those abusive patriarchal, what was it, "hierarchies" types?

Mr. Katz: Your Honour, Mr. Mariner is giving evidence and putting words in the witness's, *Professor* Skaldpedar's, mouth.

The Court: Yes, but I think she can answer, Mr. Katz. Professor Skaldpedar is a professor of law, after all. She can correct these misstatements or oversimplifications Mr. Mariner has made.

(Unofficial transcript: Let the record show that the witness does not return His Honour's solicitous smile, although Mr. Mariner somewhat audibly buzzes his lips.)

Witness: He said "dinosaur," Your Honour, not me.

Mr. Mariner: That's your view, isn't it? But as a law teacher of a whole two years' experience, you would agree with me, I take it, that whatever one thinks of the Socratic method, it has the virtue of being time-tested during more than twenty-five hundred years?

Witness: It's been around the block a few times, if that's what you mean.

Well, the old fellow's a little rusty as a barrister. Too many years in the driver's seat, I guess, or at the tiller, if not the rudder. Maybe it wasn't the most brilliant piece of cross-examination, but the point was made. Like others in the Farb's faculty and student body, Skaldpedar thinks Herskowitz is a nasty old has-been — just possibly a dinosaur who deserves to be extinct, no matter what had happened to Tony Albinoni. Justice Mariner has been successful in showing her bias, thereby denting her credibility in the cause.

✌

The Crown has updated its disclosure package — its evidence in the prosecution, all of which it is obliged to disclose to the defence — with entries from the books for Herskowitz's Institute for the Wrongfully Acquitted Criminal. Justice Mariner and Leland Gaunt pore over the photocopied pages, eating grilled vegetables in whole wheat tortillas from Bad Wrap just under the Sheraton Hotel (specialty, according to a grease-stained poster over their steam tables: "Fish'n'chips with fries"). Licking a couple of greasy crumbs from said sheets, I see, before the lawyers shoo me away:

Extraordinary expenses

Date	Expense	Re:
Sept. 01/06	$1,000	Albinoni
Sept. 03	$11,600	Buenos Aires: conference (MH+ZK)
Sept. 22	$6,800	Lyon/Paris/London/Dublin: conference, meetings (MH+ZK: itemized *infra*)
Oct. 01/06	$1,000	Albinoni
Oct. 06	$960	Ottawa panel: MH
Oct. 10-12	$1,358	Stratford weekend; dinner with local counsel, RF, DZ and spouses
Oct. 18	$225	Expenses re conference at Osgoode Hall
Oct. 31/06	see infra:	IWAC gourmet night; itemized under Meals/Entertainment, supra
Nov. 01/06	$1,500	Topo
Nov. 06	$321	Books — Amazon.ca (for library)
Nov. 11	$82.50	Expenses, MH teaching at bar admission course
Nov. 25	134.62??	(MH — expenses re ??)
Dec. 01/06	$2,000	Topo

∽✪∽

After lunch, Dougal Fergus testifies for the Crown that, during his first semester of law school, he was part of a group from Tort Law I that approached Dean Pilchard to complain about Mack Herskowitz. The gist of the student's testimony is: "Professor Herskowitz disrespected us. He never answered any questions. Instead of teaching us the material, he made us figure it all out ourselves — from the first day we walked into law school." In cross-examination, we establish that, one, law school is not junior high school; two, Mr. Fergus is an adult; and, three, adults, particularly those seeking careers in the most demanding professions, generally are meant to be self-reliant and creative in solving problems.

Pilchard follows on the witness stand, to confirm that each academic year he receives one or two such student deputations, sent out by their classmates to advise his office that Herskowitz is abusive, a bully, unfair, sexist, classist, disrespectful, arrogant, a bad teacher who makes the students teach themselves, in breach of the *Human Rights Code*, and so on. Dutifully, the dean broaches the matter with Herskowitz, who typically reminds the dean that being demanding is not bullying or unfairly discriminatory; rather, it is good training for half-formed minds who want to be fully fledged Bay Street lawyers. He is not in the business of being popular, Herskowitz always sniffs with exaggerated patience; he is in the business of working his shift at this particular legal sausage factory, grinding out market-ready barristers and solicitors. And the seasons they went round and round, until one day a particularly rebellious half-formed mind died in Herskowitz's apartment, whose occasional co-tenant was the Crown's next witness, Zipporah Kyriakos.

Again, in the way of the efficient predator, we might as well head straight for the juicy innards of Zippy's testimony. Readers who have done more than nod off in their comfy chairs are already familiar with most of what she tells the court — how she and Herskowitz hooked up amid the ruins when Herskowitz bankrupted her former boyfriend, wayward lawyer Marcus Merdnyk; her administrative and bookkeeping work at IWAC; how Herskowitz ran interference for her so she was admitted as a student in the law faculty; the events of the fateful Gourmet Night, including the spat at the table about who actually wrote the Socrates paper concerning the ancient philosopher's allegedly suicidal behaviour. But, reliably, Katz has done his spadework, interviewing other students at the Farb, who have the latest gossip.

"Now, Ms. Kyriakos, you've told us that it was you and Tony, the deceased young man, who did most of the work on the Socrates paper. And that Professor Herskowitz became insulting about that at the dinner table."

"Well, to be fair, he'd had a couple of drinks."

"A couple, Ms. Kyriakos?"

"Well, maybe more than a couple."

"Isn't it true that he had more than a couple most days?"

Justice Mariner objects. "He's leading, Your Honour. And the relevance of this topic is dubious."

"Ms. Kyriakos," Justice Cactus interrupts. "How often does Professor Herskowitz take a bit of a tipple?" Pleased with the turn of phrase, the court smirks at the students.

"Well, most nights. But not days. As sort of a bon vivant, a gourmet, I guess, he enjoys wine and spirits, but he's quite responsible — serious — about his teaching and such. And he needs a sharp mind for that."

"So we've heard. Razor sharp."

"You could say that."

"Not an easy guy to live with," Katz says.

"Your Honour," Justice Mariner interrupts again, "he's cross-examining his own witness."

"I wouldn't go that far, Mr. Mariner. I'll allow it. The witness will tell us, students, whether the professor was an easy guy to live with."

"No, but then most interesting people have an edge or two."

"Like Tony Albinoni," Katz says, leading.

The witness laughs quietly, prettily, almost hushing herself as she looks down at her feet in the witness box (a lectern with its own microphone, actually, called into service for the purpose). "Tony certainly was edgy, yes. For sure."

"Is that why he appealed to you?"

"Tony? He was a bit of a laugh. And I'm sort of drawn to the rebellious type, I guess."

"Drawn? Let's see — Marcus Merdnyk, Mack Herskowitz, Mr. Albinoni. Wasn't it sort of fatal attraction, Ms. Kyriakos?"

The witness is no longer giggling. She looks Katz straight in the face, but the blood has drained from her own, blanching her fetching freckles. "What's that supposed to mean?"

"You might well ask," Justice Mariner not-quite-whispers.

"Well, what exactly was your relationship with Mr. Albinoni?"

"Finally," Justice Mariner says, dropping his pen and not bothering to stand, "a proper question."

"You're not on the bench now, Mr. Mariner," Justice Cactus responds.

"Yes, I've noticed that, Your Honour."

"We were friends," the witness says, her voice rising in pitch and volume.

"I think you know what I'm getting at, Ms. Kyriakos," Katz says.

"Yes, all right. We·slept together." Now the freckles have disappeared as the tide comes back in, all aflush. The witness looks at her feet again, then quickly glances over at Herskowitz, before saying to her hands, clenched before her on the lectern, "Is that what you want to know? As if it does any good to make it all public. It was only twice, for God's sake." She looks up at Katz, her eyes flashing. "Twice. There was no 'relationship,' damn it, Mr. Katz. It was just twice. We'd spent a lot of time together, intense time, working late, drinking the professor's wine, bitching about how he treated us, freaking out about exams and all that. We just got carried away. It was just twice. *Twice.* There was *no* relationship. We were thrown together in a pressure cooker and we got carried away."

I turn to look at the accused prisoner, Maccabeus Theodor Herskowitz. He gazes steadily at his weeping girlfriend with what looks more like sadness than anger, resolve rather than defeat. But whether he actually hears her remains a moot question in the moot court. On which note, we make the tactical decision not to cross-examine the witness.

It was prettily devised of Aesop, "The fly sat upon the axle-tree of the chariot-wheel and said, what a dust do I raise."
Francis Bacon, *Essays*, "Of Vain-Glory"

"Let's assume you've successfully completed the bar course." Justice Mariner sits on the edge of the table in the front of the room, swinging his expensively-furnished leg (fashions by Harry Rosen of Bloor Street) as the students giggle and squirm over their anticipated careers. I sit further back, in my carrier, on the floor and against the wall, in Seminar Room 101B, Legal Profession, T-Th, 11-12, Mariner J.A. (incarceration by Canadian Tire). "My wife comes to you and says she's charged with murder. In fact, she's cut my throat with a steak knife. As her lawyer, do you want to know that detail?"

"Maybe she just thought you were really dishy," a man answers. He's slightly older than most of the students, nervous, near-sighted, balding, sitting apart from the others — a secular Chassid. "You know, real beefcake." He pulls at his bushy beard, which is going silvery at the edges.

The judge smiles. "Whether you go with some sort of insanity defence, that comes later. What I'm asking is, for starters, as her lawyer, do you want to know that she actually did it? Do you want the Truth, with a capital t?"

"Well," another student says, a young woman in winged eye-glasses with rhinestones at the tips — the style wildly popular during the heyday of Justice Mariner's mother, and a look that still seems to scream Feeb! fifty years later. "Isn't that what they say a trial is all about — the search for the truth? So, as your wife's lawyer, don't I want to know everything I can find out, in order to prepare the best defence? I need the whole truth. So I can defend with it or against it. So there are no surprises."

"Okay. But then what do you mean by 'the whole truth'? Isn't the threshold question: In law, what's truth?" Justice Mariner asks. "Anyone? Hello? What's the difference between what you *know* and what you *suspect?*" When no one hazards a guess, the judge says, "Let me read to you from the lawyer's *Rules of Professional Conduct* for our province." He holds up the manual published by the Law Society. "Rule Four Point Zero Six: 'A lawyer shall encourage public respect for and try to improve the administration of justice.' No surprises there, right?"

"I don't think the public thinks lawyers encourage respect for justice," the mature student says with a self-conscious smile. "They think lawyers try to get away with murder."

"Aha," the judge replies. "Consider also, then, the commentary on Rule Four Point Zero One, concerning 'the lawyer as advocate': 'The lawyer has a duty to the client to raise fearlessly every issue, advance every argument, and ask every question, however distasteful, which the lawyer thinks will help the client's case . . . .. In adversary proceedings . . . the lawyer is not obliged (save as required by law or under these rules . . .) to assist an adversary or advance matters derogatory to the client's case.' Do these two sub-rules square — the duty to encourage respect for justice and the duty to advance the distasteful arguments?"

"Not always," Mature Student says. "The public thinks if the guy — or the woman — if they're guilty, well, that's it. They're guilty and the lawyer shouldn't be trying to hide that. Or obscure it. They don't like tricks and technicalities."

Justice Mariner sniffs and looks around the classroom. "Do you want to know whether my wife really did it? Do you want The Whole Truth?"

"Well, if you knew she did it and you said in court she didn't do it, you'd be lying, right?" It's another young woman this time, rail thin, in a sleeveless top that shows every bone. Her face is pinched and pale, sad and long. She looks a little like a plucked chicken. You get the feeling she is in law school as some sort of defence mechanism. But then, aren't we all?

Justice Mariner holds up a finger. "Further commentary to Rule Four Point Oh One, 'The Lawyer as Advocate.'" He reads again from the *Rules of Professional Conduct:* "'Admissions made by the accused to a lawyer may impose strict limitations on the conduct of the defence . . . For example, if the accused clearly admits to the lawyer the factual and mental elements necessary to constitute the crime, the lawyer, *if convinced that the admissions are true and voluntary,* may properly take objection to the jurisdiction of the court, or to the form of the indictment . . .' Or you can argue over whether certain evidence can get in, blah-blah-blah, but — and here's the point, folks — *but,* if you know your client did it, you're not allowed to suggest somebody else did it or lead evidence that says your client didn't do it. So, do you want to know that my wife actually did the deed? And what does that say about justice, and respect for it?"

"What if you're not 'convinced' that the client is telling the truth?" Winged Victory (With Rhinestones) asks.

"What if, indeed?" Justice Mariner replies. "You can always finagle your way out of it, can't you? So what, in law, is truth? Is it all relative, a matter of subjective definition? Can we play semantic games? Can you just say, 'Well, that's her truth, my truth is something different, the jury's is something different yet again, so I can still plead her not guilty? It's all just words?' There's no absolute truth? Is that appropriate behaviour under the rule of law? Think of the O.J. Simpson case: he was acquitted in his criminal trial — the jury found him not guilty beyond a reasonable doubt of killing his wife and her friend — but in the civil lawsuit by the wife's family, the jury found that he was liable on a balance of probabilities. That is, they thought he probably did it, where the criminal jury might have thought the same thing, but they had to be almost certain he did it before they could say he did it."

The students look baffled. "For Thursday," Justice Mariner says, snapping the professional conduct manual shut with one hand, "write me five hundred to a thousand words on this proposition: 'In law, what is true is what can be proved.'"

⁓ලෙ⁓

Speaking of what can be proved: Down from the aerated heights of academe and into the real world of dead law-student researchers and the professors who might have killed them, the Crown calls Vernon Gander, Assistant Deputy Minister of Justice for Her Majesty's federal government in Ottawa

Gander repeats to the hushed court what he has told Mr. Justice Mariner some weeks earlier — basically that Herskowitz ran a sex-for-grades racket — after which, Katz asks him:

"And why have you come forward now, Mr. Gander? After all these years, with your professional reputation secured?"

"Because I couldn't live with it — in silence, I mean. It seemed like it had all gone too far. I thought Tony might have got caught up in the same sort of thing. And I couldn't allow it to continue. I didn't want to see others go through what I've suffered."

We object to that, of course, as absurdly speculative and perhaps self-serving. "Also it unfairly tends to show a supposed propensity," Justice Mariner argues, "a propensity in my client to do certain unsavoury things. There is no evidence anyone else has gone through what Mr. Gander alleges, and we have only his word on even that. From years and years ago, Your Honour. I mean, memory colours things, especially regarding experiences we've had as students. We tend to see the faculty as the enemy, sometimes, don't we — the people with our future in their hands, who don't give us the grades we deserve? And we can get very bitter about that, as I'm sure Mr. Gander would agree."

Cactus does his best to look unmoved, and instead of replying, Katz rolls his eyes as he requests another publication ban, a permanent one this time, on anything that would reveal Gander's identity. Justice Cactus solves the immediate problem of duelling submissions by reminding the students that, to preserve the publication ban as well as Mr. Gander's privacy at this point, they are not to discuss the evidence outside the courtroom. "We'll consider anything more long-term later, Mr. Katz. Let's see where this goes." Then Justice Cactus turns to the defence table and says, "Mr. Mariner? Are you still objecting, or are you cross-examining? Or making a speech, perhaps?"

"Is there really any need for us to go on, Your Honour?"

"Yes, I think he has a point, Mr. Katz," Justice Cactus allows, sitting back and making a triangle of his hands under his chin, not missing a beat. He is, in fact, a fair and experienced jurist. "I can't commit Professor Herskowitz to trial just because he was unpopular with many students and faculty. Half the world would be in jail on that standard. And what may or may not have happened to Mr. Gander has nothing necessarily to do with the charges before me. In law, Mr. Mariner is correct on that."

"But what about the evidence, Your Honour, including Mr. Gander's but not just his, on how the professor persistently engages in abuse of students? And what about the fact that Mr. Albinoni slept with the professor's girlfriend? I suspect, cumulatively, that we have the motive for murder."

"Well, yes, the young woman's evidence does supply some motive, I suppose, Mr. Katz. But Mr. Mariner, wisely, it seems, has left her testimony alone, unchallenged. It adds little to your case, Mr. Katz. We have no evidence that the professor even knew about his girlfriend's, well, intimacies, shall we say, with Mr. Albinoni. And whatever happened between Mr. Gander and Professor Herskowitz — and students, you must realize that, again, Mr. Gander's evidence is completely untested at this point; his statements are mere allegations — but whatever happened there, Mr. Katz, well, there is no necessary link between all that and what happened to the unfortunate Mr. Albinoni. I mean, unchallenged, we have what? — evidence that Professor Herskowitz was intimate with both women and men, illicitly or not, and all sorts of other things that have become more or less acceptable these days, socially, at least." Is it my imagination, or does Justice Cactus cast an accusing look here at the other judge in the room, the one who is, at least notionally, superior to him as an appeal judge, albeit outlawed to the wilds of Scarberia? "So I can't commit the professor to trial on that, either — not regarding the murder of Mr. Albinoni. We don't have much more than rumours, really about these, these, well, these alleged sexualized doings, and you haven't charged him with anything related to Mr. Gander."

"Well, but Your Honour, I have one more witness who can help make the link with much of this to Tony Albinoni, and through him, to a whole raft of offences, from murder to mischief to obstructing justice. I mean, if, or when, Justice, er, Mr. Mariner is finished with this witness, the Crown will call Ms. Deena Topo, Mr. Albinoni's spouse."

"Mr. Mariner?"

"Let him do his worst, Your Honour. We say he has no case. As Your Honour has so felicitously stated. And by the way, Katz, you haven't charged my client with a whole raft of offences. Anything but murder is irrelevant to this proceeding, as His Honour has already explained. Not to mention scandalous and malicious. You shouldn't even be mentioning it."

Meanwhile Dean Pilchard has risen to walk to the back of the moot courtroom. He calls out through the centre doors, "Ms. Topo! Deena Topo. The Crown calls Deena Topo."

Someone immediately comes in through the doors thirty or forty feet to the dean's right, the doors leading to the left aisle seats. The newcomer stands in the shadows at the top of the stairs and shouts, "That won't be necessary."

Yes, the voice certainly is familiar, shrill like Topo's, but a little deeper. The figure, in fact — if one's slightly clouded but still vital feline eyes do not deceive one — well, not to put too fine a point on it: The figure is Tony Albinoni.

∾୨୧∾

After an adjournment, during which counsel consult with Justice Cactus backstage, Cactus dismisses the charges against Herskowitz, remarking to the students that this certainly has been a unique educational opportunity for everyone involved. "Myself, as well, students. You should know that I have been at the bar of this province for over forty years. And this is the first time that I have witnessed a resurrection, inside or outside a murder prosecution. Mind you, it is coming on for Easter. And the accused man, Professor Herskowitz, is discharged, resurrected as a man with no charges hanging over his head. Meanwhile, the press shall not publish any details so as to identify Mr. Vernon Gander as a witness in this proceeding."

"I'm wondering, Your Honour," Justice Mariner wonders, unfolding his lean, somewhat feline body to its full length, "if maybe we could have a ban on his evidence, period. I mean, it's unproven, and could be very damaging to my client, without having been tested in court."

"It could be just as damaging to Mr. Gander, Mr. Mariner, even if it never goes beyond this room. And if it's true, well, it already has hurt him, hasn't it, and he has been rather brave to come forward, has he not? If he can stand the glare . . . Well, anyway, there is other recourse to clear up that matter. Perhaps the faculty council, Dean, concerning Professor Herskowitz's, well, grading methods, not to mention Mr. Albinoni's reappearing act?

Perhaps a civil action. That is not up to me. Justice must be seen to be done, as you know, Mr. Mariner. Publicly. Justice, as they say, is not a cloistered virtue. It belongs to the people. It is their right to know and see. And you have already done quite well by this proceeding, in my humble, lower-court opinion."

And there endeth the lesson. Before sweeping backstage in full judicial regalia, Justice Cactus casts a grave and significant look toward where the local press sit in a gaggle. His Honour releases Mack Herskowitz from custody, then thanks the students and administration at the Farb as Paul Frederick Katz comes up to the defence table, all elbows and miniature Napoleonic chin, trembling with righteous anger. "I don't know exactly what you had to do with this little sideshow, Judge," he says to His Lordship, choking on fury and menace. "But I'm going to get to the bottom of it. You can count on it, yes, sir. That's both a threat and a promise."

From his six-feet-something, Justice Mariner looks down on the assistant Crown with a little half-smile and says: "Same to you with bells on, Fraidy." He stretches out the e sound — *FraidEEE* — as his smile expands into a full-fledged grin.

CHAPTER 5

A much-talking judge is like an ill-tuned cymbal.
Attributed by Lord Birkenhead to Francis Bacon

In this scientific age, the conventional thinking is that truth is absolute. But truth can still be elusive, of course, or misleading. Take, for example, what financial analysts call the dead cat bounce. At first, judging by all the conventional signs, everyone thinks the stock market is recovering. Then, suddenly, it falls back. Up and down in a trice. It was just a bounce. A dead cat bounce, an illusory recovery. In other words, in the case before us, whatever was the precise number of Acadians expelled from Canada during 1755-62, however successful francophones have been in pleading their case since, the respondent Mr. Pasties relies on how perceptions of the truth . . .

I interrupt the deliberations yet again to note that, happily, we do not have personal experience of this dead cat bounce, so-called. We're still paying off the bills from the Mariner daughters' university and law school educations and therefore we remain without "discretionary income" or stakes to wager on other gambles, such as the so-called free markets. It was Justice Fierstein who first brought to our attention this infelicitously named phenomenon, this (I shudder to repeat the repugnant metaphor) shall we say deceased-feline short-term rebound. "Two days later, I lost every penny I made two days before," Marv Fierstein explained in chambers at Osgoode Hall, while we were meant to be discussing *R. v. Pasties.* "What they call a dead cat bounce. We thought the cat was a goner, and it turns out we was right." He's a bit of a joker is old Marv Fierstein.

Oh, and did I say? We (Justice Mariner and I) are back in chambers ourselves just now, at Oz, albeit exiled (again) in our own office to a little cherry-wood side table off by the radiator, given that this year's gaggle of articling students, the latest crop of clerks to the Court of Appeal, has taken over our desk and antique chair, at one time the property of John Beverley Robinson, former attorney-general, President of the Executive Council of Upper Canada, and original owner of the patch of real estate on which this very building rests. And speaking of interruptions, Sandy Pargeter, His Lordship's administrative assistant (a.k.a. secretary to unreconstructed sorts like ourselves) knocks to tell us, in true Porlockian style, that the Chief Justice is ready for us.

I of course must report this particular meeting at second hand, having been stowed for the occasion in my Humpty Dumpty box behind said desk and antique chair, to be alternately cooed over and kicked at by sundry law students. Such is life at the bar: you get your sympathetic judges, and you get your hanging ones. Speaking of which, I have pieced together what was said at the meeting with the Chief from what I have heard his Lordship tell Sandy, Penny, Herskowitz, Lee Gaunt, and so on — and on and on . . .

When Justice Mariner arrived at the CJ's office, he discovered it was to be a bit of a party, a hanging party, that is, your good old-fashioned lynch mob. Also present were P. Frederick Katz and, in his role as counsel to the Canadian Judicial Council, Tristan Chase, otherwise a specialist in malpractice litigation. Indeed, Chase likes to say that when it comes to malpractice he is an equal opportunity harasser, borrowing for his sword of Justice the physician's lancet, and for his scales of Justice the law courts' weigh-scales. Medical men, lawyers, dentists, chiropractors, massage therapists, denturists, podiatrists — his practice depends merrily upon their professional incompetence and bad faith.

This is cold comfort to Justice Mariner, of course, particularly when the Chief Justice says: "Ted. This Herskowitz business. Not to beat around the bush, Frederick's suggested to me that, well, perhaps with the best of intentions, well, there's no way of sugarcoating it. Not to beat around the bush, as I say, but, well, Ted, I hate to say it, I'd rather not say it, actually, but Mr. Katz tells me, and so I have to act on it, you know, Ted, he tells me, and this is why we're here, just to look into it, for now, anyway, he says there might have been, well, as the *Criminal Code* would put it, let's say a, I don't know, a conspiracy, uh, well, an agreement to obstruct the course of justice. With the best of intentions, perhaps, uh, I suppose the best of *your* intentions, I regret to say it, Ted."

"How could there be good intentions to obstruct justice, Chief Justice?" Ted Mariner reasonably asks, smiling. "Particularly by a judge, such as ourselves, of Her Majesty's appellate courts?"

"And," the CJ presses on, panting a little, "at the very least, whatever your role in it was, you, uh, well, Ted, for Christ's sake, Ted, you didn't even bother to report it. What in the hell were you thinking?" Now the man is angry, not so much at what Ted Mariner is said to have done as for the embarrassing position the Chief Justice finds himself in at this moment. "Not to mention, you, a justice, as you put it, of Her Majesty's appellate courts, put yourself forward to defend this man accused of all sorts of shenanigans with his students, never mind your own history in that swamp, this consorting with students business, need I bring it up again . . .

"No you needn't," I imagine Justice Mariner mutters, ventriloquist-fashion.

" . . . in that particular little swamp — and never mind, come to that, any allegations of murder or public mischief or whatever Mr. Katz has got up his sleeve at this particular point in the Herskowitz matter."

"So much, Chief Justice," Katz replies, while staring at Justice Mariner, "that I need both sleeves as well as the legs of my trousers."

"Well, Fraidy," Justice Mariner sneers, "if that's the only thing that wants to get into your pants, go for it."

"And here I thought I'd sent you out of harm's way," the CJ hastily adds, throwing old Ted a look of manifest dismay.

"Charming," Justice Mariner mutters, at least in my mind's ear, before he comes to his own defence in this particular kangaroo court (yet another sign, I guess, that we have been transported to the antipodes for imagined former crimes, and are about to be sent back there — to Tasmania by way of Scarberia — as outlaws for imagined new ones). "First of all, Chief Justice, I can tell you that there was never any intention on the part of my client, Professor Herskowitz, nor, as far as I know, the student, Albinoni," here Justice Mariner nods at Katz, "to commit the offence Mr. Katz seems to have in mind — that is, to make it look like Albinoni was dead. To mislead the police or justice or whatever. There certainly was no agreement between them as to that. We thought Albinoni was dead ourselves. Second, I can also tell you for certain that my client had absolutely no intention to harm Albinoni in any way, not even to the point of just having him look like he was dead. As you must have heard by now, this Albinoni character is a law unto himself. I've seen him in action. And now it looks to me like he's been hoist on his own petard. Honestly, that's the whole story there. And we, my client and I, are not responsible for what this kid gets up to."

"I would agree with you there, Judge, as far as that last point goes," Katz says. "You see, Chief Justice, we now know that it was Herskowitz who was supposed to have got the Mickey Finn — the knock-out drink. The professor, not Albinoni, was meant to quaff a strong dose of Percodan or Oxycontin. Dissolved, that is, in his drink."

"Those addictive painkillers, eh?" The Chief Justice nods. "Seems like they're behind nearly half the break-and-enters these days. If what gets prosecuted is any indication."

"That's right, Chief Justice," Katz says. "Those painkillers are behind a goodly number of in-your-face robberies, too — they create more pain than they kill. These are the drug of choice for the young and the clueless, and they get dangerously addicted. So they commit robberies and what-not to get the money for their habits. Anyway, Herskowitz got the drugs through Albinoni, who has told us he obtained the drugs without violence. Or rather, it was Albinoni who was to administer the drug, and his wife was the supplier. She works for a physician, you see, and she forged the prescriptions. Apparently this is a regular practice of hers. Amphetamines when hubby's law school study group wants that extra edge at exam time. A little Perc when they, and Herskowitz, apparently, when they're looking for a little extra buzz. 'You light up my life, / You give me dope to carry on' sort of thing." Katz turns briefly to Justice Mariner, smirking. "Yet another conspiracy, by the bye, not to mention several offences under the *Controlled Drugs and Substances Act* and possibly the *Regulated Health Professions Act*, Mr. Justice Mariner. Anyway, Albinoni was supposed to salt Herskowitz's drink with just enough Perc or Oxycontin so that, how do they put it, so that he was feeling no pain."

"Whatever for?" the CJ asks. "I mean, why risk lives for some stupid game?"

"Well, we don't have the whole story, which is one of the reasons we wanted to talk to Justice Mariner."

"Ever hear of solicitor-client privilege, Fraidy?" Ted Mariner asks.

"Not when the solicitor discovers his client's committed a crime, Ted," the CJ says, "or, rather, is still committing one, conspiring to obstruct justice or commit public mischief. Which you know as well as I do. As well as any bar admission student knows, too. It's stated explicitly in the *Rules of Professional Conduct.*"

"Anyway, Chief Justice," Katz continues, "Herskowitz told Albinoni that the aim of the scheme, on All Hallow's Eve, as it were, the idea was just to test out some half-baked theory of Herskowitz's about Francis Bacon. For Herskowitz's biography, the research he was doing on Bacon. Something about how some cranks say that on April Fool's Day back there in the year dot, well, Bacon didn't really die. He just wanted to escape the disgrace he'd endured when he was sacked as lord chancellor, the bribery scandal and all that, by faking his own death — so the story goes — faking his own death and then running off to France."

"And you're saying that's a crime?" Justice Mariner asks. "Sounds like academic research to me, Fraidy."

"You're saying that forging scrips for controlled narcotics is not a crime? And if you call me 'Fraidy' again, this meeting is over as far as I'm concerned."

"That's not what we're talking about, *Freddie*, and you damn well know it. You just said yourself that Mack had nothing to do with the prescriptions or procuring any drugs. And how do you know I knew any of the details of this so-called conspiracy? How do you know my client did? I told you a minute ago we didn't. And you just agreed that Albinoni's a law unto himself. Anyway, Herskowitz was knocked out just a few minutes. It was Albinoni who disappeared like the Cheshire cat, going out with a mocking grin."

Katz shrugs with a thin little smile of his own. "He was tipsy, maybe stoned, recreationally. So he mixes up the glasses. Inadvertently drinks the stuff down himself. No Perc for Mack Herskowitz."

The Chief Justice interjects. "Anyway, whether this so-called experiment was or was not a crime, Ted, justices of my court should not be involved in these kinds of shenanigans, at any level, even after the fact. What were you thinking, representing this professor, particularly when you're on an academic sabbatical? How does that contribute to public confidence in the administration of justice? I mean, this city is bursting with other over-priced briefs who would gladly have taken this, this . . ."

"Herskowitz," Katz says.

". . . Herskowitz on retainer."

"And if it was all so innocent," Katz adds, "never mind the drugs, how come Herskowitz paid off the Albinonis, and promised to pay them more after they supplied the dope?"

"You mean he was going to pay them off if everybody thought Herskowitz was dead?" the Chief Justice asks.

"Yes, sir. Then the Albinonis were to get the second half of their dirty money, according to Tony. Mr. Mariner knows this as well as I do. But when Albinoni keeled over at the party, well, that put a wrench in the works."

"Mack Herskowitz was paying Albinoni because Albinoni was his research assistant," Justice Mariner interjects, rather loudly with exasperation, one imagines. "The Albinonis needed the money to get the kid through law school. Anyway, even if any of what Fred's saying is true — and I'm not saying it is — but even if it's true, you're still stuck with the fact that it's Albinoni who faked his own death. He apparently ran out of the hospital, Chief Justice, leaving the poor sods there with the impression they'd lost not just the patient but the corpse, and then he was gone for months. Help me, here, Tris. Tell these good fellows that it just doesn't add up. My client ends up in the frame for research on British legal history circa sixteen-whatever, while some kid is running around scot-free, playing dangerous practical jokes."

"I wouldn't go that far, Ted," Chase replies.

Justice Mariner tacks back to Katz. "You've already said the kid was a recreational junkie. If he's drinking down all the dope on the premises, where's your conspiracy?"

"Well, you'd better hope it's down the tubes, Ted." Chase

chooses the inopportune moment to become more voluble, with the ominous voice of authority. Is he implying he will run Ted Mariner off the bench, just like they rousted Francis Bacon from the Woolsack — in 1621, to be precise?

Speaking of whom, and of inopportune moments, Katz adds: "They called it the Bacon Bit. Doing 'a Bacon.'"

"This conspiracy between Herskowitz and the student?" the CJ asks.

"That's right," Katz says.

"What conspiracy?" Justice Mariner shouts, in my mind's ear. "It just doesn't add up, Fred. Mack revives in situ, right before my own eyes, in fact. I was there, a few feet away."

"That's another thing," the Chief Justice grumbles. "Again you're at the scene of a crime. Seems to be becoming a habit."

"Albinoni disappears for months," Justice Mariner presses on, "then ruins his career anyway, and faces possible prosecution, by making this dramatic appearance at the end of the prelim. Maybe he was just showing off, putting one over on the legal establishment. That would be his style. He's a punk. Pinning it on Mack doesn't add up."

Katz shrugs and again shows the accused his icicle smile. "As I say, we don't know everything yet, Ted, but we'll get there. We'll get there, Judge, that's a threat and a promise."

"Maybe this whatsit, Albinoni, maybe he got cold feet, so to speak, like Francis Bacon and his turkey," the CJ says and laughs, all by himself.

"Chicken," Justice Mariner mutters, compelling the CJ to glower at him as though fisticuffs are again imminent. Shades of Pasta La Vista?

"Possibly," Chase says, nodding as if this were no joke at all. "More likely, though, when he came to, he saw it as a way to really get one over on Herskowitz. I mean, that would make him a hero with the students, after all, and much of the faculty; now he's dead, now he's not, Herskowitz has been banged up for murder, and then his little scheme, whatever it was, is in shreds. 'April fool!' Who's the outlaw now?"

Katz shrugs and says, "Or maybe the kid figured coming clean would get him absolution. Restore his career or at least some semblance of a chance at a successful life. It's been known. Albinoni's Catholic, I believe, is he not?"

"How absurd, Fred," Justice Mariner can't resist pointing out, wild-eyed and red in the face. "Tris, I can't believe you're buying this cobbled-together claptrap." As I say, as an advocate, he's sort of lost his touch, at least as an advocate in his own cause. He's just more or less called the judicial council naive and foolish, a credulous consumer of claptrap.

"So the kid made the best of a bad situation, turned the scheme to his own advantage," Katz says, "a sort of reverse Bacon Bit, where it's the co-conspirator — Albinoni — who dies and rises the same, only to suffer, mind you, the new death of all this kerfuffle."

"A dead cat bounce, you might say," the Chief Justice says, knitting his fingers on his desk. "I've heard about such things from our brother, Mr. Justice Fierstein."

"And he exposed Mack Herskowitz for what he was," Katz adds, "a deviant and a con artist, hiding behind his law-and-order pantomime — 'Ain't I the last word in demanding Socratic law teachers.'"

"How very neat," Chase says, looking dangerously contempla-tive.

"Yes, very," the Chief Justice agrees, as they all turn to gaze solemnly at Justice Theodore Elisha Mariner.

PART IV

Hemlock for Herskowitz

"This confounded Socrates," they say,
"this villainous misleader of youth!" And then,
if somebody asks them, "Why, what evil
does he practise or touch?" they
do not know, and cannot tell.

Plato, *Apology*

CHAPTER 1

The rising unto place is labourious . . .
The standing is slippery, and the regress
is either a downfall or at least an eclipse,
which is a melancholy thing.
Francis Bacon, *Essays*, "Of Great Place"

"Maccabeus Theodor Herskowitz, you stand charged that on or about October thirty-first, 2006, at the City of Toronto, you did attempt to cause the death of Anthony Albinoni and thereby commit murder, to wit: by poisoning him with the narcotic drug, oxycodone terephthalate, otherwise known as Percodan, a controlled substance under Schedule I of the *Controlled Drugs and Substances Act*, contrary to section 239 of the *Criminal Code of Canada*. How do you plead to the charge?"

"Not guilty."

"And you stand charged further that on or about October thirty-first, 2006, you did have in your possession oxycodone terephthalate, otherwise known as Percodan, a controlled substance, without being authorized by the *Controlled Drugs and Substances Act Regulations*, to wit: you did possess and administer the said substance to one Anthony Albinoni, contrary to section 4(2)(a) of the *Controlled Drugs and Substances Act*. How do you plead to the charge?

"Not guilty."

"And you stand charged further that on or about diverse occasions during the years 2004, 2005, and 2006, and particularly during October, 2006, at the Cities of Toronto and/or Ottawa, without reasonable justification or excuse and with intent to obtain money or other valuable consideration, by threats or accusations or menaces you did induce Vernon Gander of Ottawa, Ontario, to pay to you said money or other valuable consideration, contrary to section 346(1.1) of the *Criminal Code of Canada*. How do you plead to the charge?"

"Not guilty."

Yes, here we are again before His Honour Hernando Cactus, now in his new role as a justice of the Superior Court but in continuing custody of *Regina v. Herskowitz*, given His Honour's familiarity with the facts and controversy. This newer litigation also returns us rather sharply to our old stomping grounds, the courthouse at 361 University Ave. The Chief Justice is rumoured to have advised Fraidy Katz, with a stern glare, "If you're going to do this, Frederick, do it and get the whole sordid business over with and buried."

As faithful readers of my biography at the bar are aware, one can reach said courthouse, as one often has, through the underground tunnel that conjoins the courthouse with Osgoode Hall, the site of our judicial chambers — "our" meaning, of course, Justice Mariner and Your Official Court Reporter. It is no trick at all for junior counsel who stands approximately one foot (albeit on all fours) off the ground . . . no trick at all, I say, for someone who mostly goes unnoticed in any event amid the hurly-burly of Her Majesty's justice facilities, to slip out of chambers, glide past security, and secrete himself cozily at the feet of the resident court clerk or stenographer. Otherwise, where would legal history be? Bereft, obviously, of the *Amicus, Q.C. (for Questing Cat), Law Reports.*

As you have just heard, Assistant Crown Fred Katz has arranged for his personal friend, Her Majesty Elizabeth II, to lay new charges against Mack Herskowitz and, in the circumstances we have waived the preliminary hearing and proceeded directly to trial. But why in the world does "Mariner, initials T.E.," still appear for the defence, despite the Chief Justice's outrage at same? Here is how Justice Mariner has explained it to the client, Professor Maccabeus Jerk-O-Twit, and our learned junior, Leland Gaunt, Esq.: "Might as well be hanged for a sheep as a lamb." Then His Lordship sailed off to get everyone a coffee. Which conveniently permitted Gaunt the opportunity to ask the professor, "What's that supposed to mean, 'Might as well be hanged for a sheep as a lamb'?"

"I think it has something to do with poaching, or rustling. You know, 'If I'm going to get in trouble, I might as well go the whole hog.'"

"Or mutton."

"Either way, Outlaw Ted's a man after my own heart," the professor says. "He's even got it grammatically correct."

Gaunt looks even more perplexed than usual.

'Hanged,' you know," Herskowitz explains. "A lesser man would have said 'hung.'"

"Ah." Sitting in a guest chair of Herskowitz's (and latterly Justice Mariner's) office, Gaunt tries to look like the greater man, one who knew all along that you hung a picture and hanged a person. My educated guess is he considers pointing out that Parliament abolished capital punishment in 1976, and that no one's danced the Arthur Ellis Hornpipe in this country since 1962.* But then perhaps he realizes that Mack Herskowitz is aware of these facts, which anyway would be cold comfort to a fellow charged with three indictable offences (a.k.a. felonies). In any event, Leland does not seem to find it particularly surprising that His Lordship intends to go the whole mutton. And, truth to tell, His Lordship's defiant streak has a tendency to lead him into what *Homo allegedly sapiens* sometimes describe, I believe, as CLMs — career-limiting moves. To his spouse Penny the judge will later elaborate that, one, he is sick and tired of being bullied by the Chief; two, he can't get in any more trouble anyway without being altogether bounced from the bench like Francis Bacon ("Early retirement is becoming a distinct possibility," Penny interjects, nodding, in a tone not altogether hopeful); and three, he has reason to believe that, "while Mack is no angel, neither is he as bad as he's painted." And they say old-style liberalism is dead.

---

*Appointed Canada's first civil service hangman in 1913, Arthur B. English used the pseudonym Arthur Ellis, and all his successors followed that lead. English's uncle was the more notorious John Ellis (hence English's *nom de gibet*), who hanged such infamous British murderers as Dr. Hawley Crippen, Frederick Seddon, and Judith Thompson. Climactically, John Ellis topped himself after he'd executed Thompson.

English conducted more than six hundred hangings in England, the Middle East, and Canada. His career as Arthur Ellis ended when he was seventy-one, following the second time he inadvertently decapitated one of his charges. On March 28, 1935, the second unfortunate was a woman, Tomasina Sarao, convicted of killing her husband in an insurance scam. Sarao's weight was misstated on the figures officials gave English. Apparently she was at least thirty-eight pounds heavier than prison documentation said, so that English's rope was too long for the extra weight when the trap dropped at Montreal's Bordeaux Jail.

Anyway, never mind our compassionate tendencies at law, we immediately try to derail the attempted murder and drug possession counts against Mack Herskowitz. "Your Honour," Justice Mariner submits, "these charges arose on the same facts as the former murder charge did. Now we're just saying Professor Herskowitz attempted to do what Your Honour ruled at the prelim there was no evidence for his doing. If you see what I mean. You can't say he didn't kill anybody and then come back tomorrow and say, 'Okay, but he tried.' We've got a double-jeopardy thing going here. I mean, at least this is all *res judicata*, already adjudged — been there, done that, got the Law Day T-shirt, can't do it again."

"You mean he couldn't try to do what he didn't do? It seems to me people do that all the time, Mr. Mariner."

"To quote Homer Simpson, Your Honour." Katz stands, Mariner sits. "'Trying is just the first step on the road to failure.' Trying is one thing. Doing is another."

Katz sits, Mariner stands. "No. What Homer's saying, quite clearly Mr. Katz, is that it's all one path."

"Homer said that?" Justice Cactus pretends that he never watches television. "Was that in *The Odyssey*, Mr. Katz, or *The Iliad?*"

"What I'm saying, Your Honour," Justice Mariner soldiers on, "well, I'm saying that you've already ruled — when we were at the law school — you already decided there was insufficient evidence to show that Professor Herskowitz wanted to kill anyone with drugs or otherwise. Now the Crown is simply trying to relitigate that by saying Professor Herskowitz tried to kill someone with drugs. Double jeopardy."

"Your Honour," Katz replies, "there's case law on this. An attempt is distinct from an actual crime, even if it's impossible to commit the crime. There are cases, for example, about trying to pick an empty pocket, and about a man trying to have sexual intercourse with non-consenting ducks . . ."*

With a look of disgust on his usually benign face, Justice Cactus waves Katz back into his chair. "If you wanted to make that argument, Mr. Mariner, you should have gone ahead with another preliminary inquiry. We're already at trial now, and the jury has been empanelled. It's up to them to decide. Anyway, the question is different this time. We've got new facts before us, not the least of which is that Mr. Albinoni is very much alive. And trying, as the great classical poet Homer apparently suggested, is not the same as doing. Like Justice, Mr. Mariner, Homer was blind. It does not see word games, only the truth in its own heart. Justice, like Homer, is blind."

"At least he wasn't stupid in the bargain," Justice Mariner mutters to Leland Gaunt, his left-hand man.

"I'm sorry, Mr. Mariner." Justice Cactus cups his ear. "I didn't quite get that."

"I said I thought you were quoting Cupid in the Garden, Your Honour. The Garden of, uh, Paradise, Love. Love is blind and all that — with Cupid flinging his arrows all around, making all the mismatches and misalliances we see in the courts, such as Mr. Albinoni with Professor Herskowitz, perhaps, and Ms. Kyriakos, too. To quote Homer, our version of Helen of Troy and Paris."

"No, no. Mr. Katz has told us it was the great poet Homer who

---

*Katz is right, at least on this limited point. See *Where There's Life There's Lawsuits: Not Altogether Serious Ruminations on Law and Life,* ECW Press, 2003, pages 38-41.

said trying and doing or failing are distinct. Not Cupid. Will you bring in the jury please, usher?"

⁓ᘓᘔᘓ⁓

After his opening statement, Katz says: "Your Honour, I wonder if we might save some time and trouble if I just read into the evidence for this trial the testimony Ms. Kyriakos gave at the preliminary inquiry."

We are immediately on our feet, in dramatically high dudgeon. "Oh, how convenient that would be, Mr. Katz. For the prosecution, at least. Your Honour, you have just ruled that the preliminary hearing at the law school has no application to these separate proceedings."

"Ah, so now you are making the opposite argument, Mr. Mariner?" mousy little Katz sneers, springing his cheesy little trap. "First you say it covered off everything but the extortion. Now it doesn't apply?"

"I am only reminding you, Fraidy, of what His Honour has already ruled, outside the presence of the jury." Justice Mariner nods and smiles at the twelve citizens good and true. "Rather presumptuous of you, Mr. Katz, not to have Ms. Kyriakos available, isn't it? If you really think her evidence is worth hearing."

"That'll do, Mr. Mariner," Justice Cactus says. "And, sure enough, I'm not sure it's a good idea to be discussing this in front of the jury."

"The witness is attending classes and working in Scarborough, Your Honour," Katz explains, "at the law school and the professor's institute. I could have her here for the afternoon. After lunch. I mean, it's nearly eleven-fifteen now, anyway."

"Better late than never, Mr. Katz." Justice Mariner can't seem to help smirking. "You see, Your Honour, I would like to cross-examine Ms. Kyriakos on her evidence. And I am sure the jury, I'm sure *all* of us, would like to know if her evidence remains consistent with what she said earlier. And we, all of us, I'm sure," His Lordship bows to Frederick Katz, "we'd all like to know if perhaps she has anything new to tell us. Wouldn't we, Mr. Katz? Since that fateful preliminary hearing at the Farb — that fateful preliminary hearing where Professor Herskowitz was discharged because the Crown had no case against him, if you recall, on facts that were virtually the same as we have here."

Mr. Justice Mariner lays particular emphasis on this last bit.

◦◦◦

Meanwhile, back at the ranch, well, it's a dead cat bounce of a different colour, if you don't mind my changing horses in mid-metaphor. I give you Exhibit A, my transcribed excerpt of *Penelope Mariner v. Amicus, Q.C.,* another never-ending prosecution, as it transpires during the lunch break in *The Queen v. Herskowitz,* just outside the garden shed around the back of 1415 Elysian Fields North, Forest Hill Village:

Penny Mariner, for the Crown: I told you, Ted. No more pussyfooting around.

Ted Mariner, acting in his own defence and in that of the said co-accused, Amicus, Q.C.: Good one, Pen. Pussyfooting. I knew you'd see the humour in having this little guy around the . . .

PM: I've called my Auntie Bella. She doesn't suppose she has any particular objections to keeping a cat. As long as no one goes around saying she's a daft old witch with her mangy old moggy.

The co-accused, Ted Mariner: Well, no one could honestly say the cat's mangy.

PM: Now that's just cruel. What've you got against the dear old soul?

TM: Against her? Nothing at all, beyond the fact that she's a couple bagels shy of a brunch. No, really, it's just that she hasn't got room for a cat, Pen. She doesn't have room for a gerbil. She lives in an attic, for God's sake. And anyway, she's not a cat person.

PM: It's not an attic. It's a dormer flat. A nice little flat, on the third floor of a house.

TM: Of a semi-detached, you mean. And derelict at that. Bursting with the landlord's kids and in-laws and God knows who else. Illegals, probably. War criminals. Renting out illegal flats . . .

PM: They're a perfectly nice Polish family. They treat Auntie Bella like one of their own. They fatten her up with pierogies and borscht and Polish Danishes. She loves them.

TM: Polish Danishes? Must be a product of that global village I keep hearing about, which is mostly about food and restaurants, as far as I can tell, with the occasional gourdlike musical instrument thrown in. And fatten her up for what? is the question. Anyway, your spinster aunt has no time for pets, Pen. She keeps a more hectic schedule than the two of us combined. She works at COMSOC all day* and she's got her amateur theatre in the evenings and on the weekends. She's a fanatic for it, you've said so yourself.

---

*Auntie Bella, it turned out, was an administrative assistant at the provincial Ministry of Community and Social Services.

She's not a pet person, except possibly when she's playing a witch in *Macbeth*, come to think of it.

PM: But that's the beauty of it, Ted. It's perfect. I told you the other night at dinner. She's playing Grizabella in the Parkdale Library's Play-in-the-Alley Production of *Cats*, isn't she?"

TM (amid, it must be admitted, somewhat snide laughter): Play in the alley?

PM: As usual, you weren't listening. Yes, play in the alley, like, you know, play in the park, Shakespeare or whatever in the park, only this is *in the alley.* Of the library. Remember, last year, they did "Play in the Spit"?

TM: How could I forget, *Waiting for Godot* on the Leslie Street Spit?* As I said at the time, the concept was marginally better, I guess, than their "Play in the Dump."

PM: Yes, well, let's not go into all that again — how you literally had ants in your pants during her *A Flea in Her Ear.* To get back to the point, Ted, this year they're performing in the alleyway behind the library. You know, *Cats* . . . alley?

TM: I get it, I get it. Almost as ingenious as Godot and spit. What was it *Time* magazine said about Beckett and his plays? "I stink therefore I am"? . . .

PM: And Auntie Bella's playing Grizabella — you know, the former glamourpuss. So, in a sense, she is a cat, or wouldn't mind having one around the place for inspiration.

TM: Method acting amid the trash cans, you mean?

---

*Originally, the City of Toronto dumped non-toxic garbage in this landfill area to form a breakwater against Lake Ontario. Nature took over, turning the dumping ground into a large nature preserve in the city's east end.

PM: And even if she's an old eccentric, that's what old eccentrics do, isn't it? Keep cats? Herds of them.

It is at this point that defence counsel Mariner whispers to his wrongfully co-accused, off the record and subject to solicitor-client privilege: "Looks like it's the Big House for you, boy, or at least the Overcrowded, Termite-Infested House. Auntie Bella's or bust. I've exhausted my advocacy arsenal."

Rusty as it is, I say, rusty, disused, arthritic. Exiled.

"I'm afraid your only recourse might be a last-minute pardon from the Minister of Justice," the judge further advised me. "We're personally acquainted with one of his assistant deputy ministers, good old Goosey Gander, but I'm not sure he'd be anxious to put in a good word just now."

Ha-bloody-ha.

☙❧

As lunch begins to hood the eyes and slow the blood, Zipporah Kyriakos takes the stand, to outline her professor-lover's high-handed behaviour, his theft of her intellectual property concerning the death of Socrates, and Mack Herskowitz's possible role in the sort-of-death of Anthony Albinoni . . . after the lively Zippy had mated secretly with Albinoni on at least two admitted occasions.

Justice Mariner rises to cross-examine, nodding at the witness, who nods back, apparently unimpressed by the circumstances and surroundings. "Ms. Kyriakos, I have only two questions for you."

Katz exhales his silent outrage loudly enough to be understood in the back of the courtroom — a stage sigh, you might call it

(Auntie Bella take note). Justice Cactus glowers down at the defence table: "You delayed proceedings and got the girl all the way down here, Mr. Mariner, to ask her two questions?"

"Two central questions, Your Honour. Crucial questions to my client's future and his right to be presumed innocent. I'm sure the jury will understand, in the circumstances." Justice Mariner nods with a smile at the jurors. "And the first central question is, Ms. Kyriakos: As far as you knew as bookkeeper for the Institute for the Wrongfully Acquitted, the money Vern Gander gave the institute, those donations were just that, weren't they? Donations? Made of Mr. Gander's own free will?"

"Mack told me that he — Vernon, Mr. Gander — he had made some money in the stock market or some such. He said it was a couple of dead cat bounces, lucky escapes, and, as a grateful former student and Farb alumnus, well, Vern wanted to share the wealth. With donations, yes. Seeing how Professor Herskowitz had been his mentor and helped him along in his law career — and in his public service career, of course."

"A dead cat bounce, members of the jury," Justice Cactus interrupts, "is where the market looks like its recovering, but it's just a short-term sort of thing. It bounces up, you see, but then soon proves to be dead, after all. Kaboom. Back down. Kaboom. It's an illusion. An untrue recovery, as it were. Ordinary folks like you and me, we don't have experience of this, of course. We're lucky to have a pension, let alone extra money to invest at the end of the month."

"Which is something we will get to, Your Honour," Justice Mariner says, "if you'll just . . ."

Justice Cactus ignores defence counsel. "But my colleague on

high at *Mr. Mariner's court, the Court of Appeal*, where the atmos-
phere is rarefied and so are the pay cheques, well, Mr. Justice
Fierstein, up there in the mansion on the mountain, as it were, he
has told me all about it. This dead cat bounce." Having dropped
that particular bomb on the Herskowitz camp, Justice Cactus
grins in a self-satisfied manner. Bouncing around all smiles like
the semi-dead Cheshire cat, you might say.

"As to my second crucial question, Ms. Kyriakos," Justice
Mariner gamely continues his cross-examination, "please listen
carefully: Did you ever tell Professor Herskowitz you had slept
with Tony Albinoni?"

The witness's eyes flutter, but she hardly misses a beat. "No. I
never did. What would have been the point of that?"

"What indeed?"

"That's three questions, Mariner," Katz hisses and spits.

"Thank you, Ms. Kyriakos," Justice Mariner says as he resumes
his seat.

"It seems to me, Mr. Mariner," Justice Cactus says, to the jury,
"that you could have asked her that during the preliminary
inquiry at the law school and I'd have admitted it here."

His Lordship is back on his feet. "Well, again, as Your Honour
ruled previously, *outside the jury's presence*," Justice Mariner turns
toward said citizens good and true, "this is a different case than the
matter before the preliminary hearing at the law school. One, true
enough, sir, one where you cleared the professor concerning these
same events. I mean, I can understand the confusion, Your
Honour. Mr. Katz seems to be dogging poor Professor Herskowitz
so much, it's all getting mixed up. Like mixing up persecution and
prosecution."

Right — "poor Professor Herskowitz." The real reason we didn't ask this before — didn't ask Zippy, that is, whether she'd told Mack about her fling with Tony — was bald ignorance. We didn't know the answer. We didn't know the answer until during the handshaking and hugging and backslapping after Mr. Justice Cactus had discharged Herskowitz on the murder charge at that prelim in the Farb's moot court. It was only then that the professor grabbed Justice Mariner's arms, and with tears in her eyes, said, "You know, Judge, she never told me about her and Albinoni. Never. I had no idea. No idea."

CHAPTER 2

Vice lifts her head,
And sees pale Virtue carted in her stead.
Alexander Pope, *Epilogue to the Satires*

That Friday evening I am carted like a common criminal off to
Auntie Bella, a.k.a Grizabella in the Parkdale Library's Play-in-the-
Alley, Pay-What-You-Can production of — pant, pant — Cats.*
The cart in this case is, more precisely, His Lordship's beloved if
decrepit 1969 Volvo, whose ancient exhaust system suddenly lets
go a fart as explosive as artillery fire. The eruction startles a decidedly old lady with severe hip dysplasia trundling her grocery buggy
along the walkway. Although she is built like a miniature line-
backer, her sensible button-top shoes actually leave the sidewalk in
her panic. She clasps at her heart and scowls furiously at us as we
eruct past her, reviled yet again like rebels without a cause. Indeed,
in the circumstances I am reminded of a passage in Sir William
Blackstone's *Commentaries on the Laws of England*, 1765–69, lying
open in the Great Library during my salad days there, as I sunned
myself on the oak tables of the Reading Room:

---

*"**Cart** . . . To carry in a cart through the streets, by way of punishment or
public exposure (esp. as the punishment of a bawd)." *Oxford English
Dictionary*

. . . he is adjudged to be outlawed, *or put out of the protection of the law; so that he is incapable of taking the
benefit of it in any respect . . . Anciently an outlawed felon
was said to have* caput lupinum *[a wolf's head], and might
be knocked on the head like a wolf by any one that should
meet him, because, having renounced all law, he was to be
dealt with as in a state of nature, when every one that
should find him might slay him.*

So here I go again, a wolf's head in sheepish clothing to be dealt
with as in a state of nature. Adding insult to injury, if my new
landlady is herself not outlawed, she certainly is a law unto herself.
Unfortunately, being able to sing all the words to "Memory," and
mostly in key, does not by itself qualify one as official guardian to
a dependent quadruped. Between and among work at COMSOC,
amateur theatre rehearsals, and oversleeping her alarm — said
guardian leaves work rather early and theatre rehearsals very late
— Auntie Bella regularly neglects to provide one with the neces-
saries of life, as our *Criminal Code* trenchantly describes it. What
saves me from starvation, barely, are the comings and goings in
that semi-detached residence at Queen and Ossington. Though
nearby vehicular traffic has rattled and shifted its foundations so
that the poor house sags to stage right rather in the manner of
Pisa's celebrated tower (in our more modest case on Queen Street,
the porch roof sags at the middle to boot), it is so crowded with
Polish émigrés as to remind you not of the Italian tourist destina-
tion, but of the fairy-tale shoe where lived the old woman with so
many children she didn't know what to do. And, thank the Fates
and Furies (as His Lordship is wont to say), to an infant the rol-

licking, shoe-horned occupants are generally happy to share a crust of pizza, the odd fish head, or the last of the sadly skimmed milk in their cornflakes bowls, never minding whether the resident moggy comes in or out whenever they do, nor inquiring whither he goest, or whether he actually belongeth there.

For always roaming with a hungry heart
Much have I seen and known . . .

Given this new if benign form of exile in the odyssey of my melancholy outlaw's life, I am unable to relate at first hand the evidence of Vernon Gander, Assistant Deputy Minister of Justice and former protégé of Mack Herskowitz. However, I proffer the following excerpts from the trial transcript of his evidence, which I later happened upon in His Lordship's chambers. In the spirit of Andrew Lloyd Webber (and my new life in care, courtesy of *his* protégée, Auntie Bella of the other west end), I have added stage directions as I imagine they portray events in Courtroom 4-11 in so-called real time. As for the musical numbers, might I respectfully suggest that before you read the following you cue up "Memories" (original Broadway version of *Cats*) on the old CD player or ghetto blaster.

To begin with, Fred Katz for the Crown elicits from Gander what you already know: the Assistant Deputy Minister claims that, during his law school days, Herskowitz traded him sex for grades and, when he (Gander) learned of Albinoni's supposed death, he came forward out of concern that the same thing had been going on with Tony and had got lethally out of hand.

Witness [the blood draining from his visage]: I mean, I'm literally still paying for it myself.

Mr. Katz [hearing trumpets within]: You mean paying for it in terms of guilt? Shame over Professor Herskowitz's bribery of you?

Witness: Not just that. I mean, *literally,* I'm still paying for it, as well as figuratively. Mack's been blackmailing me because of it, all these years later. When I became assistant deputy minister at Justice, he threatened to expose how I "really got there," as he put it.

Several of those assembled at trial look as though they find this hard to credit. Justice Mariner for the defence, anyway, seems to be thinking: "Herskowitz might be deeply unpopular in certain quarters, but he is a man of accomplishment and influence — like Professor Kingsfield in The Paper Chase *(or Socrates or Bacon, take your pick). Plus, why would he expose some supposed dirty dealings with Gander? Didn't he have at least as much to lose if something like that came to light? Anyway, Gander exuded more than a whiff of instability about him on that afternoon he came to tell me this same tale of woe in my office at the Farb. Mind you, perhaps he was still hung over from the ill-fated High Table night chez Herskowitz.*

And so we take the transcript up again where Katz goes into the details of the alleged bribery scheme — Gander's accusations that Herskowitz extorted money from him on the threat that he would expose Gander's academic record as inflated and fraudulent.

Witness: He said all he would have to do is show the faculty my old exams. He'd kept them, see. As many as he could round up. He said they would prove that my grades were inflated, and if I then claimed he was the one who inflated them, in return for, you know, the favours to him, he would deny it. He would just say I was making it all up to cover the fact that I'd got at Mrs. Hoover somehow and persuaded her to alter my transcripts. Offered her money, or whatever. When it was really he, Herskowitz, who had done it, I mean. He said nobody would believe me because the claims were so preposterous. He had an ex-wife and a gorgeous young girlfriend, he said. Not to mention two sons. He said there were so many scandals in government these days, no one would believe me, and everyone would believe him. They'd think I was just another embittered ex-student, he said — he *laughed* — another underachiever still pathetically fussing and fuming about how demanding he had been as a teacher, and here I was a grown man with a good career trying to wreak my pathetic vengeance now that I had some minor status of my own. Where was the evidence of harm? he said.

Mr. Katz: Ms. Hoover, you said, when you were talking about your law school transcripts. For the jury and His Honour, who is Ms. Hoover?

Witness: Eureka Hoover, the registrar of the law school. She's still there, I believe — with her very solid reputation intact, for that matter.

Mr. Katz: And so you made payments to Professor Herskowitz?

Witness: Not to him. We laundered them. They were donations, charitable . . .

Mr. Mariner: I'm going to have to object to the characterization of laundering. The witness is drawing conclusions which are up to Your Honour and the jury. Ms. Kyriakos already told us clearly that the donations were donations, period.

The Court: What were these donations, Mr. Gander?

Witness: Donations to Professor Herskowitz's institute, Your Honour. His Institute for the Wrongly Acquitted Criminal, so-called.

Mr. Katz: And these were fairly substantial, I take it. The donations I mean.

Witness: Yes, several thousand dollars.

Mr. Katz: On your government salary? Several thousand?

Witness: Yes. We told Zipporah, Mack's girlfriend who was also his assistant who did the books, we told her I had made money in the stock market. That was how we kept it above suspicion. We said I wanted to share the wealth with my alma mater and mentor. When she asked me how that was possible, how I made such a profit in unpredictable economic times, with the war in Iraq and all that, I told her there had been a couple of dead cat bounces.

The Court: There goes that acrobatic feline again.

[The more thoughtful and sensitive among those assembled wince at the metaphor.]

CHAPTER 3

Opportunity makes a thief.
Francis Bacon, letter to the Earl of Essex, 1598

Auntie Bella has decided that I should earn my keep — her words, not mine. Discussion, you will have guessed, is not her forte, which she insists on pronouncing for*tay*, never mind the pregnant absence of the *accent aigu*. "At least if you were a dog, you could do something useful," she repeats as a mantra, gazing at me down her nose as she wrinkles it dubiously, "like maybe guard the place or even just fetch a little ball." When she takes any notice of her new foster feline at all, it is to talk at one like that. Other pearls from Auntie Bella's store of Wit and Wisdom: "If Penny's Ted cared a lick for his family, he wouldn't be schlepping you into Penny's lovely home with your dander and shredding the furniture and general bad habits — and he wouldn't be schlepping you into my not-so-lovely home, either." "You put even a single one of your dirty little claws into my new Don't Pay A Cent Event sofa bed from Leon's, I tell Penny and Ted you got run over by a streetcar. And I won't be making it up." Which latter assertion she repeats at double volume, in double contravention of *Criminal Code* section 264.1(1), uttering or conveying a threat to cause death or bodily harm: *"I won't be making it up."*

Be it ever so humble ... .

She has decided, Auntie Bella, that (she informs me without discussion) I can in fact make myself useful by appearing as an extra in the Parkdale Library's Play-in-the-Alley, Pay-What-You-Can production of *Cats*. To this purpose, she proposes to teach me to "meow on cue" and, "hopefully" (she'll be lucky) to wail "'Meow-mory' in a sing-songy, alleycat way." Somehow, the old witch thinks I am the least bit motivated to cooperate in this enterprise, never mind that it's not only slave labour, but by law can require a licence. During my tenure at the Great Library of Osgoode Hall, I've seen the case law that proves it. Check it out yourself, in volume 551 of the Federal Supplement, page 349 (1982), where is recorded a case out of Georgia, *Miles v. City Council of Augusta*, alias, "The Case of Blackie the Talking Cat."

In the event that you can't find your law library card, here's the gist of it: Carl Miles had displayed Blackie on the street, and sometimes in the broadcast media, as a cat he'd trained to speak English. This would strain credulity (I admit) if District Judge Bowen hadn't actually heard Blackie *in situ*, in downtown Augusta, before the judge had any idea that the matter was going to end up on his calendar.

In a footnote to *Miles*, Judge Bowen explains that, while driving downtown, he encountered a man — he couldn't say whether it was Carl Miles — with a black cat draped over his shoulder. Having heard of Blackie, the judge asked if the cat could talk. Mr. Miles said yes,

and if I would pull over on the side street he would show me. I did, and he did. The cat was wearing a collar, two harnesses and a leash. Held and stroked by the man

Blackie said "I love you" and "I want my Mama." The man then explained that the cat was the sole source of income for him and his wife and requested a donation which was provided. I felt that my dollar was well spent.

The Mileses ended up later in Judge Bowen's court because Augusta required them to pay fees for Blackie's public performances — to pay for a licence — and they didn't want to pony up. So they contended the licence requirement infringed their rights to free (literally) expression and equal protection of the law. Judge Bowen disagreed:

> The ordinance is not one designed to regulate speech or association, but merely to raise revenue. The ordinance does not subject anyone's speech or associational activity to any penalty unless . . . a tax has not been paid. Thus, the ordinance does not tread upon plaintiffs' fundamental constitutional rights.

With similar lack of success, the Mileses also argued that they were exempt from the licensing law because when they displayed Blackie they were not plying a trade, such as selling hot dogs or knock-off Rolexes on Main Street. The Mileses had a "well established" commercial interest in poor old Blackie, Judge Bowen ruled. Some might have added that this commercial interest was reminiscent of the freak show scenes in *The Elephant Man*. Indeed, Judge Bowen remarked in his footnote, "Some questions occurred to me about the necessity for the multiple means of restraint and the way in which the man held the cat's paw when the cat was asked to talk."

In any event, the Eleventh Circuit Court of Appeals affirmed Judge Bowen's view (710 Federal Reporter, second edition, page

1542, 1983), noting that "although the Miles family called what they received for Blackie's performances 'contributions,' these elocutionary endeavors were entirely intended for pecuniary enrichment and were indubitably commercial." And this was before thesaurus tools on personal computers. Anyway, while the free-speech argument seemed to apply to the Mileses as *Homo allegedly sapiens*, the appeals court stated in a footnote:

> This court will not hear a claim that Blackie's right to free speech has been infringed. First, although Blackie arguably possesses a very unusual ability, he cannot be considered a "person" and is therefore not protected by the *Bill of Rights*. Second, even if Blackie had such a right, we see no need for appellants to assert his right jus tertii [as third parties acting in Blackie's interest]. Blackie can clearly speak for himself.

Highly risible. In fiction, talking cats have got into worse trouble. You'll remember the Cheshire Cat, who offends the Queen of Hearts and presides over learned debate on whether it is philosophically possible for Her Majesty to decapitate his bodiless head (beheading the unheaded). Judge Bowen mentions the notorious Felix and Sylvester, as well as Tobermory, of the eponymous story by H. H. Munro ("Saki"). Tobermory's facility in the language proves lethal when he reveals in mixed (Has-being) company what he has learned from his shin-eye view, "creeping about our bedrooms and under chairs" at a manor house. Verbosity killed the cat.

Already outlawed and exiled, I will not make the same mistake by singing "Memory" or even "We Gotta Get Out of This Place" in the Parkdale Library's *Cats*. Suffice it to recall that I get into quite enough difficulty, thank you very much, just being a regular old "dumb" animal who happens to narrate his life's story at the bar.

⌒◌◌⌒

"Ms. Topo, at the time of the events before the court, what was your occupation?" Fred Katz stands at the lectern on the prosecution table (in my mind's eye, of course, for at the time I was roaming the alleyways and byways of west Toronto and again must rely here on the trial transcripts), holding a pencil in both hands, apparently to keep himself from thrashing about the room in a self-righteous hissy fit.

"I was the receptionist for a medical doctor, a family physician." Affectless as usual, Deena Topo gazes impassively at the assistant Crown.

"And during that same period, did you know your husband Tony to use narcotic drugs?" Katz flinches, or tics. He can't help himself.

"Occasionally. Prescription drugs, actually, but mostly for his school work. You know, uppers, stimulants, to help him stay awake and study."

"What about recreationally?"

"Every once in a while. He wasn't an addict, if that's what you mean."

"And where did he get those prescription drugs?" Katz has no particular interest in slagging off Tony.

"Several places, I think. He didn't really say."

"From you?"

"Not from me personally."

"I think you know what I mean, Ms. Topo. Let's put it this

way: Did he get the drugs *through* you, with your help?"

"Sometimes."

"How did that work?"

"Well, because of my job, I guess that's what you're saying."

"Yes . . ."

"Well, I could get drugs at work, or get prescriptions for people that needed them. But it was never anything really dangerous, like morphine or smack or whatever. It was just painkillers, like, and maybe amphetamines. Prescriptions. Harmless."

"Really? How did you 'get' prescriptions, as you put it?"

"Well, I wrote them out. On the pads we had at work."

"And the Hallowe'en High Table at Professor Herskowitz's, the gourmet night, was that one of the occasions that you supplied . . . one of the times Tony got drugs with your help?"

"Yes, I guess so."

"And what drugs would that have been?"

"Just Percodan. That's all. Just a no-refills scrip for Percodan." The witness shrugs, throwing the prosecutor a look that threatens, *I dare you to say different.*

"A painkiller?"

"Yes. It's a painkiller. Percodan. Yes."

"It's a morphine derivative, is it not?

Justice Mariner objects: "Your Honour, the witness is not a physician or pharmacologist."

"I *will* be calling a toxicologist, Your Honour." Katz turns back to the witness. "Why would Tony have needed a painkiller, Ms. Topo? Was he hurting?"

"No, not physically. Professor Herskowitz asked him to get it. They wanted to test out some theory about pretending to be dead."

"If you know, was this part of Tony's work as a research assistant to the professor?"

Justice Mariner rises wearily to his hind legs. "Your Honour, it seems to me we could have this evidence at first hand, from Mr. Albinoni himself. We're bordering on hearsay."

"And so you will have it from Mr. Albinoni, Mr. Mariner," Katz replies. "In any event, Ms. Topo, did you in fact give the prescription for the Percodan to your husband?"

"Yes."

"Your witness," Katz says, while turning his back on his learned friend for the defence.

⌘

"Ms. Topo, what is your occupation at the moment?" Justice Mariner begins his cross-examination, his tone even, all reason.

"I'm between jobs just now."

"Between jobs. But most recently you were a receptionist to Dr. Schuss, the family physician?"

"Yes."

"And why are you no longer doing that job?"

"I was laid off."

"*Laid off*, Ms. Topo. Is that what you're telling the jury? You were *laid off?*"

"Yes. Dr. Schuss has another receptionist, and he didn't like paying for two of us. He always said his practice couldn't really support it, and Helen, the other one, she'd been with him for a hundred years." Topo still shows no sign of emotion or irony.

"A hundred years. Isn't it true, Ms. Topo, that you and Helen, the hundred-and-fifty-year-old receptionist" — the jury laughs — "Helen of Troy, I guess, isn't it true you and Helen had worked together for some time?"

"Well, not some time, really. Two years is all."

"Okay, two years. You'd been working together for all that time with no so-called layoffs?"

"Yes."

"And isn't it also the case that Dr. Schuss *fired* you only on learning that you were forging these prescriptions? *Fired* you, Ms. Topo, after my client was charged with the offences we're considering today?"

"Well, I left around then. But the doctor'd been wanting to economize for a long time, Dr. Schuss was, and I was the junior receptionist. Last in, first out, as my dad used to say. He was in the construction unions. They laid people off that way when there wasn't enough work." Topo shrugs.

"Or when they couldn't be trusted and committed crimes on the job?"

"No. They fired those types of people. Layoffs were for the dependable workers. Last in, first out."

"Indeed. I'd like to take you to that dinner Mr. Katz mentioned, Ms. Topo, the High Table Night on Hallowe'en at Professor Herskowitz's home. You and I were both there, were we not?"

Topo snorts quietly. "Don't you remember, Judge?" She makes an ironic face, then adds, "I guess there was a lot of drinking, huh? So maybe you don't remember?"

"Well, the question really is what you remember, Ms. Topo, isn't it? For example, I assume you remember that the whole idea of this theory you talked about, the theory Professor Herskowitz wanted to test, wasn't the whole idea to see if Professor Herskowitz could pretend to be dead?"

"I guess so, but I didn't talk to him about it. So I don't really know."

"But you talked to Tony about it, didn't you?"

"Yeah."

"And through Tony you knew that the professor wanted to 'do the Bacon Bit,' as they called it?"

"Yeah, I guess so." Topo turns to the judge. "Isn't this, like, hearsay or something?"

It bordered on it, sure enough, as Katz chimes in: "Exactly, Your Honour. My learned friend's just said this sort of evidence should come from the horse's mouth."

Justice Mariner presses on to safer territory. "And what did that mean, as far as you know, 'do the Bacon Bit'?"

"Well, I guess it meant what you said. Pretending to be dead. Making it look like you'd cacked."

"It meant Professor Herskowitz pretending to be cacked, right? Not Tony."

Justice Cactus intervenes: "Ms. Topo. You'll have to answer out loud. The tape and the transcript can't hear a shrug."

"Like I said, the research or theory or whatever, that was between Mack and Tony. I just gave them the prescription for it."

"Well, let's go down the road a little then. The plan was for Professor Herskowitz to take enough Percodan so that his life signs were very depressed, correct?"

"I told you, I didn't discuss it with them — with him and Tony."

"But Professor Herskowitz had no idea that Tony was going to overdose on the Percodan, did he?"

"Your Honour, he can't ask her what Professor Herskowitz believed," Katz mewls. "He'll have to call his client if he wants to get that in."

"He's right, Mr. Mariner," Justice Cactus rules, "as you well know."

"Let me put it this way, Ms. Topo. After the dinner, you knew your husband was still alive, didn't you, when everyone else thought he'd died?"

"Not right after — I wasn't sure exactly what happened to him after they carried him out. Later, yeah, like a couple of weeks after that, I had, like, occasional contact with him. But he was still suffering some side effects. It was touch and go for awhile. And he was keeping a low profile."

"I'll take that as a yes. But, in any event, you and Tony were attempting to make Mack Herskowitz think that he, Tony, was dead?"

"The lowest of the low profiles," Justice Cactus cuts in.

"We didn't know what Herskowitz thought. Just like Mr. Katz said."

"You didn't tell Mack that Tony was still alive, though, did you?"

"No."

"And that was because you were blackmailing him, weren't you?"

If this is a bombshell to the jury, Topo simply puts her nose in the air. "I don't know what you're talking about."

"Neither do I, Your Honour," Katz says. "Neither does the jury, I'm sure."

"Well, let's help the jury, shall we then, Ms. Topo? Let's just have a look at Professor Herskowitz's books, shall we, for your benefit and the benefit of my friend on the prosecution side, and of course for the benefit of His Honour and the jury. Your Honour, I'd like to show the witness Exhibit 12, from the Crown's disclosure package, that part of the IWAC financial records. I'd ask you, Ms. Topo, to turn to Tab 3 in the notebook the usher is handing you, specifically to the page reading 'Extraordinary Expenses.' Do you see that?"

"Yes. But I don't know what it means."

"We'll get to that. You see several lines there marked 'Albinoni'?"

"Yes."

"Those were payments to your husband?"

"I couldn't say."

"Come now, Ms. Topo. You're trying to be clever again, aren't you? Do you know any other Albinoni who had dealings with Professor Herskowitz?"

"Your Honour." Katz stands wearily. "How can the witness know all the people with whom Professor Herskowitz 'had dealings,' as Mr. Mariner so cleverly tries to put it?"

"But your husband was Professor Herskowitz's paid research assistant, was he not, Ms. Topo? Didn't you say so yourself to Mr. Katz?"

As Topo answers, Katz stares at the wood panelling behind Justice Cactus. "Yes, but the research payments were for five thousand dollars. Half was paid at the beginning of the term, and the rest, the other twenty-five hundred, at the end. These amounts say one thousand dollars."

"Ah, funny you should mention that. So if these thousand-dollar payments were to your husband, they weren't for the research?"

"Well, alls I can say is that these are for a thousand, a series of one-thousand-dollar payments. That's not how the research payments worked. So maybe it was a different Albinoni."

"Yes, indeed, maybe it was — eventually. But is that really all you can tell us about those payments? . . . Let the record show that the witness has shrugged again. Let's move on then, Ms. Topo, shrugging our way down the road. Would you look, please, at the entry for November first, the day after your husband supposedly popped his clogs. That records a fifteen-hundred-dollar payment made to you, doesn't it? Where it says 'Topo'?"

"Yes. Professor Herskowitz was feeling bad about what happened, a little guilty, I guess. It was to help me out."

"At your demand?"

"Well, it only seemed right. I didn't twist his arm."

"No? You thought your husband was dead, and just a few hours later you go to the professor for money?"

"We're poor, Mr. Mariner. We're not lawyers, or, or judges. I was, like, whadayacall, distraught. I didn't know what I was going to do at that point. I thought Tony might have really died. I didn't know." Her face has coloured more deeply, I imagine, and her eyes dart as she speaks.

"Is that how you explain the payments in subsequent months, month after month after month? For, let's see, two thousand dollars monthly until June, then three thousand? Amounts that just seem to go up and up until the preliminary hearing at the Farb.

Amounts that seem to start out in your husband's name and end up, month after month, in yours? You just kept on being a free-lance distraught person for the Institute? Sort of a contract pretend widow?"

"I already told you. Mack was helping us out."

"He certainly was. And you also told me you had demanded he help you out."

"Like I said: what's wrong with that? My husband worked really hard for him, and practically died because of him, because of his party and that stupid experiment."

"But Ms. Topo, these payments go on month after month, long after you knew Tony was alive and didn't tell Professor Her-skowitz. They're still in your name. That's the problem with modern mores, isn't it Ms. Topo? Middle-class feminism, as it were."

"I have no idea what you're implying, Judge Mariner," Topo objects.

"Nor do I, Mr. Mariner," Justice Cactus says.

"Well, Your Honour, if she had changed her name at marriage, presumably there'd have been no name change on the books. All the payments would have gone to Albinoni, and we wouldn't have known whether it was husband, wife, or non-relation."

"And that tells us what, Mr. Mariner?" Justice Cactus asks.

"In my submission, Your Honour, it tells us that Professor Herskowitz didn't know Tony was alive. Did he, Ms. Topo? He was making payments to you, not for Tony's research, and neither you nor Tony wanted Professor Herskowitz to know Tony hadn't died, did you?"

"That wasn't our responsibility."

"But from what you've told us, if he knew, well, the payments would've stopped."

"Not necessarily."

"No? Why ever not, Ms. Topo."

"I'm just saying, they wouldn't necessarily have stopped."

"Because you had other reasons for blackmailing Professor Herskowitz didn't you, Ms. Topo? Reasons beyond the fact that Tony might have died?"

"Your Honour," Katz objects, "there's no proof that anyone was blackmailing Professor Herskowitz. In fact, the evidence shows that it was the professor who was doing the blackmailing. Of Mr. Gander."

"We disagree, Mr. Katz." Justice Mariner bows slightly toward counsel for the prosecution. "Who was blackmailing whom is a matter for the jury. And you have to prove beyond a reasonable doubt that Professor Herskowitz was blackmailing Mr. Gander. As far as Ms. Topo and Mr. Albinoni are concerned, well, odd though it may seem to the jury, you haven't charged that lovely couple with anything. The jury only has to think it was a possibility they were blackmailing the professor — and if they were, how the blackmailing could show they were the so-called attempted murderers, or pretend murderers of Mr. Albinoni. Because they stood to profit by Mr. Albinoni's Baconian non-death, didn't you, Ms. Topo? All these nice little payments from the Institute, thousands of simoleons, month after month. And it would just keep coming, so long as you could make Professor Herskowitz think Tony had died because of his research for Mack."

"Quite the speech, Mr. Mariner." Katz rolls his eyes until Justice

Cactus gives the assistant Crown a bemused look.

"Well, Mr. Katz," the trial judge says. "That would seem to be what this case is all about, isn't it? Who tried to pretend to kill whom? And why? Why oh why, Mr. Katz?"

It is the nature of extreme self-lovers, as they will set a
house on fire, and it were but to roast their eggs.
Francis Bacon, "Of Wisdom for a Man's Self"

"To caterwaul," according to *The Oxford English Dictionary:*

1. Of cats: To make the noise proper to them at rutting time.
2. To utter a similar cry; to make a discordant, hideous noise.
3. To rehearse for the Parkdale Library's Play-in the-Alley, Pay-
What-You-Can Production of Cats.

Okay, so I added that last one. In the Auntie Bella's Play-in-
the-Alley context, deriving "caterwaul" from the cat's habits and
proclivities does a disservice to rutting felines. Thankfully, the
Parkdale Library production includes very little dancing; otherwise there would ensue additional growling and wailing,
consequent upon multiple heart attacks not to mention com-
pound fractures, sprains, and concussions.

It must be said, however, that the makeup and costumes are
enthusiastically applied, and Auntie Bella acquits herself rather
well as the ageing and formerly glamourous Grizabella. She's good
at ageing and formerly glamourous, is our Auntie Bella. Is it her
fault that in the big climax at the end (right after she caterwauls

"Memory" for the last time), she's a little too portly for the fire escape she's supposed to climb to Cat Heaven (or wherever Mr. Lloyd Webber intends for her to be going in that bizarre closing scene), and she gets stuck between the railings, in Parkdale Purgatory, tearing her already tattered costume, alternately caterwauling with frustration and then laughter? Happily, Parkdale's fire department is only a few blocks away. As though anxious to accompany our amateur song stylings, the firefighters arrive with sirens wailing and lights flashing. All kitted out in their heavy heat-resistant coats, two of them ride their hydraulic ladder up to Auntie Bella stuck in Off-Broadway Purgatory, where they apply the jaws of life, splitting open the fire escape to rescue both herself and Grizabella in one go from a fate apparently worse than death. Mind you, now we'll need a new stairway to Heaven, courtesy of the municipal taxpayer. But then, that's what dress rehearsals are for, I suppose.

As for Yours Also Typecast, well, I have been allowed to roam "the stage" — which is to say the alleyway — at will, given that it is blocked at one end by the crew and their gear and at the other by a hot dog cart operated by one Marichka, a stout woman with a moustache and a large mole on her nose who has seized the rehearsal opportunity to increase her sales volume for the evening.

And speaking of seizing opportunities, it is no particular stage trick to secrete myself on the bottom shelf of Marichka's cart, among the pop cans and extra hot dog buns. Marichka is too busy flogging sausages and veggie dogs to notice. At the end of the evening, I have to stop myself caterwauling with glee as she carts me off toward the street and freedom. Unfortunately, there are aluminum sliding doors to the cart's shelves, which she suddenly slams closed, bending only so far as her heavy form and short waist will allow so that she has no idea she is locking me inside. I am trundled along like that in the dark for a time, gagging on cheap sausage fumes, consoling myself that Marichka will have to open up again during the next twelve hours or so. Until then, I can just nap.

Twelve seconds later, I am stifling. *Help!* The heat is like to roast me until my skin bursts, in the way of an all-feline hot dog on Marichka's filthy grill. *Help! I'm trapped in Salmonella Hell!* I can't breathe. I can, however, smell my own flesh on slow roast. *Help!* I'm going faint. I'm fading fast! And my blood's about to boil.

So much for catnaps. I decide to show them what caterwauling is all about. I mean, hey, you thespians, if that's what you're going to do with Mr. Lloyd Webber's musical, let's at least get it right.

I mewl and cry and piss and moan pathetically, recalling the night I watched *Bridge on the River Kwai* with Justice Mariner (goodbye, My Lord, remember Your Derelict More or Less Loyal Companion when you sit on your little derelict stool outside the old shed at 1415 Elsyian Fields North) — you know, the scene where they lock the prisoners in the sweatbox in the blazing sun? I roast. I suffocate. I am done for. Salmonella Hell.

Woozily I contemplate why it is said that *felis sylvestris* has nine lives. Well, we're survivors, of course — among extant mammals, we're the closest to our original evolutionary form, because we were already so close to perfection, as the ancient Egyptians realized in worshipping us for it. A comforting thought on one's deathbed. Less comforting is what I have read in a library — probably His Lordship's on Elysian Fields, not the Great Library of Osgoode Hall — that as "the trinity of trinities," nine is the luckiest of numbers.

Whatever luck I've had, it has reached nine-ninths, I'm afraid. Never mind that; why does *Homo allegedly sapiens* assume that survival is a matter of luck? Gasping my last, I suppose it's because this permits them to burn coal *(hot, hot, suffocatingly hot)*, split atoms *(hotter, hotter)*, run sport utility vehicles, spray pesticides hither and yon, drop bombs, rape and pave the landscape with Hell's bituminous pitch *(hot, hot, suffocatingly hot)*, alter the genetic codes in what we all consume, poison our water *(pant, pant)* as they wash their hands in it — like Judas asking What is Truth and turning a deaf ear — washing their hands of all responsibility for the planet's future. What, me worry? *I am dying, Egypt, dying!*

Somehow I cannot stop the caterwauling even when I am restored to Auntie Bella's equivocal embrace, even as the cast and crew coo at me and stroke my slow-roasted coat, now redolent of stale sausage, mustard, and sweet relish the green of pond scum. *Air, folks, air! Give the lad some air!*

"Merrawl!" says I aloud. "Merrawl!"

"Poor little fatso," Marichka grunts, her beady little eyes hidden in her own adipose tissue as she smiles. "He almost have bumpy ride, him hitched wit' mine car. In cart, I'm saying. Him hitched in mine hot dog cart, you know, wit' mine car. Bumpy bumpy."

"You should have made him into sausages, Marichka," dear old Auntie Bella replies, "a load of homemade hot dogs. Done us all a favour. He's asking for it, this one. Little furry hot dogs."

"Hot cats," says her buddy Bobby Daly, the fat and simpering assistant librarian who plays the fat and simpering Bustopher Jones in the Play-in-the-Alley *Cats*. "The new taste sensation. Of the hundreds of hot-dog vendors in the city, you'd be unique,

Marichka. Hot cats! Come and get your hot cats on a hot tin cart!"

He imagines himself a wit, an Orson Welles, does our fat little Bobby Daly.

∽◞◟∼

On the stand, Albinoni seems more haggard than ever: "Happily for us, he looked like the strung-out druggie he is," Justice Mariner later told Auntie Bella and Penny, making awkward conversation during an access visit with Yours in Care of the Reluctant Feline Aid Society (reluctance on whose part I have deliberately left ambiguous; translation: Auntie Bella and I continue our cold war of attrition). For his big day in court, Tony is dressed in his usual lounge-lizard polyester (I deduce from His Lordship's narrative), and habitually sweeps a lock of greasy dark hair from his eyes. That fool's half-smile lingers on his lips, no matter what Katz asks him.

"Let's go then, Mr. Albinoni," the latter says, his voice even foggier than usual with post-nasal drip, "to the night of the Hallowe'en dinner party at Mack Herskowitz's penthouse. It was a theme party?"

"Yes, it was a Hallowe'en party, as you just said."

"Meaning what, though?"

"Well, meaning that people were in costumes, you know? The lawyers wore their court robes, but the rest of us, the plebes, dressed up a little more imaginatively. We had more fun with it, I guess, being less tight . . . uh, tightly wound, if you know what I mean."

"Including you?"

"Well, some might say I wasn't all that imaginative, that in my case it was more a matter of typecasting. I was a court jester."

"Why do you say it was typecasting?"

"Well, I guess I'm sort of known for messing around — getting attention in a semi-serious way. The class clown in the John Belushi style or whatever. The prankster."

"You say the party followed the Hallowe'en theme. Did that include the trick-or-treat aspect of the holiday?"

"I suppose you could say the meal and wine were the treat. And we had a bit of a joke in store, too, yes. A trick, if you want to put it that way."

"Tell us about that."

"Well, it had a serious side and a fun side. It had to do with Professor Herskowitz's great interest in Francis Bacon, the seventeenth-century lawyer, philosopher, and amateur scientist. Near the end of his life, Bacon was fired as Lord Chancellor of Britain because he accepted bribes regarding law cases. So, you know, because he was the chief judicial officer, they sacked him. Woolsacked him, as Mack likes to say."

"Yes, we've heard about that," Katz advises, pausing to blow his nose in a dirty handkerchief he keeps in his suit jacket. Except he actually says: *Yes we'b heard abowd dad.* "But how does Bacon relate to the trick-or-treat, or joke, aspect of the dinner party?"

"Well, I was getting to that. See, Mack's writing a biography of Bacon. And there's this sort of wild theory that Bacon faked his own death. The official line is that he got sick after he was out in the wet and cold experimenting, you know, preserving a freshly slaughtered chicken with snow. But this one sort of wonky theory says, no, what happened was Bacon had the royal doctor inject him with opium, or some form of morphine, to make him comatose. The original conspiracy theory, I guess. Supposedly this was on April Fool's Day, around Easter time, and the idea was to make it look like he was dead. Bacon I mean."

Juror Number Two is snivelling, perhaps touched by the plight of Sir Francis. Then again, Juror Number Eight is sneezing and hacking away like he's the one who's been eviscerating chickens at winter's end. Peering hazily in their direction, Katz splutters into his filthy hankie.

"And what was the point of that, Bacon pretending to be dead?"

"Well, supposedly he then escaped to the Continent. France, I guess. You know, he was resurrected like Christ on Easter and went on with his life, escaping the disgrace of being 'thrown off the Woolsack,' as they put it. At least that's what this theory says."

"'The Woolsack' being where the Lord Chancellor sat on official business."

"I guess, yeah."

"And what did this have to do with you and the professor?" Katz sniffs, his eyes all teary and red as though he, too, is uncharacteristically moved by the saga of the Renaissance lawyer, philosopher, and essayist.

"Well, as part of our research, we wanted to see if we could duplicate something like that. For the biography. Fake Mack's death, to prove or disprove this theory. That was the original idea, anyway."

"What do you mean, 'original idea'?"

"Well, at first I was supposed to provide Professor Herskowitz some Percodan, which is a morphine derivative, you know, so he could drug himself, like in the Bacon Resurrection Theory."

"He was supposed to be the one who went comatose? And your role was just to supply the drug?"

"Yes. Well, actually, also I was supposed to arrange for him to be taken out of the room by a couple of guys dressed up as paramedics. When he went squiffy, I mean." Albinoni smirks more broadly at the memory, as he ducks his head and wipes his nose with the back of a hand. Perhaps in another fit of sympathy, Juror Number Two blows his nose (Justice Mariner has told his wife and her perpetual-motion auntie with the flair for melodrama), while Juror Number Eight clears his throat several times in succession. Juror Number Seven holds a tissue up to her wrinkled nose, mirroring the assistant Crown with his hankie.

"Who were these 'guys,' as you put it?" Katz says; or, actually, *Oo were dese 'guys,' as you puddid?*

"A couple of friends of mine, from my other life slogging away in the building trades. I work with them during the summer, and sometimes after school. I just told them we were playing a practical joke on the other guests at the dinner party, for Hallowe'en, and that they wouldn't look out of place dressed up, because it was a costume thing."

"Is that why they used a backboard instead of a stretcher?"

"Well, we, uh, we sort of borrowed that from the football team. The athletic department at Scarberia U. It was the best we could do."

"Scarborough University, you mean, I take it. But why did these young men carry you out instead of Professor Herskowitz?"

"Well, see, that's partly why I make this, uh, this distinction between what actually happened and the original plan. There was Plan A, see, where Professor Herskowitz was supposed to make a dramatic re-entry into the party once he revived. You know, after they carried him out. Then there was Plan B."

"Did Plan B call for you to collapse, or get drugged up?" stuffed-up Katz asks, only it comes out as *Plaid Beh.*

"No. It was still supposed to be Professor Herskowitz who dropped."

"So how was Plan B different from Plan A?"

"Well, Professor Herskowitz changed it. He wasn't going to come back to the party — you know, resurrected."

"You mean he was going to really die?"

"To all appearances, yes."

"All appearances?"

"That's what I said. Because, see, we — they, my friends, actually, from the building trades, my father-in-law, see, got me this part-time construction work — anyways, my friends were going to carry him out, but then I was going to drive him to the airport."

"That's why you had his car keys, which fell out of the pouch on your costume?"

"Yes."

"Where was Professor Herskowitz going? 'The Continent' — where he would pretend to be William Shakespeare, or maybe John Grisham?"

"He never said. He just explained he would contact me when he got there to give me further instructions. And I assumed he'd decided to really put the theory to the test. You know — to see if people really believed he was dead, and how that would play out."

"And when did conspiracy Plan A become conspiracy Plan B?"

"Your Honour," Justice Mariner interrupts, "no one is charged with conspiracy here. As Mr. Albinoni has said, this was nothing more than an academic exercise. Research, however unorthodox."

Justice Cactus shrugs and says, "We shall see, Mr. Mariner, we shall see." His Honour turns to the witness: "Mr. Albinoni, when did unorthodox Plan A become unorthodox Plan B?"

"Well, just a couple of weeks before the dinner party. After I got back from Ottawa."

"Ottawa?" Katz resumes command.

"Yeah. Our Intro to Legal Research and Process class took a field trip there. An overnighter to the Supreme Court and Federal Court."

"Why did the plan change, though? The Bacon Bit, so-called, or the resurrection theory?"

"Well, I don't know for sure, but I think it might have had to do with what I found out in Ottawa."

"Found out?"

"Found out from Vern Gander."

"The Vern Gander who has been a witness in this proceeding?"

"Yes, Vern Gander, the Assistant Deputy Minister of Justice for the feds. When he was in law school, he was one of Mack's research assistants, like I am. Was. Whatever."

"So we've heard. And what did you find out from Mr. Gander?"

"Well, he's a director of Mack's institute, the IWAC, so I first met him at the beginning of the school year, when Mack had a conference called 'The One That Got Away: Civil Actions Against the Acquitted Accused.' Vern and I sort of hit it off at the time, and we started keeping in touch by e-mail. I was interested in maintaining contact, because I was thinking I might like to do my articles at Justice. So he was a good contact."

"Articles — you mean do your internship in law at the Department of Justice in Ottawa?"

"Yes, as part of the qualifying stuff you have to do as a lawyer. I thought I might want to work with the Crown, you know, instead of at a private law firm. After law school, I mean. I'm interested in politics, social economics . . ."

"Okay, so you kept in touch with Mr. Gander."

"Yes. Then, well, working with Zipporah, another student who helps Mack run the institute, I saw the books."

"Zipporah or Zippy Kyriakos, who was also Mack's girlfriend?"

"Yes. Working with her I saw IWAC's accounting records. And there were these monthly payments — donations, Mack called them — from Vern. So I just sort of casually asked him about them, about why it said 'dead cat bounce' next to them. I was just curious."

"And did he reply?"

"Well, it took more time than usual, but one day I got an e-mail from Vern telling me to delete it immediately after I read it. Vern explained that he supposedly made the money in the stock market — on what's called a dead cat bounce, when the market seems to bounce back but then it dies right down again. Supposedly he sold at the top of the bounce, he said. But according to this e-mail, he didn't have any money in the stock market at all."

"That's what he said in the e-mail?"

"Yes. And he said something like, 'between you and me, Mack is really bleeding me. If you and Zipporah have any influence on him, maybe you could persuade him to ease up, give a guy a break.' Something like that. And I wrote back asking 'What do you mean, Mack's bleeding you?' and Vern responded something like, 'Well, I don't want to get into it too much, but you know Mack. When it comes to his institute and projects, he's not above putting a guy on the rack over his old law school shenanigans — to persuade a guy to keep helping him out. Mack's been very helpful to me, but he expects quid pro quo.'"

"Did you know what he meant by that, Mack 'expects quid pro quo'?"

"Well, of course quid pro quo means you get something for something. Exchange. We discuss it in first-year Contracts. And I knew that Mack's philosophy is nothing's free in this world. It's sort of his motto, really. But other than that, at the time, I didn't really know what Vern meant."

"And did you continue to discuss it with him?"

"No, but I sort of mentioned it to Mack, out of curiosity, again, but also trying to help Vern. I was joking around about it. Teasing. 'Hey, Mack,' I said, 'I hear you're blackmailing Gander.' It was a joke, you know, just to get Mack to lighten up on Vern, but Mack went absolutely ballistic. What the hell did I mean, what was I implying, what was it my business, what was I going to do about it, did I want to keep working with him, did I want to get on well at the bar? Did I want to make it even through first year? So, yeah, I may be a fool but I ain't stupid. I saw this was a pretty touchy thing, so I just left it at that. And a couple of days later, Mack changed the Bacon Resurrection plan, the Bacon Bit, to my driving him to the airport. Instead of him coming back into the room, like, resurrected. He was, well, he was going to bugger off. Disappear."

"Okay, so you joked around about Mack blackmailing Gander. Then, Plan A changed to Plan B such that, instead of coming back into the dinner party after he collapsed, Professor Herskowitz was supposed to go to the airport. But if Plan B still called for him to become comatose, or nearly so, how come you were the one who had to be taken out, while he woke up after passing out briefly?"

"Well, I collapsed and actually went comatose myself."

The testimony seems to provoke another fit on the jury of snivelling and sneezing and hacking. Katz blows his nose with a great honk.

"Yes. And why did that happen?"

"Well, there are two more theories on that."

"Whose theories are these?"

"Well, they're mine. And you agree with the second one. Because we also agreed, you and I, that the first theory has holes in it."

"Now that's what I call a conspiracy, Your Honour." Justice Mariner adopts his most reasonable tone to proffer a timely bit of constructive criticism. "The Crown and the witness canoodling to cobble together some old wives' tale for the witness to tell the jury."

Katz does his eye-roll thing. "Your Honour, for the jury's information, Mr. Albinoni is referring to our discussions when I was preparing this case against Professor Herskowitz. I hasten to say that they are Mr. Albinoni's own theories, not something I told him to say, right Tony? We did not tailor your evidence, did we? You suggested the theories to me?"

"Yes, that's right." Unfortunately for Katz, the witness goes into his court jester act again, ducking and smirking.

"Okay, Tony. Let's take your theories one at a time." Fraidy walks a few paces toward the jury, gazing at the panel with a half-smile of his own, never mind that his nose is audibly clogged and his eyes all teary. Not a pretty sight. "What's the first theory as to why you became comatose instead of Professor Herskowitz? At this dinner party."

"Well, because the glasses got mixed up. Somehow. And so I drank the spiked wine and port that were meant for Mack, as part of our Bacon resurrection experiment, by accident. I got dosed with the Percodan meant for Mack."

"Didn't you have your own glasses to drink from?"

"Yeah. But I have to admit I was also drinking the dregs left by some of the other guests in their glasses. I was helping to clean up, literally, I guess — I drank down the dregs. Cleaning up, see?"

"You said there are holes in that theory?"

"Well, for one thing, Mack was all the way at the other end of the table. At the head of it, as host. And he still had his port glass. And probably his red wine glass, too."

"Meaning?"

"Well, that's the second theory. Meaning, first, that he was too far away for me to drink his stuff. Too far away for me to mistakenly drink from his glassware. And two, meaning that someone had spiked my drinks instead of Mack's. Deliberately — or they had switched glasses on us. Or someone had spiked both my glass and Mack's, I guess."

"Or had accidentally given you the wrong glasses in the first place," Justice Mariner says, rising slowly to his full six-foot-two. "Accidentally, with no malice aforethought."

"My friend seems to have forgotten that this is examination-in-chief," Katz says.

"You'll have your turn, Mr. Mariner," Cactus rules.

"Who would have done that?" Katz asks. "Switched the glasses on purpose or dosed both you and Mack?"

"Well, I wasn't sure. But I figured Mack was still mad at me, about Vern and all that."

"So he might have switched glasses on you, or dosed you?"

"It seems plausible enough. I mean, this dead cat bounce business seemed to touch a nerve, and the more I thought about it, the more suspicious it sounded."

"So you think Mack could have switched glasses on you or poisoned you . . . *dosed* you," Katz sarcastically corrects himself as Justice Mariner rises to object, "even though he had given you the keys to his car to drive him to the airport?"

"Well, I guess he must have had another set. And I guess if it later came out I was supposed to drive him to the airport, as it has come out, well, that would throw suspicion off Mack as the one that switched glasses to try to harm me."

"How do you mean?"

"Well, he could still say he gave me the keys because he intended for me to drive him to the airport, and so it must have been an accident, that the glasses got mixed up. And if I died, well it was because the dose was meant for a much bigger guy like himself — he's twice my size, you know. And he knew that I tended to take a hit of Perc myself on occasion. So there was always the chance I would have more in my system than what I got from the glasses at the party. I mean, he would say it was all a mix-up. An accident, from a fun little experiment. Nothing intentional."

"Okay, but Back was your bentor." Translation: "Mack was your mentor."

"In a way, yes, in another way, no."

"What do you mean, 'in another way, no'?"

"Well, I was more sort of slave labour than protégé. It was a master-servant relationship, as the law puts it. You know, like Vern said, quid pro quo."

"Quid pro quo. How did the two of you get along, you and the professor?"

"Well, we didn't, really. That's what I mean, sort of."

"But, again, you were his research assistant."

"Do you like all your bosses, Mr. Katz?"

"Yet there you were at his dinner party."

"Purely in my usual role as a plebe and fool. Feudal serf for the lord of the manor. We learned all about that in property law class — seigneurs and vassals. I was part of the wait staff."

"But you had signed up to take upper-year courses from him, too." Katz consults his notes. "Business Associations. Legal Profession."

"Well, one, he's a good teacher. He doesn't mollycoddle you, and a top mark from him really means something. On the street. It gets you places. Number two, he has fantastic connections. He's quite powerful and makes a great reference for jobs and grants and all that. Yeah?"

"So you respected him," Katz sniffs, "even though it was sort of a noblesse oblige thing, master and servant?"

"Your Honour, my friend is leading the witness," Justice Mariner points out.

"How did you work together, Tony?" Katz rephrases, grimacing over his sniffles at his "friend" on the defence side.

"You're getting really sniffy, Fraidy," Justice Mariner stage-whispers.

"Mack respected me, too, I thought, not as his equal, but in my role as his assistant. And as a student. We weren't friends, but there was a mutual respect, I thought. He sort of liked it that I mouthed off, I think. He respected that, even though he said I was a smartass."

"He said that?"

"He also said I was the sort of shit disturber that ended up disbarred after four or five years."

"Not exactly high praise."

"Well, from him I thought maybe it was. I mean, he smiled when he said it. Like I might have been a wiseass shit disturber, but I was *his* wiseass shit disturber. That's why I thought I could joke with him about Vern. He admired people with guts, outspoken people, chancers. And from his point of view, it wasn't about friendship. It was business. If you could get something out of each other, mutually, well, you know, you scratch my back and I'll scratch yours. That's how Mack saw it. If you were his pal, he couldn't be so demanding of you. So he wasn't any friendlier than he had to be. You see, Mr. Katz, I don't think Mack has any friends, really."

"No? None?"

"None. It doesn't fit his life plan. Mack has enemies, like many people. But unlike many people, he doesn't have friends, too. He has rivals."

Katz sneezes violently on the jury, causing Juror Number Six to jump in her seat.

CHAPTER 5

Nothing doth more hurt in a state than that
cunning men pass for wise.
Francis Bacon, "Of Cunning"

"So you saw yourself as a rival to Professor Herskowitz, Tony? Given that, in your words, he has rivals, not friends?" A coughing fit from Juror Number Four obscures the last word as Justice Mariner begins his cross-examination where Katz left off.

"Only on a lower plane, like, say, everyday aggravation, only in that way was I any sort of challenge to him. I mean, come on, as a student, I wasn't important enough to be a true rival. But as someone who did a lot of the work for which Mack got all the credit, well, yes, I was sort of a rival."

"You sound a little bitter about that. About doing the work and Professor Herskowitz getting the credit."

The witness, I imagine, shrugs. "Not really. It's the way of the world, particularly at universities. But it made Mack a little nervous, particularly because I'm not the type to just sit there and take it."

"Precisely. It's fair to say you were at odds with Professor Herskowitz about many things, isn't it, both personal and professional?"

"Well, everyone was."

"Come on, Tony. You're not telling us the whole story, are you? It wasn't all business between you and Professor Herskowitz, was it?"

"I don't know what you're getting at."

"You knew the specifics of what Vern was saying about the Professor, didn't you?"

"Not exactly."

"But Vern asked you about your personal relationship with Mack Herskowitz, didn't he?"

"Well, he asked me if Mack had 'tried it on' with me."

"'Tried it on?'"

"Yeah. You know, come on to me. Propositioned me. You know, sexually."

"So you deduced that that had something to do with Vern's donations, didn't you? A quid pro quo, I believe you called it?"

"Well, I thought it might."

"You thought it might. And you hinted as much to Mack, didn't you?"

"I was just joking around. It didn't matter to me. We live in sexually, like, liberated times. More or less. I was joking."

"Everything was just a big joke to you, right?"

"Not everything."

"Sleeping with Mack's girlfriend, speaking of sexual liberation."

"Relevance, Your Honour," Katz growls from his trench at the prosecution table.

"The relevance, Your Honour, is to demonstrate the level of animosity this witness has for the professor. The relevance is how he might be motivated to play tricks on him, to double-cross him, even to testify against him on the very serious charges of attempted murder, possession of drugs, and extortion. The relevance, Your Honour, is how credible is this witness, this witness who pretends to be dead and is an admitted prankster."

"I didn't know it was time for closing arguments, Your Honour," Katz hisses, throwing defence counsel a predatory, chattering little frown.

"I didn't sleep with Zippy to spite Mack." The witness does his best to look exasperated.

"Oh? So maybe you did it to repay him for being your mentor, to thank him for his work with you as your teacher and research principal?"

"It had nothing to do with him."

"You sleep with his girlfriend and it has nothing to do with him? It must have occurred to you that Mack would find out. From Ms. Kyriakos or somehow else."

"That occurred to me."

"And it must have occurred to you that if you went along with the so-called Plan B, you'd be left holding the bag."

"You're losing me again."

"Well, you supplied the drugs. You were helping at the party. You were publicly always sniping at Professor Herskowitz, scoring points off him, you thought — making sarcastic remarks in his classes, slagging him off to the other students. You bonked his girlfriend. You had public shouting matches, in class and out. It must have occurred to you that if people thought he was poisoned, you would be the prime suspect. No?"

"Well, yeah, I guess that occurred to me."

"You guess. And *I* guess it also occurred to you to turn the tables, quite literally, didn't it, Mr. Albinoni?"

"I really don't know what you're talking about."

"No? Well maybe we'll get to that. For now I'd like to ask you about that e-mail you mentioned to Mr. Katz. The confidential e-mail from Vern Gander, in which he told you Mack was asking him for donations."

"Yes."

"You said you didn't follow that up with Vern."

"What I meant was, we both were really busy, Vern and I; I had mid-terms or whatever, school work and the stuff I did for Mack. Vern had his government work, and we didn't exchange any e-mails after that."

"But you saw Vern in Ottawa after that, didn't you, in early October? You said so just a few minutes ago."

"Yes, as I explained to Fred, to Mr. Katz, my law school section, first-year Section F, we took a field trip to Ottawa, with our Intro to Legal Research and Process class. We went on an overnighter to the Supreme Court and Federal Court. I had e-mailed Vern about it and we arranged to go to lunch."

"So, not only did you see him, you did in fact exchange e-mails with him."

"You're twisting it. I didn't exchange e-mails with him on the donations or whatever to the institute. I just said, 'Hey, you wanna have lunch or something?' One little, you know, question. Just a friendly get-together."

"Fine distinctions again, eh, Mr. Albinoni? I expect the jury might be wondering why you're making them. Anyone would think you had something to hide."

"Your Honour," Katz literally spits, just about having kittens, "Mr. Mariner is trying to overtake the jury's function. He's telling them what to think."

"Members of the jury," Cactus advises, smiling sadly, "Mr. Mariner can't tell you what to wonder. Mind you, you might well be wondering what he's playing at by trying to tell you what to wonder."

"I'm sorry, Your Honour. I was merely suggesting that the witness isn't quite as forthcoming as he might be."

"Your Honour," Katz caterwauls.

"I'll proceed, shall I?" Justice Mariner asks Justice Cactus, who just makes a wry face into the middle distance. "So anyway, Mr. Albinoni," defence counsel continues with his witness, "you did in fact exchange further e-mails with Vern Gander. And did you have lunch with him in Ottawa?"

"Yes. And just to expedite this so you can't accuse me of hiding anything, that's when he told me that Professor Herskowitz was blackmailing him."

"Thank you so much for expediting my cross-examination, Mr. Albinoni. I'm sure I, and the court, can use all the help we can get. You are indeed a bright law student. But the thing is, you just told me the blackmailing accusation was a joke, when you said it to Professor Herskowitz."

"Well, it was. I mean, I thought it was a bit of an exaggeration, anyways, the way Vern put it. He's a pretty intense dude, you know. Pretty uptight, which is probably why he's done so well as a senior civil servant." When the jury does not find this especially risible, Albinoni continues, "And Mack's notoriously brusque and demanding, so he gets people's backs up."

"He gets your back up too, no? A lot?"

"Sometimes. But like I say, I also respect the fact that he's demanding and very intelligent. You can't make omelettes without breaking eggs."

"Breaking eggs, scratching backs, you're up on all the clichés, aren't you, Mr. Albinoni? What about the pot calling the kettle black?"

"Sorry?"

"Well, what do you mean, exactly, you 'understood' from Vern that Mack was 'blackmailing' him?"

"According to Vern, well, apparently, when Vern was still a law student, Professor Herskowitz told him there was a way he could be sure that his grades stayed high and that he got good references for the highly competitive articling placements."

"Your Honour," Katz mewls, "he can't tell us what the professor told someone else."

"That might be, Your Honour," Justice Mariner responds, "but we've already heard the exact same evidence from Mr. Gander himself. So what's the harm? It's not exactly complimentary to my client, is it?"

"Which makes one wonder once more, Mr. Mariner," Cactus mumbles, chin in hand, "why you want to bring it up again."

"Well, Your Honour, as this case keeps showing us, not everything is as it first appears. I think the jury will find that, at the end of the day, my client was more sinned against that sinning. We don't want to be like Sir Francis Bacon's jesting Pilate, who asked what is truth and did not stay for an answer."

"Now he's telling the jury what to find, on top of what to wonder," Katz mewrawls at the moon that is Mr. Justice Cactus's big balding head.

"Well, anyway," Albinoni cuts in, impatient with being

upstaged, "what I understood was that Professor Herskowitz had a relationship with Vern."

"A relationship?"

"Well, you know how some men have a mistress, a kept woman?"

"Yes."

"Well, Mack Herskowitz has kept students, if you get my drift."

"You do tend to drift here and there, don't you Mr. Albinoni, wherever you see an opportunity to your personal advantage?"

"Your Honour," Katz whines, torquing his head eastward as though he can't contain his frustration.

Juror Number Eight sneezes so loudly, and without benefit of handkerchief, that he feels compelled to apologize viva voce.

CHAPTER 6

Suspicion amongst thoughts are like bats
amongst birds, they ever fly by twilight.
Sir Francis Bacon, "Of Suspicion"

His Lordship is in another funk. "It's a serious case of defences interruptus," he explains to Reg Holdsworth, over caffe lattes at the Lettieri under the Sheraton Centre. According to conversations I happen to hear later that same morning, Reg has come downtown expressly to watch the trial, but there will be no court today. "Outbreak of flu on the jury," Justice Mariner explains. "Right in the middle of my most crucial cross of the Crown's biggest witness. Bloody disaster." He shakes his head as he plays with the low-fat foam, a fungus on his coffee mottled with the rotting dust of cinnamon bark. "We're adjourning until next Monday, apparently." He chuffs with ironic humour. "Only silver lining is Katz's got it, too. Had him moaning about it to me this morning on the phone. Poor bugger could barely speak. I almost felt sorry him. Then again, I think he might have infected the jury with it on purpose." Reprise shaking of said head, upon which the hair grows with surprising abundance for a Has-being of his vintage. "Right in the middle of my cross."

"Yeah, I just heard. And here I came down specially for the show. That, and to tell you about my sleepless night."

"You, too? I've got a client facing eight to ten in the Kingston Pen, and my most important cross-examination has gone south. What've you got to worry about?"

"Has Albinoni ever said where he was during the time he supposedly wasn't?"

"You mean, during the time he was supposed to be dead?"

"Yeah. Something's occurred to me about that. I mean, about where he was hiding. Has he said anything?"

"Not as far as I know. We never thought to ask him."

"Actually, I wouldn't ask him, if I were you. Not just yet. I'd ask the little woman first. The very quiet little woman."

"You mean his wife, Deena?"

"Well, consider this: When we visited Zippy Kyriakos in her room at the Farb, you notice she had two bookbags?"

The judge shrugs (one imagines) and shakes his head.

Holdsworth puts on a show of being dismayed. "No, I guess not. You were too busy ogling Ms. Gappy-Robe."

"Well, no." Justice Mariner scowls in self-defence. "As you'll understand, I'm in enough trouble already for what I haven't done with students. And I can't say as I would have thought the book-bags were that remarkable even if I'd seen them. I mean . . . student, bookbags . . ." His Lordship pulls a wry face.

"Well, fair dues, I didn't think much of them at the time myself. But ask *yourself* this, as it suddenly occurred to me when I was tossing and turning last night: What use did Zippy Kyriakos have for two bookbags, and double copies of the highly expensive volumes on the first-year syllabus? I mean, she lives steps from the law school. She's just been rescued from bankruptcy. She's bonking a professor at the school, whose apartment's filled with law books and who has unlimited access to the library. What does she need one bag for, let alone two, filled with the same coma-inducing first-year law books?"

Justice Mariner laughs. "Law students can be pretty obsessive, Reg, as you well know. Maybe one's for underlining in now, the other's for underlining in at exam time. Who knows? Anyway, thinking about Zippy's no cure for a man's insomnia."

"True enough, she's a distracting young woman. But my thoughts quickly, and suddenly, turned to those bookbags. Which became even more distracting. Even though my lovely wife was right there beside me, Judge. You think I jest? Kept me up for another good hour. The bookbag, I mean, not the old . . ."

Justice Mariner laughs again, over-heartily, partly to stop Holdsworth (one would think) from using a luggage metaphor that he might regret about his lady wife. "Middle age does strange things to a fellow. You're talking to an expert on that, an expert in exile *because* of that."

"Well, Mr. Expert on the distractions of middle age, does Kyriakos really strike you as the usual obsessed law student type?"

Suddenly, Justice Mariner grows wide-eyed, his smile fading to a bemused grin. "Holdsworth, old son, I think I see where you're going with this."

"I think I see where we *should* go with this. And it's not to Zippy, if that's what you think I think."

"No. As much as I enjoy the distracting company of Ms. Kyriakos, I think we both think we don't want her to know what we think we know. Because then word could get around about that, to the wrong sort of people. And we don't want them to know we know."

"Exactly. So I think we both think we should go talk to the right sort of people."

"Deena Topo. Methinks."

"Got it in one, old man. With no distractions. If we go now, her not-so-old man'll be up at the Farb, attending classes."

"They haven't booted him out of the Farb? Like old Francis Bacon off the Woolsack?"

"There's a joint hearing pending on Tony's status, before the Student Affairs and Academic Standards Committees. Never seen anything quite like this, I don't imagine. Anyway, he's in mercy, so to say, still in school pending further measures. Accused but not yet tried. So the young and unemployed Ms. Topo will be on her lonesome while Tony's in school."

"Perfect. The day isn't a total waste, after all. And we can swing around first and pick up little Amicus. Give him a day out, poor little bugger. Living with Penny's auntie can be cruel and unusual punishment, and don't I know it. And he likes you, Reg. I can tell."

Holdsworth looks dubious — for good reason. "We can take my car. If I can remember where I parked it."

∽✇∽

"Hey, I used to have a friend that lived just one street up," Justice Mariner says as we park in front of 25 Major Street. "On Borden. The Only Falafel House used to be a few doors away, on College. Remember, Reg?"

"Ancient history, I'm afraid, Me Lud. Possibly even before me time."

This jocular response seems to depress His Lordship, as though he's thinking about exile again — physical exile as well as spiritual exile in the form of middle age. It turns out, however, that student living situations haven't changed all that dramatically in the last thirty years. Albinoni and Topo live with four, and apparently sometimes five, six, or more other young people, in a decrepit two-storey semi-detached house constructed of peeling brick facing. Resident on the second floor are two medical students, boyfriend and girlfriend, plus a Ph.D. dropout who, while waiting for the *New York Review* to declare him the next Jonathan Franzen, works as a clerk at Bloor Books, drives hack, and studies sundry Scandinavian languages (nobody knows why: maybe a female Has-being of Nordic origins has taken his fancy) at the University of Toronto. A duty counsel at the City Hall courts has the room across from the med students', while the front sitting room, just off the rotting wooden porch, serves as sleeping quarters for the more itinerant lodgers and crashers. Albinoni and Topo sleep in the back room on the main floor, just behind the kitchen with the curled-up linoleum.

The cabby-writer answers the door, having just risen for the day, though it is after eleven. Rubbing his hair and yawning stalely, he tells us we can find Deena Topo in the basement, wrangling laundry. Duelling bouquets waft from the interior walls — of charred Hamburger Helper, damp clothing, and something else sad and sour, possibly overboiled cauliflower.

"You don't mind if I bring my cat in, do you?" Justice Mariner asks, gesturing with my carrier. "It gets really hot for him in the car. In the spring sun." Incarceration with no room to turn around is just fine, apparently, as long as the temperature is moderate.

And here, supposedly, His Lordship has written the country's leading judgment on cruel and unusual punishment.

The cabby shrugs and says, "One of my housemates is allergic, but she's in the hospital."

The judge looks concerned. "Nothing serious, I hope."

"Like cat allergies," Reg adds unhelpfully. And here I'm supposed to be enjoying day parole after having committed just that supposed offence.

The cabby yawns again. "Serious for her patients, maybe. She's doing her medical internship at Saint Mike's."

Feeling our way down a dark stairway carpeted with a frayed runner, we find Deena Topo in a dank laundry room, its ceiling so low that His Lordship must duck his head. The area serves double duty as the television room, apparently, where the smell of sweet rot exudes from the concrete floors, walls, and spruce studs. Topo explains that the med students won't tolerate the "boob tube" on the main floor. The cathode-ray enthusiasts have made the best of this, no doubt concluding that in the circumstances you can never feel guilty down here about idiot-box hypnosis: It is uncomfortable enough in the laundry room that you do your penance even as you commit the sin. Perhaps as an analgesic, the tenants have put an old carpet scrap in the room, rescued from some neighbour's garbage; but it, too, exhales must, the bouquet of old people's closets. The room's windows are thick on their outsides with accumulated mud, blocking what little light might otherwise filter through. Topo has the TV going — "The Shopping Bags" obliviously advise her how to save money on prescription drugs — but you can still hear the taps dripping in the washroom just east of where we visitors sit hip-to-hip-to-carrier on transported kitchen chairs, chatting with Topo as she irons an enormous pile of clothing. Congenitally scrappy, today she looks positively anorexic.

"I do it for the whole house," she glumly says, briefly glaring up from her work at us. "That way I don't have to cook." Judging by the way the place smells, maybe she should trade jobs. "And these days it keeps me busy." The iron hisses as she stands it upright, making me thump my head against the carrier's top as I hastily rise to object for the defence. "Anyways. I thought I was done with all this, this business with Tony and Mack. I've already testified. I don't mean to be rude or that, but I don't have nothing else to say. The thing is, I told the Crown everything I know."

"Don't worry, Deena," Justice Mariner says. "We basically just want to know one simple thing that maybe the Crown forgot to ask you."

"I don't see why I should help Mack Herskowitz. Not after what happened to Tony."

"Well, but that was an accident, wasn't it?"

"Like you said in court, Judge, that's for the jury to decide."

"Is it, Deena?"

Topo says nothing, but throws His Lordship another angry look. "And you said Mack himself tried to put it right," the judge says, "by paying you and Tony for your trouble."

Topo irons more hotly, if you get my drift.

"The thing is, Deena," Holdsworth butts in, "we were wondering about how Tony so successfully made it look like he was dead."

Topo snorts like we must be really stupid and sets the iron hissing on its base again. "Well, like I said, he nearly really did die. That's how. Sheesh. You can't fake that."

"No," the judge says, "we mean after that. He was really clever at keeping out of sight. Where was he?"

"Oh, that." Topo laughs. "He stayed with a friend from law school until after the supposed funeral. Until after the coroner's office was done poking around." Topo shrugs and widens her eyes at us visitors. "The hospital thought they'd lost him, remember?" She laughs again, humourlessly, and shrugs again, sullenly. "Then he came back here." She goes back to her laundry and shrugs yet again, arching her almost invisible eyebrows.

"Did he tell you which friend he stayed with?" Justice Mariner asks.

Carefully ironing a worn striped shirt, apparently Albinoni's, Topo answers, "Yeah. Dougal Fergus. Lives near the law school, but in the basement of some house on Checkers Road."

"You sure about that, Deena?" Holdsworth asks.

"Yeah. Dougal rents the basement, in some illegal apartment, I think, on Checkers. Another criminal, eh, Judge? But I guess it could be on some other street. How should I know?"

"No, Deena," the judge interrupts. "What I mean is, are you sure Tony was staying with Dougal?"

"That's what he told me. Why would he lie?"

"Why indeed?" Holdsworth says.

"Deena," the judge says, "does Tony own a blue bookbag — a backpack, with dirty yellow stripes down the back and on the straps?"

"Yeah. Why?"

"Well, remember how I visited you at work shortly after Tony's pretend death?"

"Yeah. And basically you got me fired, thank you very much.

How could I forget? And now you want to come into my house and give me the third degree again."

"Please, Deena. It's not like that. This concerns you as much as it concerns us or Mack."

"Oh, yeah. Right."

"Yes. Yes, Deena, because, just before I came to see you at Dr. Schuss's, well, we also went to see Zippy Kyriakos. Reg and I. In her room at the LoKarb-Kola Towers, on campus."

"So?"

"Tony's bookbag was there."

Topo snorts again. "Maybe it was hers."

"There were two bookbags, Deena, both containing law books. The same law books. Expensive books that you wouldn't want to buy twice. One bookbag was blue and black, the other one was red."

Topo sets the iron down flat, leaving it hissing and spitting on the shirt, as she turns to us, her face reddening. "Maybe it was someone else's. They're common as dog dirt. They only make so many colours, you know."

"Deena, you're gonna burn that shirt," Holdsworth says, rushing over to move the iron. But it's too late. The fabric is so thin, there is already a brown equilateral triangle branded into the garment. Burning polyester lends a new spice to the dank basement bouquet.

"Come on, Deena," the judge says, putting on his most sympathetic face. "You don't believe that."

Tears literally spring out of the girl's eyes. Then she shouts as like to break your eardrums: "The prick! He told me it was a one-night stand with her! The bastard! The user! The prick! He told me he was at Dougal Fergus's."

CHAPTER 7

In the business of life, a man's disposition and the secret
workings of his mind and affections are better discovered
when he is in trouble than at other times.
Francis Bacon, *Novum Organum*

As foster mothers go, Auntie Bella makes a good wicked step-
mother. Comes the day — scratch that, comes the fourth day —
she forgets to prepare lunch for Yours in Care, let alone breakfast.
Happily the neighbourhood is chockablock with various cafés and
their lackadaisical policies on garbage maintenance in the streets
and alleyways. As Messrs. T.S. Eliot and A. Lloyd Webber put it
regarding Bustopher Jones (that fat and simpering "cat about
town") and his visits to various victual-and-alehouses:

> In the season of venison he gives his ben'son
> To the *Pothunter's* succulent bones;
> And just before noon's not a moment too soon
> To drop in for a drink at the *Drones*.

Auntie Bella's neighbourhood is bereft of gentlemen's clubs like
the Drones, so it's actually just outside the Everlasting Arms ("a
temple of refreshment," its blackboard promises, "for body as well
as soul") where I board the Queen streetcar. It is no trick at all to
obscure myself among the afternoon's first lot of dipsomaniacs and

my other assorted comrades of the alleyways (just risen to begin their long day in the urban jungle) as they shuffle through the middle doorways. Most are off downtownwards for their derelict's day's panhandling or cadging the odd swig of Liquor Control Board eighty-proof punchbowl Alcohol/*Alcool*. Fortunately our fellow passengers find it highly amusing to see "the rummys' cat" cadge a lift with them courtesy of the city's ratepayers, the Queen Street car being on the honour system and all. Some snicker or smile. Others reach out to stroke me. But mostly I avoid such infectious tributes by slinking around under this seat and that, finally stowing myself in the accordion bellows of the two conjoined cars.

Yes, this must make it the third or fourth page of my criminal record — "escape lawful custody" once again. (Arguably — as we say over at the Court of Appeal — that's my job description, ain't it?) But how did I finally evade the iron grasp of the formerly glamorous Grizabella a.k.a. Auntie Bella? The old hot dog cart number again it was, after the final Saturday rehearsal for *Cats* in the Alley, only this time *(Take notice: reader discretion is advised for the next dozen or so words)* I carefully deposited a juicy old hairball (thanks to the copious shedding of one's winter coat when summer is acomin' in) on the runner of Marichka's sliding cart door, such that the now-lubricated door never quite closed when she packed up for the afternoon and moved off to restock for suppertime traffic. Once cart-with-cat was safely out of the alley, well it was no trick at all to force the door a little further back with the old paw and then squeeze out onto Queen Street very West. Remember that little ruse, dear reader, should you find yourself in a Harry Houdini situation.

Anyway, luckily not until University Ave. does a transit cop board the Queen car, chanting "Transfer, please" like a Zen mantra. And of course that's my stop anyway, the car wheezing to rest just kitty-corner to Number Sixty, a.k.a. Osgoode Hall, my home more or less sweet home . . . away from home more or less sweet home.

✺

Thus do I become living proof that an outlaw can be *in*-lawed, and not just by acquiring through marriage a gang of relatives you otherwise would change seats on the streetcar to avoid. While during the Middle Ages outlaws were deprived of all legal rights — they couldn't own property, make contracts, sue at law — the compassionate sovereign could experience a change of heart and "inlaw" them. According to the legal historians one might happen across during one's tenancy in a law library, "If the king inlaws him [the outlaw], he comes back into the world like a new-born babe . . . capable indeed of acquiring new rights, but unable to assert any of those that he had before his outlawry."* Thus do I find myself, like a newborn kit, *in*lawed (if off my own bat) and *in*stalled once more next to the stenographer's Birkenstocks over at 361 University, a.k.a. the trial courts just north of — and conveniently through the tunnel under — Osgoode Hall. And thus do I find Mr. Justice Mariner resuming his cross-examination of Tony Albinoni.

"Now if you'll recall, Tony," His Lordship begins, "before the California influenza so rudely interrupted our conversation, we

*Sir Frederick Pollock and Frederic William Maitland, *The History of English Law Before the Time of Edward I* (2nd ed.), Cambridge University Press, 1968.

were talking about your little joke, as you put it, your little joke with Professor Herskowitz. Your joke that you'd heard the professor was blackmailing Vern Gander."

"Well, like I said, Vern was serious about it." If I'm not mistaken, there's something of a yellow hue to the skin under Albinoni's left eye. And maybe a little black-blue, too, about the size, well, of a small, bony (perhaps female Has-being) fist, although Tony's congenital swarthiness, and the shadows on his bony face, mask it. "I mean, he told me seriously that Mack was holding his feet to the fire, like. You know, threatening to expose the fact that Vern's grades were inflated. But I thought Vern was, you know, Vern was making something bigger out of it than it was. Mack is always saying outrageous things, mostly for effect, and it seemed just like Vern to take it too seriously."

"Because Vern's a pretty sensitive type."

"Something like that. One of those earnest keener guys."

"As opposed to joking keener guys like you?"

"Well, I like to have fun, but I wouldn't call myself a keener."

"No? You're not ambitious?"

"Well, not in the conventional sense."

"No, I suppose not. So was it just a little unconventional joke, 'having fun,' when you decided to blackmail Professor Herskowitz?"

"I never blackmailed Mack."

"What if I told you that I have it from someone else, someone involved in your not-so-little scheme, that you did blackmail Mack?"

"From who? I mean, look. I worked for Mack. He paid me, as a student employee. I was his research assistant."

"So the story goes. A very pat story, I might add, that we've heard a number of times now."

"Well, that's not blackmail. He paid me for work I performed."

"Okay, let's look more closely at your job, then. As far as it related to Plan B at the dinner, you say that Mack was going to pretend to be dead, as in the theory about Francis Bacon faking his own death. Then he, Mack, was just going to disappear."

"Well, I was supposed to drive him to the airport."

"Right. And had he already paid you in advance for everything owing on your so-called work for him?"

"Well, no. I mean, basically, I was working at the party. It was part of the research. The Bacon Bit, I mean. So our arrangement was ongoing. He would owe me."

"So if he was going to disappear, how were you going to get paid for what he owed you? For what was on account, so to say?"

Tony is only temporarily flummoxed — long enough, though, for the jury to notice. "Mack promised to make good."

"Come on, Tony, there's more to it than that. I remind you, I have it on good authority."

Albinoni swallows, then shrugs, not so cocky now, brushing at his apparently bruised eye socket. "Well, yeah. He said he'd send the other half of what he owed once he got where he was going."

"The other half?"

"Well, he paid half for the Bacon stunt at the party, because it was sort of extra research, he paid half up front. Because it was complicated, and involved some risk."

"Some risk. A bit of an understatement, isn't it?"

"Well, not really."

"Not really? Have you by any chance noticed where we are, Mr. Albinoni?"

"You don't have to answer that, Mr. Albinoni," Justice Cactus says.

"Mack's charged with attempted murder and drug possession," Justice Mariner presses on, "and you say 'not really' a risk?"

"Well, but that wasn't supposed to happen."

"Exactly. It shouldn't have happened."

"That's for the jury to decide, Mr. Mariner." Cactus says it before Katz makes it all the way to his hind legs.

"So, anyway," Justice Mariner continues, "you were saying Mack paid half up front for the Bacon Bit. If it was just for a few more hours' work, I don't know, forty, fifty bucks, tops, why couldn't he pay you in the car?"

"Well, he sort of owed me more. For other work, see."

"That's not what you told us earlier," Justice Cactus intervenes, ears pricked.

"Well, but I said the rest was on account, for after the party, remember? He was going to send it."

"And that got you thinking, didn't it, Tony?" Justice Mariner asks.

Albinoni takes his time again about answering, brushing at his eye, no doubt asking himself who might have ratted him out. "Well, it made me wonder if I'd ever get paid, yeah. You know, 'The cheque's in the mail' and all that."

"Yes. But more than that, it made you wonder about something much more serious. The real risk, from your own point of view. You're a bright boy," Justice Mariner continues, "a keen law student, and so you got to thinking about the plan, didn't you, good ol' Plan B? If it worked, nobody would have known Mack was still alive. Mack Herskowitz would disappear, people would think he was really dead, and he'd never pay you another dime. Why should he, if everyone thought he was dead and there was nothing on paper? Worse, people might think you killed him. You could end up being charged with manslaughter, or criminal negligence, at the very least. For killing him? Right?"

"Well, if he wasn't there to explain things, it could have looked like that. Yeah. And he might have found it amusing to watch from afar. He would have looked at it as a sort of lesson. He would have laughed."

"A lesson for talking about bribes and Mr. Gander?"

"Well, I don't know. Maybe. As I said, I was just joking."

"A lesson because you were always fighting with each other like an old married couple?"

"Well, in that spirit, yeah. We argued and messed around, but it wasn't really serious. It was mentor-student. Pedagogical, you know. Socratic."

"Well, then, he might have been amused to watch you fry because you slept with his girlfriend?"

"He didn't know that at the time."

"You sure of that? How do you know Zipporah didn't tell him?"

"Well, he'd never said anything to me about it."

"But you told Mr. Katz that Mack seemed annoyed with you — more than usually annoyed. So it occurred to you, didn't it, Tony, that if Mack disappeared maybe it even could have looked like you murdered him? Particularly if it appeared you'd given him enough Perc to kill a horse?"

"Yes, yes, I guess so, yes. I didn't have control over things, and I couldn't really trust Mack in the circumstances. Not after what

Vern told me, especially. Mack always looked after number one, and if you crossed him he could turn from being your mentor to your enemy in a heartbeat. And he's a dangerous enemy."

"Who says likes don't attract, eh, Tony?"

"Your Honour . . ." Katz begins.

"That's gratuitous, Mr. Mariner," Justice Cactus says, sitting up very straight to look genuinely offended. More likely, he has awakened from mid-trial slumber. I know the feeling.

"And so you could have been facing criminal charges," Justice Mariner carries on with his cross-examination, ignoring the interruptions. "And whatever the charge, it would have destroyed your budding career at the bar, and you'd go to prison. Payback. Because, as everybody knew, you and Mack Herskowitz were constantly at each other's throats."

"Well, yeah. What else do you want me to say? Yeah, it occurred to me that Mack could double-cross us, for whatever reason. And I realized that with all the joking and trading barbs in class and, well, Zipporah and all, well, yeah, it could look like I had a motive to kill him. Yeah."

"Meanwhile, in your mind, Herskowitz escapes from any payback, himself. Gander and you can say whatever you want about him, make any old accusation, but Mack gets off scot-free in some offshore tax shelter sipping mai tais with little umbrellas in them, because everybody thinks he's dead. And maybe the bright and lovely Zipporah's going to join him there and live happily ever after. Disappear herself. Zipporah, the girl you've got the hots for, set up for life in some tropical love nest with Mack. That's how you saw it, right, Tony?"

"Well, something like that, yeah. Except the thing between me and her was over."

"She went with money and power in the end?"

"Your Honour," Katz whines, "that's not for this witness to say."

"Move on, Mr. Mariner," Justice Cactus rules.

"So *you* double-crossed *Mack*, didn't you?"

"I told you. The glasses got mixed up somehow. That's all I can think. Or maybe Mack switched them. I don't know. Like I say. He'd gone funny, and you can't trust him. So I don't know."

"If you don't know, Tony, how come Deena, your wife, how come she dialled your friends while pretending to call nine one one? That was part of the plan, wasn't it? She dialled your friends, so that when Professor Holdsworth took the phone, they hung up. And how come those friends came straight to you with the backboard when you collapsed at the party — your buddies dressed up as ambulance paramedics? How come they didn't go straight to Mack? Wasn't that what you and Mack had planned? Plan B? Your friends, dressed up as paramedics, would take Mack out and then you'd drive him to the airport?"

"Well, I suppose they were worried about me. They saw me lying there. Or maybe they just screwed up."

Justice Mariner laughs out loud. "I can call them, as well as another witness who knows you well, Tony, to show that they didn't screw up at all. They did precisely as instructed, didn't they? You told them to come straight for you, didn't you? Because you knew you'd be unconscious? Or nearly so."

"How could I know that?"

"Because you pulled the old switcheroo on Mack, didn't you? You and Deena set it all up, right? You let Mack think you were going to play along with his game, but you turned the tables — to make it look like he killed you. You did the Bacon Bit on your-self."

"Well, if I did that, how come Mack passed out?"

"Ah, yes. Good question. I'm sure the jurors are asking them-selves the same." Justice Mariner smiles at Albinoni's supposed peers, set up like Humpty Dumpty eggs in their own little Humpty Dumpty box. "How come Mack passed out? How about Mack passed out because you're almost as smart as you think you are. You gave him enough Perc to put him *hors de combat*, so to say, enough so it looked like you were still going along with Plan B, and Mack would be out of it, unconscious, while you double-crossed him. But it was you, in fact, who was going to disappear, wasn't it? All along. You were going to pretend to be dead — you *did* pretend to be dead — and then you had your wife blackmail Mack for what he owed you and more, isn't that so? Deena threat-ened Mack that she would spill the beans on everything, the little 'Bacon Bit' game, the supposed sexual peccadilloes with Gander, all that. She threatened to tell the police he'd killed you because you knew all his supposedly dirty little secrets. That's why the names in the IWAC accounts book switch from Albinoni to Topo, isn't it? She was blackmailing Mack and then, when she'd milked Mack enough, she was going to join you, the two of you taking early retirement in Mai Tai Paradise? A double-cross right down to the last detail. More than likely, everyone would think Mack had done some sort of dirty on you. And no one would ever know the absolute truth of it. Just as some people still think Francis Bacon wrote the plays of William Shakespeare."

I'm afraid that here ends, for Yours Fugitively, this particular play in the dark, *Her Majesty v. Maccabeus Theodor Herskowitz.*

You perhaps will find the rest of the saga in the local newspapers or cbc International, or in some other cat's law reports. As for me, well, circumstances compel me to declare a rather abrupt adjournment to the proceedings. Having accidentally kicked me and startled the both of us into a shrieking duet, the court stenographer has sent for security, who fortunately are: (1) not quite as quick as I; (2) not as conversant as Amicus, Q.C., with the back exit, where the judge comes and goes, often accompanied (although usually hidden from him and all others under his flowing robe), by Yours In Extremis. And from there I'm an old hand at the quickest route to the tunnel — even as the clasp in my collar sets off several metal detectors — the tunnel that runs back to the regal shelter of Osgoode Hall.

PART V

Judicial Notice

Judicial notice: The acceptance by judges and jurors of certain facts without hearing evidence as to their validity. "Thus it has been held that, generally speaking, a court may properly take judicial notice of any fact or matter which is so generally known and accepted that it cannot reasonably be questioned, or any fact or matter which can readily be determined or verified by resort to sources whose accuracy cannot reasonably be questioned."
Lord Sumner, *Commonwealth Shipping Representative v. Peninsular and Oriental Branch Service,* [1923] Appeal Cases, page 211.

"I cannot take judicial notice of what burping constitutes."
Judge R.C. Colton, *R. v. White,* 1980, Newfoundland Provincial Court, an impaired driving prosecution.

"I take judicial notice that some boys learn how to force burps at a very early age."
Justice Robert Zelinski, *R. v. Joubert,* [2002] Ontario Judgment No. 2218, an impaired driving prosecution.

CHAPTER 1

Chiefly the mould of a man's fortune is in his own hands.
Francis Bacon, "Of Fortune"

Even sweatier than usual, none other than Wayne of the Humane is in hot pursuit as I skitter into the stairway. Happily, my dear Katrina, assistant librarian and generous patron, has opened the door, a fully robed barrister trailing her as they execute a search for the work *Naked Promises** — whose promise, considering that the volume turns out to be a history of contract law, has probably disappointed more than one young law student browsing the Great Library's holdings. The barrister stutter-steps to avoid tripping over me, effectively blocking Wayne for a crucial couple of seconds.

Well, yes, as you can see, I had made it safely back to Oz from the courthouse at 361 University, but, lulled by the familiarity of the surroundings, the following day I have let down my guard. Apparently I was nobbled because I fell asleep, as is my wont, on one of the tables in the library's grand reading room (awe-inspiring and comforting at once, with its mammoth portrait of John Beverley Robinson at one end and the twenty-foot-high alabaster war memorial at the other, about a football field away). It seemed safe

---

*Random House Canada, 1989.

enough at the time, so cozy I was that I dozed on my back, four feet north, with a similarly spread-eagle volume of the *Western Weekly Law Reports* for my mattress in a broad shaft of Old Sol's rays as they streamed through the cathedral-style windows facing Queen. But Elizabeth Bane, the head librarian (All-Biz Liz as her underlings call her when she is not in the room), espied me and raised the hue and cry, as one traditionally does with outlaws, albeit generally not because said criminals play havoc with your allergies and your law reports. As you shadow Wayne and Yours Outlawed at full throttle down the stairs and into the library's stacks, scrabbling for the tax law section — a fitting venue, I figure, to get utterly lost — consider this bit of legal history: "Hue and cry" comes from the Anglo-Norman *hu et cri*, an actual legal obligation requiring citizens to raise the alarum of "Stop thief!" and to give hot pursuit to criminals. If the criminal made it unscathed across municipal boundaries, denizens of the second village took up the merry chase, and so on through each region, until the outlaw was in hand. Then, usually, his captors executed him summarily. "He wears the wolf's head!"

Or no head at all, I can well imagine, in abject horror, as I feel so-called Animal Rescue's retractable hoop-on-a-pole brush gently — euphemistically, you might say — down my whiskers and then begin to decapitate me as the noose cuts into my throat. Collared, I believe the jargon has it, again. Lynched, more like. I can't breathe. The musty room and its shelves and shelves and shelves of musty dusty fusty volumes and volumes and volumes volumi-nous tombinous ruinous spins and spins and upsy-daisy ass-over-teakettle spins. Objective vertigo, I believe is the technical term. Ring around the outlaw's not-so-rosy life. I gasp for air. It's the coup de grass — given that I shall never again see Osgoode's park-like lawn, which His Lordship and I have admired on so many occasions from the window of his chambers three stories above. *Goodbye, dear Ted, I hardly knew ye!* One last time my pupils dilate like time-lapse petunias and my eyelids flutter shut. Oh, well, a fitting end, one supposes, to Yours Most Unwanted. I am dying, Egypt, dying. Adieu, friends. His Lordship will have to finish this tale for you where I have left off. Parting, as His Lordship's favourite author has said, is such sweet sorrow — the sweet amid the bitter being that at least Auntie Bella will never have me in her amateur theatrical clutches again. As Oscar Wilde said of the wallpaper on his deathbed, "One of us has got to go."

CHAPTER 2

Truth may perhaps come to the price of a pearl, that showeth
best by day, but it will not rise to the price of a diamond or
carbuncle [ruby] that showeth best in varied lights.
Francis Bacon, *Essays*, "Of Truth"

*In 1987, this court considered the case of a man who wrote pamphlets
saying the Holocaust never happened. This court ruled that it was
necessary to put the Holocaust itself on trial in order to resolve whether
the denier was correct. That is, we said the trial judge could not "take
judicial notice" of the Holocaust as an historical fa*

"In my beginning is my end," said Mr. T.S. Eliot, albeit not in his
Old Possums Practical Book of Cats, a.k.a. (with certain melodic
amendments) plain old *Cats*. Old Tomcat Eliot borrowed the
phrase (with certain melodic amendments) from Mary Queen of
Scots, who said, "In my end is my beginning," no doubt shortly
before Queen Elizabeth relieved Mary of her head — where it all
began. The phrases anyway spring to mind as I await my fate yet
again in the firm grasp of Wayne S., Animal Control Officer — at
the portals of 1415 Elysian Fields North, Forest Hill Village, Toronto.
Yes, he really did collar me in the end, as in the beginning.

"We've injected a microchip into his neck, the scruff, you
know? — so's we can keep track of him from now on." Thus
Queen Mary isn't the only outlaw with a mortal pain in the neck

as Wayne of the Humane wheezes away at His Lordship through his chronically blocked nasal passages. And yes, his muddy shoes and sweaty mien again crowd Penny Mariner's foyer with the French leaded glass and the Sheridan Nurseries potted laurel on the Italian marble floor. In fact, it was Wayne of the Humane *banging* on the French leaded glass that brought His Lordship to the door forthwith, as we like to say at the Court of Appeal when we mean "pronto" — as in "You'll soon be getting an invoice for eighty dollars on the chip, Mr. Marinara. Plus one hundred and twenty for this service call."

"Eighty dollars!" His Lordship is inspecting said leaded glass, which would probably cost fifty times eighty dollars to repair. "That's more than you folks charge for a whole stray cat."

"No, sir, it's a good deal, actually, for you and us. It means one more cat we don't have to warehouse or euthanize. That's where the real expense comes in. And anyways it's priceless to us to make sure the companion caregivers keep track of their adopted animals, sir. They are no different from your children in that respect." No doubt the Animal Control Officer has been coached by his employer in these set-speeches of public relations. Cambering his eyebrows and tilting his head, Wayne S. does a fair job, for Wayne S., of managing a look of mild chastisement. *Odour in the court!*

His Lordship is familiar with the gesture, having performed it often from the bench. "Children? Yes, well," he replies, not visibly chastened, peering doubtfully at me through the bars of my portable cell, "they're certainly as much trouble."

∽ळ∾

"Fred, gimme a break. It was Albinoni all the way. If anyone was trying to kill anyone, Albinoni was trying to kill Mack, one way or another. And it was Albinoni who possessed the drugs, too, old son. I mean, nice try, but, you know, gimme a break." His Lordship is on the speakerphone, attempting to convince Fraidy Katz that his case against Mack Herskowitz has fallen apart. I am under the divan, still outlawed from the matrimonial home at 1415 Elysian Fields North, Forest Hill Village. This doesn't stop His Lordship from secreting me in the backyard shed after working hours. Happily, the days are lengthening, the earth is warming, but the trail leading to Amicus, Q.C. (for Quietly Concealed) remains cold: When Ted putters around and about the shed on my behalf, Penny assumes he is pushing the season, gardening in the mud amid the last grey crusts of snow.

Katz snorts, then squawks from the little box atop His Lordship's desk in chambers. The articling students have skived off somewhere — Starbucks most likely, or Mountain Equipment Co-op, where they seem to purchase the latest fashions — providing us the perfect opportunity to reassert ownership of said beloved workspace. Adverse possession, they call it in Property Law I, Balfour, MW 9–11 a.m. at the old Farb. "Give you a break? At the very least, Herskowitz was a party to it all. *All of it.* That makes him just as guilty. An accessory, as they say in the States."

His Lordship mugs across his desk at Lee Gaunt, who nods his simpleton encouragement, clicking his double-jointed jaw. "Face it, Fred. You don't have the evidence for attempt murder. Not by anyone. I'm a more likely suspect than Mack is." Justice Mariner fingers a volume of the Dominion Law Reports, left on his desk by one of the articled clerks.

"Don't tempt me, Judge," Katz says. Then, after a wet, sniffy pause, the assistant Crown adds, "Tell you what, you plead guilty to the extortion, I'll withdraw the other charges."

"Freddie, Freddie. I just said, you won't get a conviction on the other charges anyway. You got the wrong guy. Period."

"Take it or leave it, Judge. I won't offer a better deal, not with this sweetener. C'mon. We'll make a joint submission to the judge on sentencing. Your guy gets five years for the extortion. With time served doubled in his favour, he'll be out in eighteen months, tops."

❧

Justice Mariner has put Katz's offer to Herskowitz, who decides to take his chances. Mack is making no concessions or deals. It is his style to brazen it out, and Justice Mariner gives him a sixty to seventy percent chance at stonewalling the charges. Herskowitz gazes calmly from the dock — arrogantly, some might think — as the court clerk informs Mr. Justice Not-That-Prickly Cactus, "The jurors are all present, Your Honour. Mr. Foreman, will you please stand? Members of the jury, have you agreed upon a verdict?"

The jurors mutter that they have.

"Mr. Foreman, do you find the prisoner at the bar guilty or not guilty as charged in count number one?" That would be the attempted murder.

"Not guilty as charged, but guilty of the included offence of administering a noxious substance."

Ah, yes. Justice Cactus gave them that idea, in his instructions: "You may decide that Professor Herskowitz did not intend to kill Mr. Albinoni, nor did he intend to cause him bodily harm knowing that it was likely to result in Albinoni's death. You may still then decide that Professor Herskowitz intended to and did in fact administer to Albinoni a noxious substance, namely this Percodan drug . . ."

"And on count number two?" the clerk asks. Count two would be the drug possession charge.

"Not guilty."

"And on count number three?" The extortion.

"Not guilty." Not enough evidence, I guess — or at least it was ambiguous what was going on with those, er, extinguished feline rebound "donations."

"Members of the jury harken to your verdict as the court hath recorded it. You say the prisoner at the bar is not guilty as charged on count number one, but guilty of administering a noxious substance, and not guilty as charged on count numbers two and three. So say you all?"

❧

And so it is spring coming on for summer and the bleeding hearts are in bloom. Reinstalled more firmly at our desk in chambers (or upon said table, in Your Official Court Reporter's case) we finally have a head of steam up on *Her Majesty the Queen against Ian Luther Pasties*. The articling students are in the library, perhaps, or more likely planning their weekend at the cottage in their new fashions from Mountain Equipment Co-op.

> *without any evidence that the Holocaust was an historical event. That is, we said the trial judge could not "take judicial notice" of the Holocaust as an histor*

Yes, you guessed it, there is a knock at the door. His Lordship gazes upon one, who happens to be sitting on the completed portion of his judgment, keeping it warm as the judge sighs, "Yes, come in." The visitor opens the door and stands at the threshold, looking uncharacteristically reticent. "Have you got a minute, Judge?"

"Mr. Albinoni," Justice Mariner responds, not making much effort to hide his surprise. "You have a way of popping up when least expected. Please. Have a seat."

⁓◦∾

"I wanted to explain."

"I would think I'd be at the end of the queue for that duty, Tony. And it's a very long queue, I reckon."

"Yes, I understand that. But that's partly the point. You know how they say at Alcoholics Anonymous that you should seek forgiveness so you can move on and heal and all that?"

"All that. Yes. But again, you've done nothing to me — which can't be said regarding several other people who trusted you. And, anyway, I thought you said it was all just a joke."

"I know, Judge. I was wrong. I got carried away. I'm taking responsibility now. I'm trying to fix things, as much as they can be repaired. And, well, I wanted your advice."

"Advice?" His Lordship is not for softening. "I'm not even sure we should be speaking. I'm still Mack's counsel, you know, at least technically."

"This isn't about Mack or any of that. Well, not exactly, anyway. I mean, well, what I wanted to ask is, do you think my career in law is finished?"

Justice Mariner makes a wry face and slumps back in John Beverley Robinson's restored chair. "What do they say about that up at the Farb?"

"The decision of the Academic Affairs Committee is pending. But I think they might give me another chance, if I stay on the straight and narrow. So does my lawyer. Do you know Izzy Finster?"

"Oh, yes, quite well, in fact." Finster, one of the country's most celebrated divorce counsel, looked after us before the judicial council regarding the Pasta La Vista and articling student, uh, misunderstandings.

"Well, he gives me a good chance. My grades are good . . ."

"I think you should probably take it one step at a time. If they find against you and you're still interested in getting your degree, I imagine there's an appeal process. If you succeed at that, well, a law degree can be very useful even if you don't go into law practice."

"So you think practice is out for me now?"

His Lordship looks helpless, and anyway not completely willing to help. "Not necessarily, but I really don't know, Tony. I mean, the drugs, the extortion, that's not exactly fun and games, is it? Most people don't see that as a joke. I don't think the Law Society does, anyway."

The two men stare at each other for an uncomfortable interval, until Justice Mariner continues. "And you could've killed Mack, you know, Tony. Not to mention yourself."

Looking genuinely chastened, but otherwise rather healthier than usual — there's more flesh on him, the bruise under his eye has healed, and he has more colour — Albinoni is silent for a moment longer. At last he says, "I see that now. But we tried to be careful. We didn't want anybody to get hurt. Actually, we were trying to stop all that."

"By extorting money from Mack?"

"As I said in court, it wasn't like that, Judge. And he wasn't exactly blameless in all this himself, you know."

"I'm not going to talk to you about that."

There is another silence.

"All right. I know it looks bad," Albinoni begins again, "but I called it off, didn't I? I mean, it was getting way out of hand. I can see that now."

"Yes, but I assume it also became obvious to you that you could never have pulled it off — the disappearing trick, I mean — taking off with the money and the girl, or with Deena. You knew you'd get caught anyway. You're still a kid, Tony, a bright kid, but a kid. You're not a well-connected and experienced lawyer like Mack, assuming he really was planning to disappear. And I'm not saying he was."

"Well, yes, I realized I was in over my head. But it wasn't just that, Judge. There was Deena. I couldn't have left her out there, holding the bag like that, the poor sap, dealing with it all by herself. I mean, I know I'm selfish, but I'm not heartless. Like you said, I'm still a bit of a snot-nosed kid."

The judge relents a little. "Well, true enough, it's a mitigating factor, as the criminal law puts it, that you came forward, even if you were just showing off. I assume that's why Katz hasn't charged you with anything — your cooperation, I mean. And compassion for your wife is generally a desirable thing." The judge can't resist another dig. He's only *Homo allegedly sapiens*, after all. "In all the circumstances."

"I know, Judge. I get it, honest. I've been an asshole. A complete asshole. But I still think I'd make a good lawyer. I really do. I mean, that's what I'm trying to say. I'm still young. I think I could have a good, successful practice and really help people. Make amends, maybe, you know?"

Justice Mariner abruptly sits forward, to signify that time is running short. "That's entirely possible, I'm sure." And sure enough some of the world's biggest, well, anal sphincters have highly successful law practices. But His Lordship doesn't say that. He says: "So here's what you can do, all right? Keep your nose clean from now on, study hard, work in the legal aid clinic at the Farb, show that you've learned your lesson. Cultivate people you can use as references, and work your butt off for them. Once you get to third year, assuming that all pans out for you, contact the Law Society and tell them about it. Be forthcoming. Explain to them that once you were young and foolish, but that's all water under the bridge. Show them your references. Ask them what they think, how they might look at you as a candidate. Show them your good record after all this. Prove to them you've rehabilitated yourself. Make your good faith 'plain and obvious,' as we redundantly put it at the Court of Appeal. All right?"

As Albinoni opens the door to leave, Justice Mariner adds, "And Tony."

"Yes, sir?"

"I'll be watching to see how you make out."

CHAPTER 3

It is a strange desire to seek power and to lose liberty.
Francis Bacon, "Of Great Place"

Well, in my experience you can make your bona fides as plain and obvious as a boil on their noses and still find yourself an outlaw. I remain *sylvestris non grata* at Osgoode Hall, and Penny Mariner, the chief judicial officer at 1415 Elysian Fields North, remains oblivious that I am again in residence, albeit hidden in the garden shed come evening. In my beginning is my end.

And as long as we're meting out poetic justice of the circular kind, you will want to consider one last time the sad case of Maccabeus Theodor Herskowitz, formerly professor of law and head of the Institute for the Wrongly Acquitted Criminal at Scarborough University. Having been "wrongfully acquitted" — or at least discharged — at that preliminary hearing in the moot court at the Farb, he now has received a "conditional sentence" upon his conviction for administering a noxious substance to Tony Albinoni. Yep, house arrest for twelve months, conditional (Justice Cactus has ordered) on his resigning his post at IWAC. And he might even have to wear one of those electronic collar thingies — on his ankle mind you, not on his neck, more's the pity. Then again, I suppose they could inject a microchip below his skull. In my beginning is my end.

Of course Dean Pilchard has fired Mack from his teaching position at the Farb, and the Law Society is looking into disciplinary proceedings. "Disbarment is almost a certainty," His Lordship advises Penny. I can hear them through the open windows as they consume toast and coffee in the breakfast nook, just off the deck.

"But what will he do for a living, Ted?" Penny asks, unaware that the springtime backyard still might have ears. "I mean, if they strip him of everything? It seems counterproductive." It's not for nothing that she's spent thirty years married to a civil libertarian. "How's he supposed to rehabilitate himself?"

"Well, he should have plenty of time to complete his biography of Francis Bacon, and to consider how the mighty have fallen. And he could disappear to France, I guess, and write Harold Pinter's plays or something."

"No, seriously, Ted. How's he supposed to live?"

"He can do some consulting, I suppose — if anyone will have him."

"Not likely, is it?" Penny shakes her head. "How sad. A bright man like that. A living death."

"Yes, he certainly doesn't have to fake it any more. He's fallen all the way down that winding stair, in full public view. Death in life. The truth in shadows."

All rising to great place is by a winding stair. In my beginning is my end.

⟨∞⟩

And speaking of rising to great place on winding stairs, Auntie

Bella's reviews, at least in the Mariner Household Daily News, were unusually positive. The Parkdale Library's Play-in-the-Alley, Pay-What-You-Can production of *Cats* was "enthusiastically attempted," the Household reviewers opine, with singing and "adapted" dancing that "wasn't always terrible, for amateurs," not to mention plastic lawn chairs that left hardly any noticeable creases in the audience members' backsides and thighs. ("Although I don't feel it was really necessary for you to creak around and sigh loudly in yours," Mrs. Mariner has advised her long-legged co-reviewer, "through every one of the quiet songs in Act Two.") It was heartily agreed, anyway, that the climax, starring Auntie Bella, lived up to its name, and was truly the stuff of "Memories." Said conclusion featured, after all, the same hook-and-ladder engine that had rescued Grizabella from the fire escape during rehearsals, wailing in on cue, its lights flashing in the summer night as Auntie Bella herself scaled the truck's hydraulic lift. Then, as Penny's aged relative gesticulated as best she could twenty feet up, harnessed to a narrow stairway of wobbling aluminum and attempting to make "Memory" even remotely audible above the racket, the firefighters in full regalia propelled her toward the stars and crescent moon on that perfectly crisp and clear spring evening.

Rating: Two thumbs sort of ambivalently wiggled back and forth by your seasoned critics, Mariner and Mariner.

CHAPTER 4

If a man will begin with certainties he shall end
in doubts; but if he will be content to begin with
doubts, he shall end in certainties.
Francis Bacon, *The Advancement of Learning*

In 1987, this court considered the case of a man who wrote pamphlets
saying the Holocaust never happened. This court ruled that it was
necessary to put the Holocaust itself on trial in order to resolve whether
the denier was correct. That is, we said the trial judge could not "take
judicial notice" of the Holocaust as an historical fact; he had to hear
evidence before he could determine whether it took place. Otherwise,
we agreed, assuming the truth of the Holocaust might have caused the
jury to prejudge the issue they were meant to decide — had the
accused deliberately lied in saying the Holocaust never happened? —
(1987), 31 Canadian Criminal Cases (3d) 97.

We did a little better, but only just, in 1990. The same man was
before the court, having been convicted again of spreading false news
about the Holocaust. This time we said a trial judge could take judi-
cial notice of the Holocaust itself — that, in the trial judge's words,
"the mass murder and extermination of Jews of Europe by the Nazi
regime during the Second World War is so notorious as not to be the
subject of dispute among reasonable persons." This was different, our
court claimed, from accepting without hearing evidence that the
Holocaust reflected "any policy of the National Socialist government

and/or Adolf Hitler, . . . the specific numbers of persons who died and . . . the use of gas chambers": (1990), 53 C.C.C. (3d) 161. We said courts still could not take judicial notice of the politics and mechanics of the Holocaust, but that the existence of the Holocaust itself was capable of judicial notice.

Unfortunately, I believe we were still wrong. Whatever was government policy under Adolf Hitler, and whatever the number of people he murdered, the Holocaust was not on trial. What was on trial was whether the denier knew he was telling lies about the Holocaust. The distinction we made is itself an insult to history and to the victims of the Holocaust. Like all truth, the truth of the Holocaust is not equivocal, whether ten million died, six million, or some other number. Truth is absolute.

In that light, assume that three hundred years ago, as part of an official military policy and based on international law, an ethnic group was forced at gunpoint to leave what is now maritime Canada. In 1987 there are no survivors of the actual expulsion, and no film, newspapers, radio, or television footage documenting the event. Neither are there any other living witnesses — soldiers from the other side, neighbours of the expelled people — to tell the story. And despite this attempt at ethnic cleansing, descendants of the expelled people still flourish in this country and nearby.

This describes, of course, the expulsion of the Acadians by their British governors in 1755–62, and — nonetheless — their continued vibrancy here and in the United States. Would any modern Canadian court, or any reasonable person, dispute the historical veracity of these events, including the fact that the expulsion was official policy of the ruling forces, never mind that the expulsion occurred not fifty years past, but centuries beyond the memory of anyone still alive? I think not.

I therefore take judicial notice that the expulsion of the Acadians in 1755–1762 from what today we call maritime Canada is a fact of history. I also find that the appellant, Mr. Ian Pasties, intended to spread, and did spread, the false news that the expulsion was somehow fabricated by the descendants of the Acadians.

For these reasons, the appeal is dismissed and the conviction affirmed.

— T.E. Mariner, Justice of Appeal

I concur with the disposition of this appeal by my colleague Mariner J.A., but wish to add that I do not believe the Holocaust denial cases are wrongly decided.

— P.E. Brossard, Justice of Appeal

I concur with the reasons of Mariner J.A. in this particular case, but would add that whether the politics and mechanics of the Holocaust are capable of judicial notice remain questions for another day.

— S.F. Fierstein, Justice of Appeal

I concur absolutely and unconditionally with the reasons of Mariner, Justice of Appeal, but would add that it's well past time for lunch.

— Amicus, Q.C. (for Questing Comestibles)

And so at last we conclude our most thoughtful reasons for judgment in *R. v. Pasties*, just as Penny Mariner discovers His Lordship and Your Prodigal Son sitting in the garden shed.

"Ted!" There she is on the deck again, some fifty yards away, frowning, waving her trusty portable phone. "It's Auntie Bella! She says she can't find your bloody cat anywhere!" Penny mugs at us in an ironic sort of way, silent again with her ear back at the phone. So begins the case for the prosecution.

"She says she put posters on the utility polls!"

Silence as Penny rolls her eyes.

"She says she's extremely sorry but she thinks it's for the best, really, and we should just accept that it's not going to work between her and it."

Silence.

"She says it's just one of those things. She says she's done her best but the little outlaw keeps running off on her."

His Lordship and I exchange bemused glances as Penny performs a little pantomime of her aunt gabbling on. Then she rings off and brings me half a can of her best water-packed tuna.

It is late springtime in the back garden of 1415 Elysian Fields and — as I say — the bleeding hearts are beginning to bloom. Stooping to conquer, Her Ladyship pats my head as she sets the meal down near the little garden fountain as it gurgles away. When Justice Mariner makes his "Will wonders never cease?" face, Penny replies: "Well, I suppose the little outlaw's got to eat, doesn't he?"

"Yes," His Lordship concurs, eyeing me dubiously, "I suppose he does."

"Ted. Did you really think I didn't know you were hiding him back here?"

His Lordship doesn't reply, patting and cooing at me as a diversion. Instead, he says, "Yes, even outlaws deserve a break now and then."

He's learning, His Lordship.

And so, for now, the verdict is unanimous. Mind you, Her

Ladyship has served said tuna in an old plastic margarine tub, washed and dried so many times that its yellow has faded to off-white — just like the lardy-looking margarine you see in Quebec, where the farm lobby ensures that it's illegal to make the stuff look like butter. What is truth, indeed, one asks, and fully intends to stay for an answer — at least until dinner.

Afterword

To read for yourself how the Ontario Court of Appeal originally refused to accept the truth of the Holocaust without evidence to prove it (in the jargon, how they refused to "take judicial notice" of the Holocaust as an historical event), see the "spreading false news" case reported at (1987), 58 Ontario Reports (2d) 129. As my fictional Justice Mariner explains in *Murder on the Rebound*, the court reasoned that "if the trial judge had taken judicial notice of the existence of the Holocaust [it] would have been gravely prejudicial to the defence [of the Holocaust denier] in so far as it would influence the drawing of the inference concerning the appellant's [the denier's] knowledge of the falsity of the pamphlet" he had distributed. Translation: If the trial judge had told the jury to assume the Holocaust was established fact, this could have caused them to prejudge whether the denier had deliberately lied about that fact. In other words, assuming the truth of the Holocaust might have led them to prejudge the very issue they were supposed to decide.

Not surprisingly, this ruling was widely viewed as not just illogical but worrisomely equivocal, or even racist. Many lawyers pointed out that the court had misconstrued the issue while purporting to recognize it: the Holocaust was not on trial. What was on trial (as Justice Mariner points out) was whether the man accused of spreading lies about it did so knowing the "news" was false. In other words, the gravamen of the offence, as lawyers call it, was, did the man intend to lie about the Holocaust? This had nothing to do with the historical validity of the Holocaust itself.

In light of such criticism, following the man's second trial, the appeal court retreated, accepting the Holocaust itself as an incontrovertible historical event. The court finessed the apparent contradiction in its two rulings by distinguishing the Holocaust *per se* (in the second trial judge's words, accepting that "the mass murder and extermination of Jews of Europe by the Nazi regime during the Second World War is so notorious as not to be the subject of dispute among reasonable persons") from details reported about it, such as whether millions of Jews died in gas chambers and whether this extermination was official Nazi policy: [1990] 53 Canadian Criminal Cases (3d) 161. This novel assumes that the court's retreat came a little later, and more sympathetically, in Justice Mariner's reasons in *R. v. Pasties.*

The free-speech dilemma posed by historical revisionism did not become academic, by the way, when the Supreme Court struck the offence of spreading false news from the *Criminal Code.* Similar issues arise in prosecuting those who promote hate or genocide (which remain *Criminal Code* offences), and of course judicial notice is a vast area of evidence law history itself, involving (again, as Justice Mariner notes) the very nature of truth — is the sky really blue and the sea really green, and, as Wittgenstein implied: Can we ever truly know whether a hippopotamus has entered the room?

Readers interested in the broader legal history of "spreading false news" might like to consult my own *Where There's Life, There's Lawsuits*, ECW Press, 2003, pages 248-252.